Deadly Traffic

Other titles
by David Crosby

Million Dollar Staircase
Book One, Will Harper Series

Guilty Money
Book Two, Will Harper Series

Florida Burning
Book Three, Will Harper Series

The Florida Shuffle
Book Four, Will Harper Series

Keeping Us Afloat
A Trip Down the Intracoastal Waterway
& A Journey Through a Marriage
(Non-Fiction)

Deadly Traffic

A Will Harper Novel

David Crosby

Published by

CROSBY Stills

Thanks to the Plantation Writers Guild for their input and especially for their encouragement in the writing of this book, and to all my beta readers for their help with catching errors. Any that remain are my own.

This book is dedicated to my wonderful wife, Marilyn.
You are always my inspiration.

Table of Contents

Prologue

Fifty miles from the Mexican border, miles from the nearest town, the driver of the tractor-trailer struggled to control the wheel as a blowout destroyed his right front tire. He managed to get it stopped, then he panicked. He left the truck running and ran into the grassy fields on the side of the road. He had a bottle of water. It was more than he left his passengers.

The sun was setting when a Texas State trooper drove by and spotted the abandoned truck. He called it in and requested assistance from the Border Patrol. He waited nearly an hour for the two BP agents to arrive in their SUV.

They got out, introduced themselves, and said, "So, what's the story, Officer Robinson?"

"I was driving home at the end of my shift and saw this truck idling by the side of the road. There's no sign of the driver. I was going to check in the trailer for contraband, but I have no way to open it."

"We carry bolt cutters with us. Shall we?"

Robinson carried his Maglite to the rear of the trailer, shining his light on the lock as the agents cut it off. When the door was opened, three bodies fell out onto the pavement.

Robinson jumped back. "Damn! What the hell happened here?"

Agent Sanchez leaned over one of the bodies. He touched the man on the neck to check for a pulse and yanked his hand back. "This guy is frozen." He checked the other two bodies. "Their fingers are bloody, and their nails are ripped apart. It looks like they were trying to claw their way out."

Robinson shone his torch into the trailer. "Holee shit, there's dozens of bodies in here."

Sanchez removed his radio from his belt. "I'll call it in. " When the dispatcher answered, he said. "We're going to need backup. Got a truck full of bodies out here on highway 9. Looks like a bunch of illegals. Damn smugglers brought 'em in a freezer truck."

* * *

Carmelina was sad and exhausted. She took in the luxurious surroundings that were a part of her daily life, but they were not for her to enjoy. They were for her to clean, fourteen hours a day. The house servants, butlers and kitchen help only worked ten hours a day, but Carmelina was of a lower status. She was a slave.

When she'd departed her home in San Antonio des Nubes, Guatemala, with her brother Pablo and younger sister Leilani, her parents had cried. Not because they wanted them to stay, but because they wanted them to live.

The rugged patch of land they farmed would not support a family of five, and there were no jobs to be found for a hundred miles. Going to America was their only choice. Mama and Papa had scrimped and saved for more than a year to raise the $5,000 that Pablo would pay to a coyote to sneak them across the Mexican border into the U.S., then across the country to Florida.

With a large colony of Guatemalans in the state, the three siblings hoped to find work and housing. That had been the dream, anyway. It had been a long trek, fifteen hundred miles from their mountain home to the United States border on foot. Pablo had been excited when he handed the five grand to the smiling man with a mustache who would spirit them over the river to freedom.

They'd been surprised when he led them to a parking lot where rows of big trucks were lined up. Leilani was terrified as the man and two helpers placed her in a cardboard box inside one of the trucks. She was given a blanket and a bottle of water, then sealed inside. Carmelina trembled as she saw the box lifted by a forklift, then slid to the front of the empty trailer.

She went in the next box, sweat pouring off of her in the stifling heat. Alone in the dark, she felt the movement of the forklift sliding her box next to her sister's. She heard Pablo speaking with the coyote, then heard a sharp warning to stay quiet before he too was sealed in a box and slid into the truck.

We will die before this truck even gets to the border, Carmelina thought. Then she heard the rumble of an air conditioner. The forklift worked for two more hours loading boxes of beef parts. She had no way of knowing, but cows that provided that beef had already crossed the border more than once.

The Mexican cattle are sent to the United States to be fattened on corn and alfalfa, then sent back across the border for slaughter. The prime cuts are sent back across the river to feed American consumers, and some of the parts that are considered "beef byproducts" by the U.S. stay in Mexico, where they are popular delicacies.

Beef tongue, oxtail, stomachs and even the head, nothing is wasted. The head of the cow, you put it to boil, and you get the cheeks for barbacoa. You save the eyeballs for special gourmet tacos.

None of this mattered to Carmelina, Leilani or Pablo. They sat in the dark, feeling the motion as the truck rolled onto the highway. They'd finally gotten relief from the sweltering heat when first the temperature dropped from over one hundred degrees to a comfortable seventy. The problem was, it kept dropping, all the way to thirty-five degrees.

Soon they were shivering, barely helped by the thin blankets they'd been given. They tried to stay quiet when the truck stopped at the border, but Carmelina was afraid the chattering of her teeth would give them away.

It didn't, and the truck drove for another forty-five minutes before finally stopping. She heard the sound of a metal door opening, then the truck moved again briefly before stopping.Without the noise of the truck, Carmelina tried whispering to her brother in Spanish.

"Pablo."

"Shhh."

"Where are we?"

The metal door squealed on rusty tracks again

She heard a low voice through the heavy cardboard. "We're across the border, but I don't know where."

The sound of the truck door opening stopped the conversation. Carmelina could hear the forklift starting up, then a lift gate rising to the back of the truck. After more than an hour of hearing boxes moving out of the trailer, she was startled to feel her box being lifted. After a few moments the motion stopped, and she felt it settle to the floor.

She cowered on the bottom of the box as a blade cut through the packing tape at the top, then squinted at the sudden light as the box was opened.

"Come on, get up."

She struggled to her feet, stiff after the cold and the hours of confinement. She was in a high-ceiling room lined with metal shelves, huge boxes covering most of them. Two men stood by a box.

One of them, a burly man with a large, black beard, reached over and grabbed her arms, lifting her from the cardboard.

The smaller man said, "Stand over there and be quiet."

She watched as first Pablo and then Leilani's hiding places were taken from the truck, opened, and her siblings came blinking into the overhead lights. The three of them hugged, then Leilani whispered to Pablo.

He turned to the men. "Please, sir, we need to use the bathroom."

The bearded man cursed, but the other one said, "Come this way." He led them to a door into a dirty restroom with four stalls, then waited outside as they relieved themselves and washed.

Leilani whispered to Pablo, "Do you think they will feed us?"

"I don't know. I'll ask."

There was a pounding on the door. "Hurry up in there!"

The three siblings hugged again, then walked out the door back into the warehouse. They followed the man into a room with tables, benches and vending machines. Leilani looked hungrily at the snack machine, but they had no dollar bills or coins.

Pablo asked, "Could we have something to eat and some water?"

"Wait here."

They sat, and a few minutes later the man returned with three bottles of water and several peanut butter and jelly sandwiches. "This is all we've got. They'll feed you a proper meal in the morning."

The three of them ate, drank the water, and then lay on the benches, exhausted. An hour later, the thin man returned.

"Let's go. Your ride is here."

Groggy, they followed him out into the warehouse where a rust-streaked van with "Smith Brothers Electrical" painted on the side waited.

The bearded man opened the rear door. Empty shelves for equipment lined the walls, but that wasn't what they looked at. Four men, dirty and weary looking, were sprawled on the floor on sleeping bags. There was very little open room on the floor.

He said, "Find a place and get comfortable." He tossed in three more sleeping bags. "It's a long drive to Florida."

* * *

The next twenty-four hours were a blur. They sat on the sleeping bags, crowded between the shelves and the men. The three siblings took turns sleeping, Leilani with her head in Pablo's lap. The four men talked among themselves, and more than once Carmelina saw them looking hungrily at her younger sister.

Only once when they stopped for gas did they receive anything to eat, bags of fast food and sodas which they devoured. Pablo asked the thin man if they could get out to use the bathroom and stretch at the next stop, but he shook his head.

"Too risky, someone might see you." He pointed to a plastic utility pail near the back door. "Use the bucket."

Growing up on a farm, the bucket wasn't too shocking to them, but the lack of privacy was an issue. Pablo held up a sleeping bag in front of each of his sisters as they took turns at the bucket.

Finally, after a long and mostly sleepless night and much of the next day in the back of the work van, they arrived in Florida. The two men in front changed drivers at the welcome station, and they gave the passengers each another bottle of water.

Carmelina asked, "Is this our destination?"

The bearded man laughed. "Close. Only about five more hours." Then he shut the door.

Pablo leaned over to the older of his two sisters. "Remember the paper I gave you with the family members in Florida?"

"Yes, our Morales cousins, and phone numbers for two of them. I still have it."

"If we get separated for any reason, get to a phone and call them. They will be expecting us."

Her eyes widened. "I don't want to go without you!"

"I want the three of us to stay together, but I'm trying to plan in case something goes wrong. Be sure and watch out for Leilani. She is young and pretty, and that could be dangerous for her."

He saw the hurt look in her eyes and touched her cheek. "Ah, my Carmelina, you are pretty as well, but her youth puts her more at risk. You are the wiser one."

She gave him a weak smile. "Please stay with us, Pablo."

"I promise."

It was a promise he could not keep.

* * *

Finally, the van arrived in West Palm Beach and pulled into another warehouse facility. The passengers heard the engine stop and waited anxiously for freedom. The rear door opened.

The bearded man who had done most of the talking told Pablo and his sisters to wait by the van . They watched while he unloaded the four men from the back and sent them off with the thin man. Then he turned to Pablo.

"Okay, I got you over the border and into Florida. Now pay me the rest of the money."

Pablo looked shocked. "But I already paid you!"

"You paid the coyote his fee. He gave you to me. My fee is $10,000. I usually charge $5,000 each, but I'm giving you a discount." The man gave him a nasty smile. "I'm a generous guy."

Carmelina said, "Sir, please, that was all the money we had."

He crossed his arms. "Then you'll have to work off your debt."

Pablo started to object loudly, and the bearded man pulled a pistol from his pocket.

"No arguments." He gestured towards a corridor. "This way."

They walked in front of him to a small room with an empty desk and two chairs. There was a window looking out of the warehouse, but it had metal bars on the exterior. Once they were inside, he said, "Wait here," and closed the door and bolted it from the outside.

Carmelina hugged Leilani and looked over her shoulder at Pablo. "What are we going to do?"

"They have laws in this country," he said. "He can't keep us prisoners."

Once again, he was wrong.

After several hours, the bearded man opened the door and gestured at Pablo with the pistol.

"You. Come here."

Pablo followed him into the hallway, and the door was closed and bolted again. After a few minutes Carmelina saw movement outside the window and rushed to see what was happening. It was Pablo, being led in handcuffs towards an old pickup truck with a big red tomato painted on the door. A man in overalls opened the passenger door and shoved him inside, then got in the driver's side and drove the truck out of the compound.

Leilani and Carmelina cried together for an hour before running out of tears. Two hours later, they came for Leilani. The buyer was a man with slicked-back blond hair and a slight paunch.

He said, "Mmm, tasty. She'll work out just fine on the party boat."

Carmelina flew at him, clawing at his face until she was dragged away by the bearded man and thrown to the floor.

"Bitch! I'm gonna have a hard time getting anything for you with that attitude. Keep it up and I might have Capn' Willy here take you out and toss you overboard."

The blond man dabbed at a scratch on his check with a handkerchief. He glared at her. "I'd be glad to."

The bearded man shook his head. "Not today. I know someone who might take her. Cheap bastard, too. He'll be happy to get a bargain."

Their American Dream had become a nightmare.

David Crosby

Chapter One

I watched Jimmy's back as he pedaled in front of me. We were on the last leg of a twenty-mile bike ride, and I'd stayed with him the entire way. As we made the last eighth of a mile, I poured on the speed, powering past Jimmy just as we crossed the imaginary finish line.

I threw my arms in the air. "Yes!" I said, declaring victory.

Jimmy grinned. "If I'd known you were that close, I'd have never let you take me."

I gaped at him. "No way did you *let* me win."

"I'm just ragging you, Will. You did great. Quite an improvement from where you started."

When we'd begun riding together a few months ago I did well to even finish seven miles. Now I was riding twenty miles, kayaking for hours, and had become a star in the ladies self-defense class. That means I no longer got my ass kicked, about which I was very relieved.

"Thanks, Jimmy. You've helped me a lot with my conditioning."

"You've worked hard, that's what did it. You'll be ready the next time someone comes after you." He laughed. "Of course, kicking Axel Winter in the balls worked pretty well!"

I grinned. "One thing you taught me is all's fair in a fight."

"Absolutely. It's about survival, not style points."

We put the bikes away and sat on the front deck of Jimmy's houseboat.

He said, "Now that we've been virtuous and exercised, how about a beer?"

"Sure thing." I'd been trying to cut back on my Red Stripe consumption lately, but I felt like I deserved this one.

"How are things with Callie?" Jimmy knew that we'd had some issues lately.

"We're okay. She's pretty happy about the new job with the Bradenton Journal. Even though it's not an office job they gave her a new MacBook Air and a dedicated iPhone for contacting the editors and Dillon Haverhill. Having a sense of purpose is doing her a lot of good."

"Is she working on anything big yet?"

"No, she's been poking around some of the environmental problems in the state, but doesn't have any new information yet to hang a story on."

Jimmy took a sip of his beer and looked over the bottle at me. "You don't seem in a big hurry to start something new."

"Hey, I haven't looked for stories since I moved to Florida. They keep dropping in my lap. I'm perfectly happy just working out, doing a little creative writing, and sitting around on the boat the rest of the time. I'm not looking for projects."

He toasted me with his bottle. "To doing nothing."

"I'll drink to that."

✳ ✳ ✳

Carmelina was exhausted. The days of vacuuming, ironing, dusting, seemed to go on forever. The Palm Beach mansion had thirty rooms, and even with the help of two other immigrant workers they finished cleaning the house only to start over again.

She got one twenty-minute break for lunch, and at night she was locked in her room in a distant wing of the massive house. There she would lie in her single bed and write endless letters to her sister, Leilani and her brother, Pablo, telling them of her daily life.

She feared she would never get the chance to give them the letters, but it gave her hope to write them.

The other thing she feared was the master of the house. He was gone much of the day, working in the office where he ran the giant sugar company, but he was home most nights. His wife traveled alone often, and when she was away there was a steady stream of pretty young girls who were brought to the house by the chauffeur.

They were for the entertainment of the master, and Carmelina had no doubt about what that meant. He generally left her alone, barely noticing her existence. One night that changed.

She had heard the master talking to one of his attorneys as she cleaned in the hallway, seemingly invisible to them.

"Listen, sir, with the big sting that went on in Jupiter, I'd advise you to cool it with the female 'visitors' for a while."

"What the hell does that have to do with me, Carson? I'm not stupid enough to go to those storefront massage parlors like the idiots who got arrested."

"No, sir, but the authorities are attempting to track the girls themselves, and you certainly don't need that kind of negative publicity."

The master cursed and complained but had apparently acquiesced. That was when he began noticing her.

"Hi, honey, are you new to the staff?"

She answered in her heavily accented English. "No, sir, I've been here for ten months." One of the other girls had helped her pick up some of the language.

"How old are you?"

"Almost eighteen years, sir."

Ah, old enough. "Why don't you take a break for a few minutes and come sit with me in my library."

She looked at him nervously. "Sir, Mrs. Lopez, the head housekeeper, she will punish me if she sees me sitting instead of cleaning."

"Bah, she works for me! If I say sit, it's fine to sit."

Carmelina followed him into the library where she watched as he sat on a short leather couch. He patted the cushion next to him. "Come, sit down."

She sat as far from him as she could, perched on the edge of the cold, leather cushion, ready for flight.

The master said, "Let's have a drink." He got up and filled a tumbler from a crystal decanter, then poured a second tumbler with a smaller amount and handed it to her.

"Sir, I have never had alcohol before. I should not drink this."

"What's your name?"

"Carmelina, sir."

"Well, I don't like to drink alone, and I'm the boss, *comprende*?"

"Si." She took a small sip and coughed violently as the fiery liquid burned her throat.

"Dammit, girl, you're wasting expensive liquor and getting it on the leather!"

"I am sorry, sir, it burned me."

He took the glass from her, diluted the amber liquid with water and handed it back. "Try it this way."

She reluctantly tried it again. She winced, but managed to keep it down without coughing.

"See, that's better, isn't it?"

"Yes, sir."

He leaned into the corner of the couch and turned to look at her. "You fill out that uniform pretty well, honey."

She didn't know if a reply was called for and kept silent while taking another sip of the diluted whiskey.

The master downed his glass, shook his head to clear it, then stood and poured himself another tumbler full. "Drink up. Things are lot more fun with a little lubrication."

Carmelina took one small sip, then another. Before long, her head was swimming. She barely heard it when the head of housekeeping came into the library.

"Sir, would you like me to return this girl to her room for the night?"

"No, I'll take care of it. I have a key."

He saw the disapproving look on the woman's face, but he didn't care. He paid all the staff he didn't own. Every person in the house. *I'll do what I damned well please.*

The master slowed down his own drinking but poured another glass for Carmelina. He needed her pliable but awake for what he had in mind.

"Come on, honey, I'll show you my private wing of the house."

Through the fog of alcohol her hopes rose. Only the most trusted servants were allowed into that part of the sprawling mansion. Maybe she'd find a way out from there.

* * *

Sweat poured off Pablo in the Florida heat. He'd been picking tomatoes ten to twelve hours a day, seven days a week. When he was sold to the foreman who ran the crew, he was told he'd be paid fifty cents per thirty-two pound bucket of tomatoes. He needed to pick just over three tons of tomatoes every day to make $50. It was only possible to pick that much when the days were long and the fruit on the vines was healthy and plentiful.

The pay didn't seem all that bad at first, until he discovered the charges that were being withheld from it. He shared a broken-down mobile home owned by the packing house with nineteen other immigrant pickers. He was charged $50 a week for that. The food was miserable, often just dry tortillas and water. Another $50 a week for the meals. $5 a day for the sixteen mile ride to the fields in the elderly school bus.

It would be impossible at that pace to pay off the $5,000, the amount the smugglers told him he owed for his freedom.

He saw what happened to workers who tried to escape. One picker who couldn't take it any more ran off. The crew boss saw him and chased him down in the old pickup truck the supervisors used to roam the fields. They returned without him an hour and a half later. They'd beaten him so badly that they just dropped him off at the hospital

The man never recovered, and a message was sent to the rest of the workers. There is no escape.

Pablo kept his head down, trying to get through every day the best he could. His arms had become strong from the work even as his knees and back suffered. There was no day off for pain.

Those who were identified as troublemakers were shackled, making the work that much harder. Pablo did his best to avoid that, but one day he'd had enough. Boss John, the crew boss, had spent the morning following him around, kicking him in the ass and calling him a worthless spic. Pablo had stumbled over a tomato-sized rock in the field, a rarity in the heavily cultivated soil. He picked the stone up and put it in his pocket.

When the crew boss started in on him again, Pablo rose up, pulled the rock from his pocket, and struck him in the side of the head. The boss fell to the ground, blood pouring from the wound. Pablo dropped the rock and ran. He ran like his life depended on it, and it did. With Boss John down, no one followed him.

Hours later, he finally reached a main highway, and began the long, slow walk to freedom. Now he had to find his sisters.

* * *

Leilani had lost track of day and night. She spent most days locked in the cabin, moving with the rocking of the boat. The lights were on, and she had no way to turn them off. When men came through the door, she wished she could turn off the lights, but the lights stayed on. When they left after they had used her, she kept her eyes closed, praying for darkness to overcome her.

Chapter Two

Carmelina awoke in the softest bed she'd ever felt, covered by a silken sheet. For a second it felt heavenly, until she became aware of the pain in her head and between her thighs. She turned her head and saw the master beside her, huge belly rising and falling as he snored.

She almost screamed but stifled it before it escaped her throat. She needed silence to escape. She put her feet on the floor, trying hard not to make any move that would awaken the beast in the bed. She rose, found her discarded clothes on the floor and dressed quietly.

Looking around the room, she saw a dresser against the wall, with the master's wallet laying atop it. She removed a hundred dollar bill and four twenties from the billfold, leaving the rest. She was not a thief, but she needed money to get away. She had earned it.

Carmelina eased the bedroom door open, peeked into the hall and found it empty. The bedroom clock had said 7:45 am, and all the staff knew not to awaken the master this early. He often entertained the women who were brought to him in his bedroom, and she knew that the women arrived and departed through a rear staircase into the upper hall.

Carmelina had to find a way out. Hesitant to open any doors and raise the alarm, she noticed that several of them seemed less ornate than the master's bedroom entry. Trying the first of the plain doors, she found it opened into a storage closet. The second one was a linen closet. The third disappeared into a staircase heading down.

She entered and closed the handle quietly, then stopped to listen. The house was silent at this early hour, by order of the master. She tiptoed down the carpeted stairs, past a landing, then further to a door that latched from the inside. Carmelina prayed that it didn't lead to the kitchen or anywhere else she would be seen by the staff.

She was in luck. It opened onto a covered porch at the side of the huge house, shielded by hedges. The very spot that helped the master sneak his women into the house was helping her to escape from it. Now the question was where to go next.

She hid in the bushes, afraid to walk into the open. If she was spotted, she'd be returned to the house, punished and locked up again, with no hope of future escape. This was her only chance.

At 8:15, a pickup truck towing an open-topped trailer with enclosed sides drove on the pebbled driveway past her hiding space. Limbs trimmed from the hedge surrounding the outside wall of the Palm Beach estate filled it nearly to the top of the sidewalls. Two men got out of the pickup cab and spoke to each other in rapid Spanish.

"Jorge, you trim the side by the pool, I'll do this one. Remember, work quietly. When the trailer is full, we'll make a trip to the landfill, then take a lunch break, okay?"

"Si," was the only reply.

Carmelina watched as the man nearest her walked to the end of the row of shrubs, turned away from her hiding place, unzipped his trousers and urinated. She took advantage of the moment and raced to the trailer, climbed over the side and wormed her way under the brush inside. The slight clatter of the trimmer from the far side of the hedge was enough to cover the sound.

She lay under the scratchy limbs, blood welling from small scratches on her arms and face, and she prayed.

* * *

Things had been going smoothly with Callie and I since we'd returned from Key West. At least *I* thought so. We'd worked through her feelings of being smothered by my fears for her safety, and now, with her new job at the *Bradenton Journal*, I was prepared for a period of calm in our somewhat stormy relationship.

After my morning's exercise with Jimmy and a nice nap after lunch, I woke to find Callie at the salon table on the WanderLust, pounding furiously on the keys of her laptop.

"Working on something good?" I asked. It seemed like an innocuous remark.

"Yes. One of us has to get some work done for the *Journal*."

"Whoa, what's this all about?"

She pushed her laptop away. "It's been more than a month since we were offered a deal to write and research together by Dillon Haverhill, and nothing is happening, that's what."

"Callie, we can't just manufacture a story from thin air. The facts have to present themselves."

"Well, they won't present themselves to you while you're out riding bicycles with Jimmy."

"Let me remind you that Haverhill said there were no deadlines, no editors pushing us. That means we have the luxury to wait until the right story comes along, not try to force one that isn't worth the time it takes."

She glared at me. "Is that what you think, that I'm trying to *force* a story to happen? I just think there are enough serious problems in the state of Florida that I don't have to *force* myself to pick one."

"Calm down, Callie, this isn't worth fighting about."

"You think my job with the *Journal* is a joke, don't you? Well, I take it damn seriously, and it's about time you took it seriously too!" She stomped off the boat, setting it rocking in the slip as she skipped the boarding steps and jumped over the side onto the dock. *Good grief.*

As I watched her stomp down the dock, I heard Captain Rick coming from the other direction.

"Trouble in paradise, Will?"

"That's one way to put it. Can I offer you a beer?"

"Sure." He stepped aboard. "Looks like you could use one yourself."

I opened two Red Stripes and handed one to Rick. We went to the covered rear deck and sat down.

He said, "Callie sounds pretty riled up. What'd you do now?"

"That's just it, *nothing.*"

"Didn't sound like nothing."

"Callie is mad because we haven't started on a new story series since the *Bradenton Journal* hired us."

"Well, why haven't you?"

I sighed. "Because I haven't found the right story, and because Dillon Haverhill said we could take as long as we please. There's no rush to work on something that doesn't catch my interest."

He shook his head. "Will, you are a slow learner sometimes."

"What did I do?"

"You helped Callie find her purpose in life, and now you're keeping her from doing anything with it."

"Nothing is stopping her. She's been researching a couple of things, but none of them have grabbed my interest yet. I can't just make up something to write about."

He laughed. "She's got her race car revving at the starting line and you're back in the garage polishing the hood, dummy."

"Hey, that's not fair."

"If you want to hold on to her, you'd better find something constructive to do. She's not gonna wait around forever for you to get motivated."

Well, hell. There goes my vacation.

* * *

Carmelina had waited more than an hour lying under the branches in the trailer as more debris from the bushes was dumped on top of the pile. She held her breath every time as dust and clippings filtered down on her, trying to stifle a sneeze. Once she held her breath for more than a minute, holding her hand over her mouth to mute her sneeze until she finally heard the trimmer start up its clatter again.

The piles of leaves weighed down the branches on her body, and when the workers spread a tarp over them and winched it tight, she thought she might suffocate. When the truck began to move, she bounced off the trailer floor, but relaxed when she felt air flowing between the boards as they sped onto a highway.

After a half an hour on the road the truck drove into a parking lot far from Palm Beach. She heard the landscape workers open their doors and slam them behind them, then heard the phrase "Descanso del amuerzo." *Lunch break.* They walked into a restaurant.

This is my chance. She struggled free of the press of the branches, and reached up to the tarp itself, only to find it attached from the outside. Forcing her body through the tightly packed branches, she felt all around the edges until she came to a loose section where the eyelet had ripped free. Carmelina covered her eyes and pushed upward, ignoring the scratches, getting her back against the tarp, then pushing with all her strength until she felt the fabric rip.

Freedom! She climbed out of the trailer and made her way to the gas station next to the diner. She needed to wash her face and rinse the blood from her scratches before she asked anyone for help. The last thing she needed was a Good Samaritan calling the police.

Carmelina kept her head down as she walked into the mini mart, made her way to the restroom and locked the door behind her. She looked in the mirror, startled at the scratched and bloody face that looked back at her. It took her ten minutes, during which someone grew tired of waiting their turn and began pounding on the door, but at last she felt presentable.

She walked to the drink cooler, reached in and got a soft drink and walked to the register. The woman behind the counter looked Latina. Carmelina put one of the twenty-dollar bills on the counter to pay for her drink, and said "Iglesia?"

The clerk said, "What? Speak English."

She tried again. "Church? Close?"

"Ah, you need to find a church. Looks like you might be on the run, honey. I know just the place for you. Let me call em." She saw the confusion on Carmelina's face. She held her hand to her ear. "Telefono. For help."

Carmelina nearly collapsed with gratitude. "Si, Gracias."

* * *

Captain Rick left after one beer, I think because he didn't want to be there when Callie came back after our fight. Can't say I blame him. I spent the afternoon catching up on all the Florida news of the day on my laptop, and there was, as usual, plenty of it. Police shootings, new Disney projects, a small plane crash, wildfires, you name it. The most interesting was the usual weird-Florida news, a woman walking naked across I-95 to help a stranger retrieve a dog that had escaped his car.

No one had any idea why she was naked in her own car in the first place, but the video that a passerby captured made it go viral. Only in The Sunshine State. I was about to give up my research for the afternoon when Callie returned.

She stepped into the cabin, saw me at my laptop and said, "What'cha working on?"

"Just scanning the headlines, seeing if there's anything worth pursuing."

She sat at the table, leaned back in the chair and said, "Pastor Marlee called. She's got something she needs our help on. She wanted to tell us about it in person, so I invited her to dinner at the Riverhouse. We'll go eat after sunset drinks on the boat. I didn't think you'd mind."

I felt a reprieve coming. "Callie, you know how much I want our new working arrangement to succeed. Sorry I've gotten off to a slow start, but I felt a little fried after everything that happened with the sober homes, the opioid stuff and all that drama in Key West. I needed a break."

"Okay." She paused. "Had enough of a break, now?"

"Yes."

"Good. Let's see what Marlee's got for us."

Chapter Three

When Pastor Marlee arrived at the WanderLust, Callie had already set up a cheese and veggie plate on the rear deck. She hugged Marlee, and said, "It's good to see you again. How's Zoe?"

"Oh, wild as always."

I jumped into the conversation. "Hi, Marlee." I gave her a hug.

Callie said, "You should have brought Zoe with you!"

"I would have, but since we're going to dinner, I didn't want to leave her on your boat. It took me a while to dog-proof the motorhome, and I wouldn't want her chewing up anything on this beautiful boat."

I added, "You know we love Zoe. Next time we'll make dinner on the boat so you can bring her."

Callie said, "Chardonnay for you, Marlee? Or would you prefer a beer?"

"Wine is good. It's appropriate for a sunset, and for the story I have to tell you."

I said, "We're anxious to hear it. Why don't you and Callie grab a glass and go to the rear deck and I'll bring the wine."

Carrying the open bottle and my own glass, I joined them around the table and filled the three glasses.

Marlee lifted hers in a toast. "To sunset with wine and friends." Then she leaned back in her chair. "This afternoon I got a call from St. Mary's, where they have the immigrant's shelter? They have a young woman from Guatemala, just eighteen years old. Her name is Carmelina. She was smuggled across the border in a refrigerated meat truck with her brother and sister."

That caught my interest. "Three siblings together? I don't think that happens very often."

"No, but what happened to them is all too common. They paid a coyote to bring them to Florida, but the man on the US side delivered them here, then told them his fee was an additional ten thousand dollars."

I whistled. "Pretty steep. I'm assuming they didn't have it?"

"Of course not. They'd given him all the money their parents could scrape up, five thousand."

Callie said, "Well, what can he do about it? You can't get money they don't have."

Marlee shook her head. "That's the problem. He sold them."

I was stunned. "Sold them? You mean like slaves?"

"Exactly. He sold Pablo to a tomato grower, Carmelina to a rich man as a housekeeper, and their younger sister, Leilani, to a man who has something he calls a 'party boat'."

"That's outrageous. We should contact the authorities and get them released." I knew how naive that sounded even as I said it.

Marlee said, "First of all, we don't know where they are. Carmelina saw her brother being put handcuffed into an old truck with a big tomato painted on the door. We're assuming it's to a grower but have no idea which one. There are hundreds of them across this part of Florida. Carmelina only knows her younger sister was taken by a man called Cap'n Willy and that he said he ran a party boat."

She paused, then added, "The other problem is that they're illegal. If we contact the authorities, they'll call ICE, and Carmelina will be detained until she can be deported. She can't help find her brother and sister if she's locked up."

I shook my head. "Yeah, I don't know what I was thinking. Dumb."

Callie looked angry. "The problem is our screwed up immigration policies. The government is so busy locking up all the asylum seekers at the border and taking their kids away that sneaking across sounds like a better option. Who the hell do they think is going to fund Social Security in their old age if they shut down immigration! It's the only thing that keeps the population from declining with the low birthrate."

I looked at her. "I didn't know you were so passionate about the subject."

"Well, you do now. An editor and I have talked about it a lot while you've been off riding bicycles."

"What editor? Someone at the *Journal*?"

"His name is Alvaro Romero." She sniffed. "*He's* been very interested in my work."

"I thought this was *our* work."

Marlee looked worried. "Hey, you two, do I need to come back later? Let you talk this out?"

Callie looked embarrassed. "I'm sorry, that was my fault. I've been a little out of sorts lately."

A little? At least I was smart enough not to say it out loud. "Please stay, Marlee. We're fine. What can we do to help?"

"For starters, come talk to Carmelina. I think you'll find her story fascinating. She's a perfect example of what's wrong with current immigration policies. She's a hard-working young woman who only wanted freedom and a chance to make a living but fell into the hands of unscrupulous smugglers."

I said, "It's a lot like the drug war. Making drugs illegal makes the black market inevitable."

Marlee said, "Just like what happened in prohibition. We saw how that worked out."

Lifting my glass, I said, "I'll drink to that," then downed my wine. "Anyone ready for dinner?" I hoped dinner would go smoother than drinks had.

* * *

Pablo was exhausted. He'd been on the road for days, and with no money for food he'd only eaten what he'd scrounged from dumpsters behind restaurants, washing it down with water from garden hoses.

He'd been amazed at the bounty he'd found. The amount of food that Americans discarded shocked him, and while some of it was spoiled, many things seemed to have been tossed in the garbage untouched. *This is truly a rich land. Why are they so unwilling to share it?*

He'd grown up on the hard-scrabble farm in San Antonio des Nubes, and while they didn't have much, neither did they forget their neighbors. They helped each other as was needed. When the man in the farm across the ridge broke his leg, Pablo and his father had helped till and plant his field, along with other neighbors and family.

When that field grew, its corn was shared between both families. It was their way. Pablo was having a difficult time with the idea of discarding unspoiled food in the garbage. *Are there no pigs to feed in this country?* It would be better than wasting it as they did. The first food he came across was at something called a bakery, and he'd gorged on the piles of bread and sweets that were piled in one of the trash cans.

It was a meal he regretted. As hungry as he'd been, his stomach rebelled against the sweet, rich pastries. Some of them tasted so wonderful, but his belly disagreed and rejected them. Only the water he took from garden hoses got him through that painful night.

Pablo learned to be more judicious in the foods he chose, sniffing things he found in dumpsters first for freshness, then for sweetness. Unspoiled food was essential, but he found slightly old vegetables and fruits to be much more nutritious than the sweets and fried foods that Americans seemed to prefer.

No wonder so many of them are fat! Pablo had lost much weight under the working conditions at the tomato farm, but he had no wish to grow a large belly. Finding a place to sleep hadn't been much of a problem so far. The nights were so mild in this land of Florida that he only needed a place to lay his head.

The dumpsters usually held cardboard that he put between his body and the hard ground, and newspapers from the trash covered him against the morning dew. America was a land of plenty. He had but to find work, and he knew he could survive here. But first he must find his sisters.

* * *

Eduardo Alvarez was angry. "Where is that bitch?!" he howled.

The head housekeeper cowered. "Sir, I am sorry, but we've searched the house and she is not here."

"Don't you keep her locked up at night?!"

She dreaded the words she must say. "Sir, I offered to lock her in her room last night, and you told me to let her stay. You said you had a key, so I thought you would return her to her room when you were...finished with her."

His eyes were slits as he approached her. "Are you blaming me for her escape, Mrs. Ramirez?"

"No sir!" she stammered. "I, I just meant that it was, you know, why she was not locked in her room. Sir."

Alvarez had awakened in his sumptuous bed to find himself alone, and to discover money missing from his wallet. "*No one steals from me, is that clear?*"

"Yes, sir. Shall I call the police?"

"Don't be stupid. She has no papers. How do we explain that to the police? Call my head of security."

She said, "Yes, sir," and scrambled out of the room. She was relieved to have a reason to walk away from his anger. *I'm glad not to be Carmelina*. There would be pain when she was caught. Alvarez would make sure of it.

Eduardo threw on a robe and went down the stairs to his study where his attorney, Chadwick Carson, waited. He slammed the door to the study, sat behind his desk and took a sip of the coffee that sat on a tray on his desk. His arrival had been anticipated.

"What the hell do you want this early, Carson?"

"Mr. Alvarez, I have the papers from the Goodland acquisition for you to sign. We discussed it yesterday, remember?"

"Right. Put them on my desk, and I'll sign them after I've had my coffee."

He hesitated. "Sir, I heard shouting earlier. Is everything all right with the household?"

Alvarez glared at him. "No, everything is NOT, you imbecile. One of my maids has run off, and she took money out of my wallet on the way out the door."

"Um, not to be indelicate, sir, but how did she gain access to your wallet? I know you keep close track of it." It was an understatement. Alvarez was tight as a tick, and always knew where *all* of his money was at any given time, including the exact amount of cash in his wallet.

Alvarez reply was subdued. "She spent the night in my bed."

Carson couldn't keep the surprise off his face. "But, Mr. Alvarez, we discussed avoiding, uh, complications with ladies during the Jupiter investigations."

Alvarez looked smug. "No, you said not to *bring* any ladies here while the cops were looking into the sex trafficking sting. I didn't bring anyone. She works here."

Carson hated to say it, but it was his duty to protect his client. "Sir, is she legal?"

"She said she was almost eighteen. No problem."

Oh shit. "Um, Mr. Alvarez, the legal age of consent in Florida is eighteen, not seventeen."

"That's ridiculous."

"No sir, it's the law."

"Well, damn!"

The lawyer stood and looked down at his shoes but stayed silent.

"Come on, Carson, spit it out. What's got that stick up your butt?"

He stood straighter. "When I asked if she was legal, sir, I meant is she a citizen or does she have a green card." He knew Alvarez liked to hire the cheaper illegals.

The smug look was gone. "No. She doesn't."

This just keeps getting worse. "You'd better hope she keeps her mouth shut when they catch her."

Chapter Four

The atmosphere was a little strained aboard the *WanderLust* the next morning as we prepared to make the trip to St. Mary's to interview Carmelina. Callie had been defensive when Pastor Marlee left after dinner. She felt her degree of involvement in writing the story of the three sibling immigrants was in question. I decided to make a peace offering.

"Listen, Callie, it sounds like this young girl, Carmelina, has been treated pretty badly by men. Maybe she'd be more comfortable if you took the lead on questioning her." I couldn't help but notice the sparkle my suggestion brought to Callie's eyes.

"Do you think so? I guess I might be less threatening to her. Plus, I'm closer to her age."

Ouch. "That works for me."

"I mean, it's fine if you want to jump in with any questions."

"Sure thing." My ego is pretty secure, and I don't need new bylines all the time to boost it. If taking the lead on this story helped Callie build her self-confidence, then I was prepared to take a back seat.

That didn't mean I was going to step away from the project. I have a lot more experience than Callie in digging out the stories, and I haven't really seen anything she's written. She'd have to walk before she could run.

We arrived at the shelter, and Pastor Marlee was there to meet us.

"I'm so glad you're both here. Carmelina is anxious to tell her story, but she's scared, too."

I gave her my best smile. "Tell her we don't bite."

"It's not that simple. She's worried about her brother and sister, and afraid that publicity might give ICE a reason to come after her. Would it be possible to leave out any mention of St. Mary's and the shelter? If they don't know where she is, they can't try to arrest her."

"I don't see why not. We can just say we were introduced to her, without saying where or by whom."

Callie jumped in. "Won't the publicity help the shelter, though?"

Marlee said, "Not really. It's supported by private donations, mostly from within the parish. Plus, there are some in the community who don't like the idea of giving sanctuary to illegal immigrants. They think we should turn all of them over to ICE to be deported. Keeping a low profile can be a good thing."

Callie looked crestfallen. "Guess I still have a lot to learn."

Marlee tried to soothe her feelings. "Hey, this is how you pick up new skills, by doing it. On the job training is the best kind."

"I second that," I said. "When I got out of journalism school, I thought I knew everything about the newspaper business. It took me about three days to realize I didn't know squat. It was a steep learning curve, but the experience came fast. The hours were long and the pay was crappy, but I knew how to track down a story and write it on deadline by the end of the first year."

Callie grinned. "Oh, well, at least I can't complain about the pay."

Dillon Haverhill was paying us well to write anything we thought was worth our time. It was an enviable position to be in.

Marlee said, "Ready to get started? Carmelina is waiting in the library."

"Lead the way."

* * *

Listening to the session with the young immigrant was painful. She began with her story of leaving her parents in the mountains of Guatemala, not knowing if she'd ever see them again. Then there was the long march on foot to the US border, to what she saw as the land of opportunity. The long, frigid ride in the meat truck as it crossed the border should have been the end of her fear, but it was only the beginning.

After emerging, shivering from a box in the back of the truck, Carmelina had been reunited with her brother, Pablo, and sister, Leilani, then hustled into the back of a van for the long drive from Texas to southern Florida and their expected freedom. Instead, on arrival they were told by the smugglers that they owed another ten thousand dollars.

Carmelina said, "My brother, he tried to fight them, but they pointed a gun at him and took him away. I could see out the window when they put him in a pickup truck with a big tomato on the door. If I could find that truck, I know I'll find Pablo."

Callie said, "We can search for it, that will be a good start."

I hated to see her get Carmelina's hopes up. "It might be a needle in a haystack kind of deal, finding that old truck."

Carmelina said, "Needle in haystack?"

"Sorry," I explained. "It's an American saying. It means looking for something small in a very crowded place."

Callie jumped back in. "Don't worry, the internet makes it a lot easier to do that kind of search these days. We'll find it." She gave me a dirty look as she said it.

Pastor Marlee said, "Tell them what happened next, Carmelina."

She looked sad. "They took my little sister, Leilani. The way that wicked man looked at her, I knew what he wanted. I hit him and scratched his face, and that made him very angry."

"Do you have any idea where she was taken?" I asked.

She shook her head. "Only that the man I scratched was named Captain Willy and that he had something called a party boat. I'm scared for Leilani. She is beautiful, but innocent. I know what men like that want. They'll hurt her."

Callie tried to be encouraging. "At least with a partial name and having an idea of what kind of boat he's running we can search the docks. Surely there aren't that many Captain Willys who run party boats around."

Marlee caught me rolling my eyes at the statement. She said, "Carmelina, tell them the rest about your own experience."

"After I scratched the man, the bearded one said they would sell me to a 'cheap bastard.' I was taken to a beautiful home, but the woman who worked there, she locked me in a small room for two days. They brought me food, and only let me out three times a day to use the toilet. On the third day, she came and gave me a maid's uniform, and told me I was to clean."

She sighed. "The house, it was very big, and filled with fancy furniture and statues to dust, thick carpets to vacuum. I'd never seen a vacuum cleaner before, and when she switched it on the noise frightened me. I dropped it, and it fell onto a table and broke an expensive vase. The master saw it and he beat me. Then she locked me back in the room.

"I was locked in until the next day without food. When the woman returned, she said I only had one more chance before I would be sold onto the streets."

Callie was open-mouthed. "That's outrageous! They can't do that. You're a human being!"

I put a hand on Callie's knee to slow her down, but she shook it off.

"Will, back off. I've got this." She turned to Carmelina. "Tell what happened after that."

"I did my best to stay out of trouble. I was very careful not to break anything, and I worked very hard. Fourteen hours every day, then I was allowed to eat with the other servants in the staff kitchen before they locked me back in my bedroom.

"There was never a chance to escape. I was afraid if I tried, they would sell me again. At least I had food and shelter. Then came the night the master took me to his bedroom. He gave me alcohol and then he used my body. I was frightened and ashamed. No man had ever touched me before." A tear ran down her cheek as she stared at the floor.

Pastor Marlee said, "Don't blame yourself for that, Carmelina. You were held as a prisoner by evil people. You are not responsible for anything they did to you. Do you understand?"

She sniffled. "Yes, but it made me feel dirty. When the church gave me shelter here, the first thing I asked for was a bath and some clean clothes." She grimaced. "They will never make me wear the maid's uniform again. I will kill the master before that happens!"

Callie was silent, so I spoke up. "Did you hear anyone say the master's name?"

She looked grim. "Yes. Mr. Alvarez. Eduardo Alvarez."

Her statement shocked me. "Eduardo Alvarez? The head of United Cane Inc.?"

Carmelina nodded. "That is his name, but I don't know of this United Cane."

I grabbed my phone from my pocket, googled his name, and pulled up an image from the UCI web site. I showed it to her. "Is this the man who kept you locked up?"

Her lip curled in disgust. "Yes. That is the filthy pig who raped me."

Holy crap.

* * *

Callie and I sat with Pastor Marlee in the staff lounge after we were finished hearing Carmelina's harrowing tale.

I was angry, and it showed. "We need to nail that bastard, Alvarez!" I fumed.

Callie shook her head. "The first thing we need to do is find Leilani and Pablo. Carmelina is safe here, but who knows what might still happen to her sister and brother."

"You don't know that she's truly safe. Alvarez has lots of connections and deep pockets. He may have the authorities looking for her already," I said.

"You just want to go after him because he's a sugar company exec. I still think looking for her siblings is the first priority."

"Fine. Then I'll go after Alvarez and you can search those haystacks for Pablo and Leilani."

Callie stuck her nose in the air. "I'm sure Alvaro, my editor friend, will be glad to help me."

Marlee looked dismayed. "What is going *on* with you two? You're not going to help any of those three kids if you spend all your time fighting!"

Callie blushed bright red and I could feel the heat on my own face. I said, "Sorry, we've both been a little tense with each other lately."

Marlee said, "A *little*? Looks more like World War III to me."

Sighing, I turned and said, "Callie, it's not just a vendetta against sugar companies, okay? It's true that I don't like the way they operate, but my concern here is about taking out a rapist who is imprisoning young girls. Who knows how many others he has locked up?"

She wasn't about to surrender the point. "I'll bet if you got Alvarez's house raided *today* you wouldn't find a single underaged girl or any illegals. His lawyers will have made sure of that."

"Let's go back to the *WanderLust* and you can start looking online for leads to where Pablo and Leilani may have been taken. I'll make some phone calls and see whether there's any chance of a raid on Eduardo Alvarez based on Carmelina's testimony."

Pastor Marlee spoke up. "Don't forget, Will, she's illegal. The first thing the police would do is take her into custody. That won't help anyone."

I ran my hand through my hair. I wasn't tracking well. "Okay, I'll see what I can do to keep her out of it."

We got up to leave, and Callie said, "Drop me off at the *Bradenton Journal*. They have a faster internet connection than you do on the boat. It will speed up my research. I'll get an Uber to bring me home."

Marlee's sad look as we walked out mirrored my own.

Chapter Five

I dropped Callie off at the newspaper as requested after a silent drive over from St. Mary's. As she got out she said, "Don't wait up," and slammed the door.

Things were as tense between us as they'd ever been, and I wasn't sure why. I knew she'd been upset that I was reluctant to jump into working on another story, but now we were doing exactly that. She'd acted upset at her inference that I somehow respected her journalistic efforts less than my own, and I'd bent over backwards to let her take the lead with Carmelina.

All it got me was the silent treatment and a slam of the door.

I cared for Callie deeply, but I wouldn't put up with this forever. On arriving at the WanderLust, I opened the rear cabin doors to air the boat out, popped the cap off a Red Stripe and climbed to the upper deck to stare at the stars and contemplate life.

It was ironic. The first thing that came between us was my concern for her safety. She felt suffocated by my protectiveness, never mind that she'd nearly lost her life twice in the course of the Florida Shuffle investigation. What was I supposed to do? Stand back and let her die so she wouldn't feel overprotected?

All I wanted in a relationship was a partner, someone who wanted to be with me every day. It seemed to me that keeping her alive was a reasonable concern.

My woes must have been sending signals into the darkness, as I soon heard Captain Rick coming up the dock.

"Yo, Will, you up there?"

"Yes, come on up, Rick. Grab a beer on the way if you want one."

"Don't mind if I do."

The boat rocked as he stepped aboard, and I heard the cabin door open and then slide shut as he headed for the fridge. A moment later he climbed up to the flybridge.

"Beautiful night, Will. Why are you up here by yourself? Callie not speaking to you?"

"That's pretty much it. We had an argument after meeting with a young Guatemalan refugee, and Callie told me to drop her off at the newspaper on the way home. She said not to wait up."

"Damn, Will, sounds like you're about to run another one off."

"It feels that way. We seemed to be so close at first, but that stupid job at the rehab center changed everything. She was tense and jumpy all the time. When it sounded like it was getting dangerous, what else could I do but ask her to quit?"

Rick stared off into the night. "You know, Will, I'm probably not the best one to be giving advice about women. I sure don't claim to understand 'em. Guess that's why I'm single now."

I said, "It feels like the harder I try to fix things the worse they get."

He chuckled. "That sounds about right. Maybe you should try just living your own life and let Callie figure hers out for herself."

I thought about it for a minute. Truth is, I was pretty happy with how my own life was turning out. Relationships with women were another matter. Most of my friends were other guys. That gave me a thought.

"Hey, Rick, maybe I should talk to Pastor Marlee. I'll bet she does couples counseling."

"Might not be a bad idea. Don't count on her to fix everything, though. Maybe she can help you get things straight in your own head, not Callie's."

I clinked bottles with him and took a drink. "Worth a shot."

* * *

Pablo was dreaming of the green mountainsides of his parent's farm at San Antonio of the Clouds. In the dream he was resting on a steep pasture, staring at the clouds as he watched over the sheep. When a boot crashed into his side, he was shocked into wakefulness.

His eyes flew open and he saw that boot coming for his face. He threw his arms up, grabbed the foot and twisted. The man attached to the boot howled in pain and fell to the ground.

"You little bastard, I think you broke my ankle! Teach him a lesson, Jimbo."

Pablo scrambled to his feet, facing off against a large man who circled him, sizing him up.

The man named Jimbo said, "Looks like I'm gonna have to teach you not to mess with 'Amuricans', you dirty spic." He lunged, and Pablo leapt nimbly aside, pushing the big man to the ground as he rushed by. Jimbo got up, breathing heavily, and pulled a knife from his belt.

Pablo waited until the man made a move towards him and sidestepped again, kicking the man's wrist as he took a wild swipe at him with the knife. The knife flew to the ground, and the man went to his knees, holding his wrist.

"Damn you! I'm gonna kill you next time I catch you around here."

It wasn't much of threat with the two men incapacitated by their injuries, but Pablo decided he should leave before the police showed up. He picked up the knife from the ground, and the man on his knees flinched when he stepped towards him.

"Hey, I didn't mean nothing by it. We were just horsing around."

Pablo told him, "Lay on the ground."

"Man, there ain't no cause to do this. We didn't hurt you."

The pain in Pablo's bruised side told a different story. "The only reason you didn't kill me is because you are clumsy and stupid. Now, lay down."

Slowly the man lay down, cradling his damaged wrist.

Pablo gathered his meager belongings, and then spoke to the two men. "If I see you again, I will use your knife on you." Then he resumed his trek up the highway, sleep forgotten for the rest of the night.

* * *

Late that night I felt the movement of the WanderLust when Callie returned. I heard her move quietly through the main salon, her steps down to the master cabin, then the rustle of clothes as she undressed. I was facing the wall with my back to her, and when she slipped under the covers I expected the same from her. She surprised me by gently putting an arm across me and snuggling against me, skin on skin.

"Are you awake?"

"Sort of. What time is it?"

"One-thirty."

"Late night."

"Yeah, we got a lot done."

We? I didn't have the energy for questions. We could talk in the morning.

"Will? I love you."

I mumbled, "Love you too," then drifted off to a troubled sleep. My last conscious thought was, *Did either of us mean it?*

The next morning I was up before Callie, having gotten at least a little more sleep. I was sitting on the rear deck, sipping coffee. My iPad was closed and sat on the table. I'd pretty much read all of the news of the day I could stomach.

When I'd been up an hour, I felt the boat rock as Callie stumbled from the bed to the marine head. I heard the flush, water running in the sink, then the sound of the spoon clinking in the mug as she fixed her coffee. There was a moment's pause, and I wondered if she was going to join me.

I wasn't sure whether I was relieved or unsettled when she sat down next to me at the small table.

"Good morning."

"Good morning. Catch up on your sleep?"

"Yeah. Sorry I got in so late."

"Well, you said not to wait up, so I didn't."

"Right."

The silence was not a comfortable one. Five minutes went by with the only sounds coming from passing boats on the water, and our coffee mugs being set down after a sip.

Finally, she spoke. "Do you want to talk?"

I took a deep breath. "Only if you have something to say."

When I looked at her, I thought she looked as down as I felt.

"I guess not."

"I'm going to see if Pastor Marlee has time to talk with me today."

That seemed to perk her up. "Oh? Would you like me to go with you?"

I shook my head. "I think I'd like to talk to her alone. Don't worry, it's not about the story we're working on."

"I wasn't assuming anything."

"Okay." I stood up. "Guess I'd better get cleaned up and head out."

Callie sighed, sipped from her mug, and said, "Okay. Can we maybe talk when you get home?"

"Sure." I kissed the top of her head and walked back into the WanderLust. This day wasn't starting off well. Once inside, I called Marlee.

"Hey, Will, what's up?"

"I wondered if I could come by and talk to you sometime today?"

"Sure thing. Is this about Carmelina?"

"No." I didn't want to say it was about Callie with her close by.

Marlee caught on quick. "Is it about you and Callie?"

"Yes."

"Ah, I thought so after last night. Want to come by the motorhome about eleven? Zoe will be glad to see you."

"That's great, thanks."

"See you then."

Maybe she'd have some answers for me. At the moment, I was fresh out of them.

* * *

Right at eleven I knocked on her door. When she opened it, I stepped inside to a whirlwind of gray and black-furred Shih Tzu.

"Zoe! Did you miss me?" She scrambled in circles around my ankles, and when I reached down to pet her, she rolled onto her back, paws stretched wide and presented her pink belly for rubbing as her tongue dangled from her mouth.

I laughed, and Marlee said, "Zoe, you are shameless!"

While I was rubbing her belly briskly, Zoe was in heaven, but as soon as I stopped she scrambled up on her feet to jump on me some more. I headed for an upholstered recliner, and as soon as I sat down I was besieged with kisses from the little fur ball.

I held her at arms length. "Enough!" I put her in my lap and scratched her behind the ears, which seemed to calm her down a bit.

Marlee said, "Sorry. You'd think she'd never seen another person before."

"That's okay, it's nice to be loved unconditionally."

She put her hands in her lap. "Sounds like you've been missing that feeling."

"It shows, huh?"

"Oh, yes. So, what's going on with you two?"

"I wish I knew. It seems to come down to her feeling overprotected. I've been doing my damnedest not to act that way, but it's like she doesn't want to get over it."

"Have you tried talking to her about it?"

"Some, but it always seems to turn into a fight. She didn't come home until one-thirty last night, then she wanted to talk this morning. Frankly, I wasn't up to it, in part because I knew it wouldn't end well."

"Oh dear. That doesn't sound good at all."

"Have you ever been married, Marlee?"

She laughed. "Only for twenty-four years!"

"Oh, wow, I didn't know."

"I figured that's why you asked. My husband, Ben and I got married when I was eighteen and he was thirty-six. At sixty he hit his head on a sailboat boom mid-ocean, fell in the water and drowned."

"So sorry to hear that."

"It's been a long time ago now. As he always said, 'It's all part of the legend.' He led an exciting life."

"It sure sounds like it. Must have been a lot of fun for you."

"Yes and no. I was really young, and I felt intimidated by all of the wonderful adventures he had. Some of the travel we did together, but he was also gone a lot. When he died, I realized I hadn't built a life for myself."

"What did you do?"

She grinned at me, "I finished college, and then I went to seminary. I was forty when I graduated and was ordained."

"That's wonderful."

David Crosby

"Yes, it has been. Bottom line was, I built my *own* life."

Chapter Six

Leilani sat in the locked cabin and made a decision. She'd struggled against her captors, resisted every time she was assaulted, and it had gotten her nowhere. It was time for a new approach.

She washed her face, brushed her hair, and was ready when her breakfast of toast, oatmeal and coffee was delivered. The guard warily opened the door, saw her sitting quietly on the edge of the bed and moved to restrain her.

"Señor, you don't have to hold me down."

He nodded to the cook, who took the tray and set it on the small dresser.

"Last time I brought food in here you threw it at me."

"I am sorry. I have been frightened at being locked up. I will be good now."

The cook backed out the door, unwilling to take his eyes off her until he was safely outside.

The guard said, "If you start cooperating a little, it will go easier on you."

"Yes, sir, I will try to do better."

He left, and she heard the lock click. It would be difficult, because she hated these men and the things they did to her, but she would charm them. They had to believe she had been tamed. It was the only way she would get a chance at freedom.

* * *

After meeting with Pastor Marlee I was feeling restless, and not ready to face a talk with Callie. It was lunchtime, and I decided to treat myself to a lunch on the waterfront. I put the top down on the Z4 and took a leisurely drive towards Cortez and the Star Fish Co. It's not fancy, with picnic tables and paper plates, but you can't beat the fried clams and hush puppies.

It was a little past the lunch rush, so I didn't have to wait too long. I sat at a table with a cold Corona, powered up my Kindle, and enjoyed my lunch in the sunshine as I read Wayne Stinnett's latest Jesse McDermitt Caribbean adventure. It's always fun to escape into someone else's life rather than live your own.

After a second beer, I finished eating, closed the eReader, and bussed my table. It was time to go back to the *WanderLust* and face the music.

I parked the BMW in my shaded spot at the marina, locked it up, and walked down the dock. There's something wrong when you dread going home to a beautiful boat on the water. My problem is that I don't like confrontations. I'm an easygoing guy, and I try to treat others the way I want to be treated. It makes it hard to understand when things get crossed up in a relationship, but this wasn't the first time it had happened to me.

When I boarded the *WanderLust*, I found Callie with her laptop open on the salon table, notes strewn across the wooden surface as she talked on her cell phone. She held up a finger to indicate she'd just be a minute.

"Right. That sounds good. Let me know when you have it. Bye." She put down the phone. "Hey, how did it go with Pastor Marlee?"

"Oh, good. I got lots of licks from Zoe."

She smiled. "She is the happiest little dog."

"Yep." I didn't know where to start this conversation.

"Did she have any suggestions? About us?" she asked.

"Indirectly. Did you know Marlee had been married?"

"Yes, to Ben. Sad about the way he died."

"I guess she's talked to you a lot more than me."

"We've shared our stories."

I paused. "Rick stopped by for a beer last night."

"I haven't seen him much lately. How's he doing?"

"Good, he asked about you."

"What did you tell him?"

"The truth. That we weren't doing so great."

"Oh."

"Yeah. He said I should live my own life and quit worrying about yours. Marlee said the same thing in a round-about way. She told me about her husband dying, and that she'd been so wrapped up in his life and adventures that she hadn't made a life for herself. After he was gone, she became a pastor."

She looked a little sad. "So, what are you saying?"

I took her hand. "Look, Callie, I'm not ready to give up on us. Can we call a truce? I'll try not to worry so much, and I'll do my best not to crowd you. All I ask is that when we *are* together, let's not fight. I miss that look in your eyes, the one that made me feel like I was special to you. Now I kind of feel like an annoyance."

"Oh, Will, I'm sorry, I haven't meant to make you feel that way. I've just been so excited about finding a new career, I want to run with it. I'm not running away from you."

She put her arms around me. "I've always been an independent person, and living on your boat sometimes makes me feel like I don't have my own space. I mean, I love it here, and I love sharing this all with you, but it's *yours*, not mine."

Now I was confused. "Do you want to be a joint owner of the *WanderLust*?"

"No, you dolt. Sometimes when a couple gets married and they each have their own places, they buy a new place so it's theirs together. Understand?"

Married! "Not at all."

She sighed. "Let's just drop it."

"Can we still declare a truce?"

Her lips touched mine. "I *do* love you, Will Harper."

I wasn't sure who she was trying to convince. Me, or herself.

* * *

Eduardo Alvarez sat in his study, drinking coffee. His butler entered the room.

"Sir, Mr. Carson is here to see you."

Damned attorneys. They buzz around me like gnats. "Send him in."

A moment later, Carson entered and closed the door behind him. "Good morning, Mr. Alvarez, you're looking well."

"Cut the crap. Have you found that girl?"

He looked startled. "Uh, not yet, sir. I've checked discreetly with a contact in the police department, but they haven't run across her. She's likely hiding out with relatives. Either that, or in one of the shelters for illegal immigrants. "

"Well, hell, can't you find out? What do you think I'm paying you for?"

"Um, we don't know who her relatives are, and the shelters protect their identity. They aren't going to tell us if she's there. They don't even cooperate with the police or ICE."

"Be creative. Hire someone with the right looks and age to claim they're illegal, and get them inside the shelters. Do I have to do all the thinking around here?"

"Sir, sending someone in under false pretenses could look really bad if it came out that you were involved. It would be better if you could just forget about this girl. She'll probably be too scared to go to the authorities about being forced to work in your home as a prisoner."

"I told you, *nobody* steals from me. I want her *found*, and I want her sent *back* where she came from." He grinned without mirth. "With a few extra scars as my gift to her." He stood and said, "Now get out of here, and don't come back until you've found her."

* * *

Pablo knew he was close. He'd memorized the name on the roof and tried to pay attention to the road signs and landmarks as he was driven away in the tomato picker's old truck. Even on foot, he'd spotted several of those landmarks. The church with columns and the big white steeple, the pawn shop with the big guitar on the sign, the tire store with the large inflatable gorilla in the parking lot.

This was a strange land, but these things were guiding him to his destination. After two more days of walking, Pablo had found his way to the truck depot where he, Carmelina, and Leilani had first arrived in South Florida.

He found a spot in the brush alongside the chain-link fence and settled in to wait. He would know the man who sold them when he saw him again. It was a face he could not forget.

* * *

I'd taken a walk on the docks to clear my head, and when I got back to the *WanderLust,* Callie was still hard at work, her notes spread out on the salon table. She looked up as I walked in.

"Will, I'm glad you're here. Alvaro just emailed me a list of the tomato pickers in the region who have a history of using illegals as labor. Seems like every company gets complaints against them, but I thought we'd start with the ones who are repeat offenders with a long list of violations. Sounds like the pickers keep the local ICE office busy."

"What would you like me to do?"

"I'm going to search for an online presence for the companies, see if any of them have a logo with a big red tomato on it. Would you be willing to drive around some of the packing houses, and see if you spot anything like that?"

Groan. "Would you mind if I got Jimmy Wilkins to do that? He's been looking to pick up some extra cash, and we do have a budget to pay others to do some of the leg work. I had plans to do some background research on human trafficking in Florida."

"Can't you do that online?"

"Yes, but Hanna McBride at the ACLU knows an immigration activist group that works out of West Palm, and she offered to set up a meeting with them for me." I had briefly dated Hanna before I met Callie, but things hadn't worked out.

"And how is Hanna these days?"

Uh oh. "She seems to be doing well. I haven't seen her lately."

"Then how do you know she's fine?"

"We talk on the phone every now and then."

"How nice of you."

I was getting irritated. "Look, Callie, Hanna is a friend, okay? I told you when we met that I have friends all over the place, and some of them are women. The fact that you and I are together doesn't mean I have no interactions with women in my work."

"That's fine with me. Go have your *interactions*, and I'll call Jimmy to help me with the tomato pickers." She paused. "Wait, isn't he dating Hanna?"

"No, that didn't last very long. She was looking to settle down and start a family, and Jimmy isn't ready for that."

"Good, then he'll be available. To help with the pickers, I mean. You can go have fun with Hanna."

"Callie..."

"Tell her I said hello." She turned towards the papers on the table and seemed to be engrossed in them again.

I'd been dismissed.

There didn't seem to be much point in hanging around the boat, so I headed for the Z4. Driving is always a good distraction for me, and I decided to go to the ACLU office and see if Hanna was in. She really had offered to set up a meeting with the activist group for me, and I thought it might be nice to see a friendly face.

She and I had managed to remain friends after we stopped dating, and it truly was just friendship. This human trafficking story seemed to be a big topic, and I wanted to find more individual stories to humanize the series. The three siblings were our starting point, but so far, Carmelina was the only one we could talk to. There was no way to know if we'd ever find Pablo, much less Leilani.

It sounded like the youngest sister had been taken and put to work on a party boat by someone named "Captain Willy." Searching tomato farms for Pablo might end up being a waste of time, but the odds were better than those of finding Leilani.

We'd only need to find one boat in all of Florida.

Chapter Seven

Hanna wasn't in her office, but I got her on her cell phone and arranged a meeting for the afternoon. Still restless, I decided to take a drive over to Jimmy's houseboat dock to see if he'd like to get in on the research for the human trafficking story. It was late afternoon, and I found him puttering around the boat doing maintenance projects. He saw me walking from the driveway.

"Hey, Will, come aboard."

I stepped onto the deck and felt the waves from a passing fisherman create a rhythmic roll under my feet. "What are you working on?"

"Replacing the lines on the stanchions. The cable railing is original on this boat, and I was getting tired of catching my fingers on the places where the old cable was unraveling. Those little steel points are like needles."

He was wearing heavy leather gloves for the work of pulling the old cable out, and I could see why. He already had a pile of it on the dock. "Looks like a nasty job," I said.

"Yeah, but keeping this old boat in good shape makes my rent low. No complaints from me."

Captain Rick had found Jimmy a deal as caretaker for a waterfront property on the Manatee River, and part of the package was being able to live on the houseboat parked out back in exchange for keeping it in good running order. An unused boat goes downhill fast.

"What brings you out this way, Will? Too late in the day to take the kayaks out."

"I have a little research project I'd like your help on. You remember me telling you about Carmelina, the Guatemalan girl who was imprisoned by a sugar baron?"

"Yeah, pretty outrageous. You making any progress on nailing that guy?"

"Not yet, but in the meantime, we're trying to locate her brother, Pablo. He was sold to a tomato picker, and our only real clue has been Carmelina's description of an old pickup truck with a logo on the side showing a big, red tomato."

"How can I help?"

"Callie has put together a list of tomato growers and pickers who've had run-ins with ICE over immigrant labor, and we need to have them checked out in person, partly to see if you can spot that truck with the logo."

"Sounds right up my alley. I'm glad to help."

"It does help, but it's also a real job. We have a budget for research assistance. It even pays mileage."

"Damn, Will, that's awesome. I can sure use the extra cash."

"Hey, you've helped me out plenty of times. I'm happy this one comes with a paycheck."

"That makes two of us. Let me finish pulling this old cable out and I'll join you for a beer. I'm almost done."

"Anything I can help with?"

"Nah, I've only got one pair of gloves, and this stuff has sharp edges. Help yourself to a beer, and I'll be right in."

I took him up on his offer and checked out the fridge. He had Corona's and Yuengling, but no Red Stripes. I went for the Yuengling. After popping the cap, I found a Koozie in the drawer and made myself at home on the bow seating. After about ten minutes, Jimmy joined me, wiping his face with a towel and carrying a Corona.

He clinked bottles with me, "To paying projects."

"I'll drink to that." We both took a sip.

He said, "Sorry I don't keep any Red Stripes for you. It may be the local cheap beer in Jamaica, but it's pricey at Publix."

"No worries, this Yuengling is actually pretty good."

We drank in silence for a moment, then he said, "How are things with Callie?"

"She's fine. I guess we are too. It's been a little tense lately, but it's starting to smooth out. I have hope."

"Callie has been good for you, Will. I hope it all works out too."

"So do I. It seems like there's been a revolving door of women in and out of my life. They're the ones who decide when it's over. That gets old."

"You thinking about settling down, making things permanent?"

"We're not there yet. I found out the hard way with my ex that marriage only makes things worse if you're not in sync with each other. I'm not sure Callie wants the same things I do."

"How so?"

I took a long pull on my beer as I gathered my thoughts. "She's got a lot of ambition, and I don't. I kind of feel like the years in the newspaper business scratched my itch for having my name in print. Now I really want to spend more time relaxing on the boat and cruising. The stories I keep getting dragged into make me feel good, but it's not something I *need* to do.

"Callie is more driven. Apparently, not needing to have an income just made her feel like she wasn't paying her own way. Hell, neither am I! My Aunt Dotty's generosity in her will is the only reason I can live on the *WanderLust* and not in a crappy apartment in Atlanta."

He laughed. "You've got a point there. Maybe it's because she's younger than you, and she still feels like she needs to prove herself in the world."

"Hey, I'm not *that* much older than she is."

Jimmy shook his head. "No, but you had a career, and you got tired of it. She hasn't made her mark yet."

"I didn't get tired of the work, just sick of the people in charge. It's the same thing that keeps pulling me into doing stories around Florida. I see injustice, and I want to call out the bad guys publicly. Getting the credit for it isn't a big deal to me."

"And therein lies the problem. The spotlight has never been on Callie. She wants her moment in the sun."

Now I was feeling glum. "Maybe you're right. We're not in the same stages in our lives." It was something to think about.

* * *

Things were quiet when I got back to the *WanderLust*. Callie was deep into her computer research, and we said a perfunctory hello and goodnight to each other before the day ended.

I'd been reading the latest *Breeze* book from Ed Robinson, and when my eyes got gritty, I decided to turn in. It was late, and I said, "Callie, I'm heading to bed. Are you coming?"

She said, "Yes, as soon as I finish this. I'll be just a few minutes."

When I crawled in the bed with my Kindle, the other side was empty.

I woke just before dawn, eReader still on my chest. Callie was snoring softly next to me, but I didn't remember her coming to bed. I got up, shuffled to the galley, and put the coffee on. I read the day's headlines while the pot brewed, then poured a cup and headed to the rear deck to watch the sun rise over the water.

The sky was filled with streaks of pink and yellow, the sun lighting the clouds from below, but the promise of the day felt empty to me. I thought of the many hours Callie and I had shared at this table, sunrises and sunsets, talking of hopes and dreams, hands touching.

She was still on the boat, snug in my bed, but it felt like she was gone.

* * *

Callie woke at 8:30, and I swear it all seemed to have returned to normal. She walked up behind me and put her arms around my neck.

"Good morning, lover." She kissed the top of my head.

"You're in a good mood today."

"Let me get a cup of coffee and I'll be in an even better one."

She walked into the galley to fill her cup, and was back in a moment, taking the chair next to mine. She took a sip, holding the mug in two hands, scrunched her shoulders together and said, "Ahh, perfect."

I wasn't sure where this bubbly version of her was coming from, but I liked it.

"Sounds like you slept well," I said.

"Oh, I did. Sorry I came to bed so late. I got caught up in reading about the way immigrants are treated in the tomato picking operations. It seemed like one link led to another, then another, and next thing I knew I woke up with my head on the laptop and it was 2 a.m."

"I'm surprised you're up this early after getting to bed late."

She yawned, covering her mouth at the end. "Have to be. I told Alvaro I'd meet him at ten at the *Journal*. He thinks he might have a few leads for me."

And just like that, my hopeful mood vanished.

"You're spending a lot of time with him lately."

She bristled. "Of course I am! He's helping me with the trafficking story."

"I'm not complaining, but I was hoping we could spend some time together this afternoon, maybe take the boat out?"

"This might not be a good day for it. Speaking of boats, have you made any progress towards finding the boat captain who took Leilani?"

"Not yet, but I'm meeting Hanna at the ACLU office later this morning. She's arranged for the head of the pro-immigrant activist group I told you about yesterday to be there. They apparently have some ideas of how to track the party boat."

"That sounds promising. I'm going to see Carmelina this afternoon to give her an update on our progress. Want to come?"

"I'd better pass." In truth, I was disappointed at Callie's lack of interest in an afternoon out on the water with me. *At least she won't be spending the whole afternoon with this guy, "Alvaro."*

She set down her coffee and said, "I'd better get a shower and get going."

Callie tended to take over the space when she showered, so I grabbed a towel and my shaving kit, donned my shower shoes, and walked up to the marina bath house. No sense in waiting my turn. Showers don't take me that long, but trying to share the head in a boat is an exercise in futility. There's barely room for one person, let alone two.

By the time I returned, Callie was in front of the mirror, donning makeup and humming to herself. She turned when she saw my reflection. "Where did you go?"

"I went to the bath house to shower. No sense in the two of us dancing around each other in here."

"Oh, gosh, I didn't even think about it. I guess I should have let you go first."

"It's not a big deal. I needed to get going, and the walk sure didn't hurt me."

Even with her head start, I was dressed and out the door before she was. I kissed her goodbye, said, "See you tonight," and walked up the dock.

Twenty minutes later, I was in Hanna's office, being introduced to a stunning woman. She was obviously Latina, and her clothes seemed to be having a hard time containing her curves.

"Will, this is Isabella Calderon with Worldwide Rescue."

She took my hand and stared deep into my eyes. "It is so nice to meet you, Will. Call me Bella. I understand that you work on behalf of the immigrants as I do."

My hand seemed to tingle where she held it. "Um, not exactly. I do write about injustices in Florida, everything from environmental destruction to prison abuses and government corruption. This is my first immigration story since moving to the state."

Her eyes never wavered. "So, you have campaigned against injustice, and now the injustice you write about is human trafficking. You are working on their behalf, si´?"

She made me feel awkward. "I suppose you could look at it that way." She gave my fingers a final squeeze and withdrew her hand.

"Then we shall do this together."

Oh boy.

Chapter Eight

I sabella made me a little nervous with the way she'd said we'd do this investigation "Together," but I really did need her help.

"Will, I understand you are looking for a young immigrant girl who you believe is being held on a boat here in Florida."

"Yes, her name is Leilani Saucedo, and she was only fifteen years old when she arrived in the US. I think she may be sixteen by now, but I'm not exactly sure of her birth date. We know that the smugglers who brought her to Florida sold her to someone named 'Captain Willy,' and that there was mention of a party boat. I'm assuming that means they bought her for sex work."

She shook her head in disgust. "There seems to be an endless supply of men who will pay to be with a young girl. With the months that have gone by, her innocence will be gone. We must hope that she is at least still alive."

"Do you think there's any way to find her?"

She nodded. "Worldwide Rescue has a mission to find and free girls that have been sold into the sex trade. Florida has become a hot spot because of all the college and professional athletics in the state."

"What does that have to do with it?"

"Every time there's a big sporting event, many thousands of fans gather in one city, days in advance. The girls are all brought from around the region to that city to service the men with money in their pockets. It's a big business."

"That's terrible."

"Yes, it is. It saddens me that so many men with their own wives and daughters put their conscience aside to have sex with young girls. Sometimes I think the violence of the games they watch on the field makes them a little reckless."

I was getting quite an education myself. "Why don't the police crackdown on the sex trade?"

She shook her head. "It's not that easy. The Russian Mafia is behind a lot of the sex trade. They are a brutal bunch, and it's been nearly impossible for law enforcement to infiltrate their ranks. Last year the FBI managed to get a Russian recruited as an informant, and his body turned up on the shore in Palm Beach minus his head and hands. The coroner had to ID the remains with DNA."

"That's pretty gruesome."

"Yes, and that's the point. Anyone would be terrified to testify against them."

"Her older sister, Carmelina, told me the man who took Leilani spoke like an American. Maybe it's not the Russians."

"They run things at the top, not on the street. Alexsei Semenov is behind most of the sex trade in South Florida. He brought a bunch of Eastern European girls into the US to work at his night clubs. When the police closed a couple of them down, he started the string of party boats. They are mostly stocked with girls from the former Soviet block countries, but he occasionally buys a girl from south of the border if she's beautiful enough."

"So, how do we track down one lone girl?"

"Do you have a picture of her?"

"Yes, but it's not recent. Carmelina gave me a school photo she kept of Leilani. She was twelve when it was made." I handed it to her.

Isabella looked at the photo sadly. "She was a beautiful little girl." After a pause, she continued, "The eyes and the shape of the face should still be the same. It helps. We will use facial recognition software to check the mug shots of anyone in the right age range who is arrested for soliciting or prostitution. The problem is the party boats. Almost no one ever gets arrested off the boats."

"Why not?"

"Surveillance is nearly impossible. Nothing ever happens at the dock. The girls are locked below decks, and the customers are taken out past the twelve-mile limit so the Coast Guard can't stop them without cause."

"You make it sound pretty hopeless."

She put her hand on my arm. "Don't give up yet." She pulled her hand away and sat straighter. "I'll put the word out to look for party boat flyers that mention a Captain Willy. If we can get a lead on which boat it is, we'll at least have a place to start."

That surprised me. "You mean they advertise?"

"Yes, they call the party boats 'A place to relax on the water, served by beautiful women.' Everyone knows what they mean by 'served', but saying that is not illegal. The clientele is mostly rich businessmen, and South Florida has its share of those. It's why we seem to have Asian massage parlors on every corner."

The conversation had gotten depressing, and I decided to wrap it up.

"Thank you for helping me, Isabella. I promised Carmelina I'd try to find her siblings, and so far all I've found is a lot of dead ends."

She stood when I did, and took both my hands. "I'll do my best for you. Stay in touch, okay?"

The moment lingered as she looked into my eyes. There seemed to be more going on behind them than what was being said. I mumbled my thanks, retrieved my hands, then turned and left. She was an intense woman, and I knew I'd have to stay focused on the work when I was around her. I didn't need any more problems.

* * *

After a day and a half of watching the truck depot, Pablo was getting impatient. He'd left his hiding place in the brush by the chain-link fence surrounding the compound several times in search of food and water, and to relieve himself.

I may have been away when the one I seek was here. This feels like a foolish plan, but I have no other.

He settled back into waiting and kept watch.

Three hours later, his patience was rewarded. A refrigerated truck pulled through the open gates of the compound and parked near the building where Pablo and his siblings had been held. The smuggler who sold them got out of the cab of the truck, opened the back, and a man with a forklift began off-loading crates and driving them through the roll-up door of the warehouse on the left.

After forty-five minutes of watching the tedious work, Pablo saw the driver climb into the rear of the trailer carrying a box cutter. He emerged a few minutes later leading a young girl who was holding her hand over her eyes, blinking at the brightness of the sun after hours of being sealed in a box.

Pablo's anger consumed him, and he sprang from his hiding place, ran through the open gates and tackled the truck driver, knocking all three of them to the ground. He rolled on top, punched the man in the gut, and as the air whooshed from his lungs, Pablo struck him on the jaw. The man fell unconscious.

He helped the girl up, and she yanked her hand back, terrified.

"Come. We must go before they stop you."

Her eyes were wild. "No! Leave me. I have bought my passage into this country. Go away!"

He grabbed her arm. "Trust me. They will sell you into slavery. Hurry."

She looked scared and confused but allowed herself to be led through the gates and into the trees and brush next door. When they were concealed, out of site of the compound, he showed her where he had hidden food supplies and bottles of water.

"Here, drink."

She took the bottle from his hands and quickly drained it. He saw the tenseness leave her body as she began to trust him. She looked directly at Pablo.

"Who are you?"

"My name is Pablo. What is yours?"

Shyly, she said, "Francisca." She looked at the ground, then gazed up at him again. "Why did you think that man wanted to make me a slave?"

"Because he's the one who sold me and my two sisters."

* * *

Carmelina was restless. The shelter at St. Mary's church had been such a relief after the endless toil of the master's house, but in a way, doing nothing was worse. She felt hopeful when Pastor Marlee had brought Will Harper and Callie Lovett to speak to her about her experience. They made her believe that they could find Pablo and Leilani, but still, she waited.

Marlee visited her every week, but there had been no news of them. When the pastor arrived on this Wednesday, she had to ask her.

"Pastor Marlee? I have heard nothing for weeks. Are Mr. Harper and Callie any closer to finding my brother and sister?"

She hesitated before answering. "I... haven't gotten an update recently on their progress. When I get home, I'll give Will a call and see if I can get a report for you." *The last time I talked to them it was all about Will and Callie's relationship issues. I hope their differences aren't keeping them from the search.*

"I feel lost, Pastor. And I feel like my brother and sister are lost, too. I sit in this place all day, watch TV, eat the food, and I don't even know if Pablo and Leilani are alive."

Marlee put a hand on her arm. "I know it's hard, Carmelina, but I trust that Will and Callie are doing everything they can to find your family members. It just takes time."

A tear ran down the young girl's cheek. "Please. Find them soon."

* * *

Jimmy Wilkins had spent the day working his way through the list of tomato growing and picking operations and set up a map of the most likely targets. They were spread far and wide over South Florida, and he realized he was looking at days of travel just to get to the top five places on the list. Nothing to do but get started.

At least he enjoyed driving in his silver Camaro, a present to himself when he got out of the service. He'd nearly lost it when the Grove County deputies had locked him up for a month on a phony assault charge and impounded his car. He'd managed to bail it out just two days before it was to be auctioned.

Bastards, he thought. *Deputy Snyder probably gave that alligator indigestion when it ate him.*

Jimmy hadn't planned on the deputy dying when he had snatched him. All he'd intended was to give the deputy a taste of the solitary confinement he'd inflicted on Jimmy. *I told him there were gators in that swamp behind the shed.* But Snyder's little bail scam had fallen apart after he disappeared, and that was a good thing. *Good riddance. One less crooked official in the state.*

He felt much better about the work he did now, helping Will expose the corruption in Florida. It amazed him how such a beautiful place could have so many dishonest people trying to tear a piece off its carcass for themselves. Bribery, pollution, fraud, outright theft and now modern slavery. He could only shake his head.

He thought, *The people basting themselves in coconut oil on the beach have no idea of the crime surrounding them. Well, at least not until green sludge in the water chases them off the beach.* Jimmy was determined to do his part to help Will expose the rot.

By mid-afternoon, he needed a break. He'd visited two tomato growers so far, and neither of them had been very cooperative. "We don't hire illegals," was the mantra he heard from them. The babble of Spanish spoken everywhere he walked through the fields told him a different story. For all the complaining about illegal immigration, the tomato industry depended on it for cheap labor.

Bleary-eyed from staring at the two-lane road and tired of being stuck behind logging trucks, Jimmy pulled into a truck stop for gas and a cold drink. He didn't see the old pickup truck with the big red tomato painted on the door as it pulled onto the road behind him.

Chapter Nine

Pablo and the girl he had rescued moved through the darkness, back towards the place where he'd been able to find discarded food. When they arrived at the overflowing dumpsters behind the restaurant and market, Francisca curled her lip at the smell.

"What is this? You expect me to eat garbage?"

"Listen, there is good food here. The Americans throw away much of what they serve. In my home, nothing was ever wasted."

"Well, I'm not eating that! Until the drug lords killed my family, we had a good life. We did not eat *garbage*."

"Drug lords? Where are you from?"

"Culiacán, in Mexico. It used to be a wonderful place to live, but the drug cartels have taken over. My brother got involved with them, and when he angered one of the bosses, my whole family was ordered to be killed. I'm the only one who escaped."

"That's horrible! I am so sorry about your family."

Tears rolled down her face. "My heart has been broken. My papa sent me to a cousin in the countryside before the killers got to Papa and shot him. Even the cousin's farm was not a safe place, so I had to come to America." She dried her tears.

"Now I get here and find the coyote could not be trusted either. Most of them work for the cartels, making money from smuggling."

"You are free now. We need to find you a safe place."

"I thought I was to stay with you?"

"No. I was watching that man so I could capture him and make him tell me where he sent my two sisters. When I saw that he was about to do the same to you, I was angry and had to stop him."

She touched his arm. "Thank you. I'm sorry I wrecked your plan."

"You didn't wreck it. I will go back and try again."

Francisca looked frightened. "No! I cannot go back there again, not if he will sell me."

"I won't take you with me. We will find a place to hide you, where someone will help. Perhaps a church."

"I haven't been to the church in a long time. We grew up Catholic, but the streets became too dangerous to attend mass. One of the priests brought us communion at home a few times, but even he was frightened away when we were marked for death by the drug lords."

Pablo said, "It is different here. There are still bad people, but it is mostly safe to walk down the road. I had bandits attack me, but they did not fare well."

"That's awful! I did not think America had bandits."

He laughed. "Francisca, every place has bandits. The world has many bad men, but perhaps there are not so many in this country."

That would turn out to be an empty hope.

* * *

After my meeting with Isabella Calderon, I decided it was time to do a little networking. I called my friend and editor Ben Carlson at the *Journal*.

"Hi, Will, good to hear from you. Working on anything for me to get excited about?"

"Yes, actually. Is it okay if I stop by and talk it over with you?"

There was a pause, and he said, "It's five o'clock somewhere. How about meeting me for a beer at Pier 22?"

Groan. "Let me guess, I'm buying?"

"Of course! After all, you're the one with the big expense account."

"Okay, I'll meet you there in about twenty minutes. Let's sit on the patio. It's early enough that it shouldn't be too crowded."

Even though it was a short drive, the day was sunny and mild, so I put the top down on the Z4. I hadn't bothered with the top lately, and I'm not sure why. Ever since Callie and I had returned from Key West it seemed that all of my rhythms were out of sync.

As I drove with sunglasses on, I looked up at the puffy clouds in the blue sky and got the feeling that all was right with the world. The feeling wouldn't last.

When I arrived at Pier 22, Ben was already at a table, beer in hand. He waved me over.

"Hi, Will, haven't seen much of you lately."

"Yeah, I've been trying to dig into this human trafficking story, and I've been struggling with it. It's just such a big topic."

"I'll say. Ever since they found that freezer truck full of dead immigrants in Texas, trafficking has been a big story."

"That was pretty awful stuff. I saw that they found the runaway truck driver dead a few miles away. He left them to die in the back of that truck, then died of dehydration himself. Karma."

"So what's your new story about?"

I filled him in on Carmelina, Leilani and Pablo's journey, then told him about my morning meeting with Isabella Calderon. He was definitely intrigued.

"I've met her before, she's an intense woman."

"Boy, intense is the word. When she stared at me and held my hand, I was glad Callie wasn't with me. She'd have been pissed."

He took a drink of his beer, then said, "How are things with you two?"

I sighed. "It's been a struggle lately. First, she was feeling like she needed a job, then when your boss put us on the payroll, she threw herself into the work. We were supposed to be writing and research partners, but it feels like she's gone out on her own."

"Uh, not really on her own, Will. She's been spending a lot of time at the newspaper offices with one of the other editors, Alvaro Romero."

"She told me about him. What's his deal?"

He looked uncomfortable. "He's a nice guy, early thirties, good looking. Actually, he's a great editor, hard working too. He seems really interested in working with Callie on her story."

"Yeah, so am I, but lately she seems to prefer working with this guy, Alvaro."

"Will, are you and Callie heading for a split?"

That's when the waitress showed up with my beer and took our appetizer order. I had skipped lunch, so I got a dozen oysters.

When she left, I said, "To answer your question, I don't know. Two months ago, I thought we couldn't be closer, but it's been rough lately. It's almost like nearly dying twice in the last six months made her want to put her life in high gear. To not waste any time."

"I've seen that happen with people before. Tasting their own mortality gets them motivated."

"Could be. Anyway, I'm getting fed up with her being testy all the time. I thought Callie and I had long-term prospects, but if she's that unhappy with me, maybe she should just go."

I couldn't believe I'd said that, and neither could Ben.

"Whoa, this sounds serious."

My throat closed up. Suddenly, I didn't want to talk about it anymore. "So, about this story. Isabella told me that the sex trade part of human trafficking in Florida is run by a guy named Alexsei Semenov. Have you heard of him?"

He sat up straighter. "Hell yes. It makes me cringe just to hear his name. Did she tell you about the informant who washed up minus a few body parts?"

"Yeah. Sounds like Semenov is a nasty guy."

"That's an understatement. He's a monster. The *Journal* has written about the Russian mob in Florida, and we always have to increase security when a series runs. We had a kidnapping attempt on a reporter about two years ago, and the cops thought the Russians were behind it."

"Damn, that's terrible! That was before I moved to Florida. I must have missed the story."

"It was scary stuff. Two guys grabbed him and were hustling him into the side of a van when a cop pulled up behind it. The cop saw what they were doing and hit the lights and siren. They dropped our guy like a hot rock and took off."

"Did the cop chase the van?"

"No, he called in the tag after he checked on the reporter, but the van was stolen. They found it abandoned and all the prints wiped."

"So the guy was okay?"

"He was pretty shaken up. We had to take him off the story, and he took a three-month leave. Now he does human interest pieces."

Ben really had my attention. "Sounds like we need to be careful. Me and Callie both."

"Definitely. I didn't know about the Russian angle on this. I'll talk to Alvaro and make sure he knows that could be treacherous ground to cover."

"Thanks."

My oysters and Ben's blackened grouper sandwich arrived, and I ordered another beer. I quickly downed a couple of oysters and chased them with the beer.

"You okay, Will?"

"Yeah, pretty much, anyway. I'm okay with all the excitement of covering stories, even when they are dangerous, but not knowing if Callie will be there when I get home is wearing on me."

He shook his head. "You do have the worst luck with women, Will."

"Don't I know it. Maybe I should be a monk."

He laughed. "I've got a big picture of that, my friend. You like women and beer too much."

I couldn't help but grin. "At least the beers are always there when I need them."

* * *

Leilani sat on the upper deck of the big sport fisherman, soaking up the sun in a small bikini as she sipped a Bloody Mary. So far, her new strategy of cooperation was working well. She was now allowed on deck, and while the men still came to her cabin to lay with her, she was not restrained.

Leilani had learned to slip into another world when the men were with her. She let her mind drift, remembering playing with goats on the hillside of her parents small farm on the mountainside. The men used her body, but they did not have her mind. Her mind was elsewhere, back in Guatemala, in San Antonio in the Clouds.

Once she had been asked if she was awake by one of the men who lay with her. He was irritated that he made no impression on her with his sexual prowess.

73

"Dammit girl, I didn't pay to screw a mannequin! At least pretend you're enjoying this. Move a little or something!"

Leilani smiled at him, then let her mind return to the clouds.

At least the crew of the party boat was happier with her. After months of having her food thrown at them, kicking, biting, screaming her resistance, her new compliance was a relief to them. She'd even managed to befriend a deckhand named Leo. He was nearly as young as Leilani, just a teenager who'd needed a job when a friend's older brother sent him to the party boat.

Leo enjoyed his boat-related duties on the not very originally named *PlayTime*, but the many women he saw being taken into cabins disturbed him. He'd grown up as an altar boy, and this wasn't something he felt comfortable around. He'd been ready to quit and disappear for a while when Leilani was brought aboard.

He was struck by her beauty, and even as she screamed and fought with her captors, he'd attempted to help her. Small things, like sneaking her food after she'd thrown her meal at the cook. Leaving cookies for her on the dresser when she had been taken out of the cabin to shower. Just ways to let her know someone cared.

She'd spoken to him when she only screamed at the others. Now, the rest of the crew believed he had tamed her with his kindness. But they had talked on the deck in the dark of night, sharing their stories and their secrets. He knew that she hated the men who came to her cabin. He knew she did not lay with them willingly.

And he knew that the first chance she got, she would escape from her waterborne jail. He would be the one to help her.

Chapter Ten

Eduardo Alvarez sat in his study, drinking strong Cuban coffee and smoking a cigar from his native land. He had a source in Canada who bought the banned cigars from the island and shipped them to him. The door opened, and the butler spoke.

"Sir, Mr. Carson, your attorney, is here to see you."

"I *know* who he is. Idiot."

The butler retreated and held the door for Carson.

"Good morning, Mr. Alvarez."

"What have you got for me, Chad?"

The use of his first name was a good sign. "Well, sir, I was able to arrange for a pair of teenage immigrant girls to make the rounds of the shelters asking for help. Between the two of them, we hope to get at least one inside all of the seven area shelters long enough to see if Carmelina Saucedo is in any of them."

"Excellent."

"I cautioned them both about the need for secrecy in this, and they are being paid well for their silence."

"Just be damned sure they don't let her know I'm looking for her."

"Understood. What's the plan for after she's found?"

"Just tell me where she is. I'll handle it from there."

The lawyer asked, "Ah, sir, you don't mean her any physical harm, do you?"

Alvarez's grin said it all. "That's not your concern, Carson."

* * *

Jimmy Wilkins was bleary-eyed by the third day of driving the Florida backroads. He'd worked his way through the five tomato growing operations most-likely to be using illegals without spotting the old pickup truck with the big red tomato on the side. Now he was searching out smaller operations, and they were in even more remote locations.

"This is starting to feel like a waste of time," Wilkins grumbled to himself. Just then, he gripped the wheel as an oncoming tractor-trailer blew by him in the opposite lane. He almost didn't see the old pickup following close behind it. He barely caught a glimpse of a red patch on the door.

"Crap! That's it." Jimmy looked for a place to turn around as the truck disappeared around a turn in the road. Not seeing a good spot, he pulled onto the shoulder, turned across the road, and was able with a little backing up to get onto the pavement heading in the right direction. He needed to catch up to that truck before it turned off.

He was half a mile behind it when he saw the pickup turn onto a dusty dirt road. He slowed to give the truck time to get further down the road, then made the turn himself. The rutted road bounced his car around as he skirted the potholes and rocks, and Jimmy pulled the Camaro into an opening on the side of the road and stopped.

He turned the Camaro back towards the highway. When he got to the main road, he saw the small sign at the turn that said, "County Landfill".

Damn. Missed that on the way in. He drove onto the two-lane highway, found a boarded up country store, and pulled into the drive facing out. The wait was short.

The old pickup truck drove by, headed back the way it came. Jimmy waited a minute, then followed behind.

* * *

The meeting with Ben Carlson had left me feeling depressed. The news that Leilani was likely in the hands of a murderous Russian gang was a scary complication. Almost worse was my realization that things were coming apart with Callie. What was it about me that made it so easy for women to leave?

I tried to shake it off and get back to work on the story. Sitting in the salon, I opened my laptop and began searching for charter boats along the coast that offered more than fishing.

It didn't take me long to see that was a dead end. There were hundreds of listings for fishing excursions, and while many of them sounded like they were part fishing boat and part drinking and cruising, none of them mentioned providing female companionship.

My knowledge of the ways men search for women online was limited. I've never sought out a paid companion and don't understand why anyone does. The connection I need to be involved with a woman is much more than just physical. It's hard for me to imagine anyone paying a stranger for sex, much less paying to have sex with an unwilling participant. It's just not in my DNA.

Researching the topic showed me that the usual way to find sex online had been the CraigsList personals and a site called BackPage. All of that crashed to a halt with the passage in 2018 of a pair of controversial bills, the House bill known as FOSTA, the Fight Online Sex Trafficking Act, and the Senate bill, SESTA, the Stop Enabling Sex Traffickers Act. Advocates praised the bills as a victory for sex trafficking victims, but they had negative effects as well.

By stripping away the protection of Section 230 of the 1998 Communications Decency Act, which protected websites and providers from being legally liable for things posted by their users, they damaged the web as a whole. FOSTA/SESTA was passed primarily to shut down BackPage, but the bills passage drove many web sites and companies out of the practice of hosting ANY remotely sex based content for fear of prosecution under the act.

This had the unintended consequence of driving independent sex workers, many of whom took up the work out of economic necessity, back to the streets. Along with the sex traffickers, it targeted anyone selling sex. The traffickers have lots of money, so they went further underground, not out of business.

Leave it to the United States Congress to pass laws with unintended consequences. It often seems that the purpose of many laws is more to look good and play well in a sound bite than to actually accomplish their stated purpose. And the politicians can all say they did something.

I shut the laptop in disgust. This was getting me nowhere. *Maybe I should harness the resources we'd been offered through the Bradenton Journal.* I dialed their number and asked for Alvaro Romero.

✳ ✳ ✳

Pablo and Francisca were both getting tired of walking. They'd stopped at every Spanish speaking business they could find, but still had no leads on a shelter that would take her in for safety. She was nearly ready to give up.

"Maybe if I just turn myself in, at least ICE will give me food and a bed to sleep in until they send me back. I could try to seek asylum."

Pablo shook his head. "I heard stories from other illegals standing around campfires. It's a bad time for those crossing the border."

"What do you mean?" she asked.

"The border detention compounds are nothing more than prisons. They lock them up in cages, take away their children, don't let them shower and barely feed them. Better to hide than to go through that."

Francisca nervously bit her nails. "But where?"

"We'll keep asking until we find a place for you." He put a hand on her shoulder. "Don't give up, okay?"

For the first time, she dropped her angry mask. "Thank you, Pablo."

"For what?"

"For saving me, for taking me with you, for trying to help me. Everything."

He blushed, and mumbled, "No problem." He shook his head as if to clear it. "Let's keep going."

After another hour and four more inquiries at Spanish speaking shops, they were tired and thirsty. Pablo said, "Let's stop at the MiniMart. Maybe someone there speaks Spanish."

They entered, and because it was a woman at the register, Francisca spoke to her.

"Habla Espanol?"

"Nope, sorry. Only English here." At least she smiled when she said it.

Francisca tried her broken English. "Need shelter. Church maybe?"

"Ah, another one of those." She looked at Pablo. "For both of you?"

"No. Sólo yo."

"Well, I understood enough of that. Hold on and let me make a phone call." She looked at Francisca's frightened face as she picked up the phone. "Hey, honey, it's okay, I'm just calling the church to see if someone can pick you up. No Policia."

The two weary immigrants stood in front of the MiniMart as they awaited a van that was sent to pick up Francisca. They were primed to run if they saw a police car instead. Twenty minutes later, a van with St. Mary's Catholic Church painted across the side pulled into the parking lot.

Pablo said, "They have come for you. Time for me to go."

She put a hand on his arm and said, "I hope you find your sisters. God be with you." Then she kissed him on the cheek, stepped away, and got into the van.

* * *

Alvaro Romero sounded surprised that I was calling him. "What can I do for you, Mr. Harper?"

I tried for a casual approach. "Please, call me Will. I know you've been working with Callie on the human trafficking story, and I wondered if I could get your help as well."

He was cautious. "What kind of help?"

"I've been trying to locate the boat where Leilani was taken after she arrived in Florida, and I keep hitting dead ends. Ben Carlson spoke highly of you, and Dillon Haverhill said I could use the resources of the newspaper when Callie and I were pursuing stories." I couldn't resist the "Callie and I" part.

"Oh, uh right. If Mr. Haverhill said so, then certainly I'll help however I can. What do you need?"

"I'm trying to find a party boat, a place where men go to find compliant women for a price. It seems like all of the ads for sex have gone underground since the new anti-trafficking laws were passed, and I haven't had any luck with the search."

He thought for a minute, then answered. "Instead of looking for the boat, maybe we should look for the girl. Callie has shared a photo of Leilani with me for the file, I can run a face recognition search across the web and see if anything pops up."

"Hey, that sounds like a great idea. How long will it take?"

"I'm not sure, let me check with our IT department. They'll do the search for us."

"Thanks, Alvaro. I promised Carmelina that we'd do our best to find her sister and brother. I have to keep trying."

"Glad I can help, Will. Callie has been working hard on it from her end, and with the three of us all pulling on the ends, we'll unravel the truth."

The three of us? I shook my head. "I need to tell you one more thing. A contact I made with an anti-trafficking group locally told me that most of the trade is run by a guy named Alexsei Semenov. Have you heard of him?"

Alvaro said, 'Oh, yes, I've heard many stories about the Russian mob in Florida. You need to tread carefully around him."

"Um, okay, I wanted to make sure you knew he was likely involved."

"Don't worry, I already warned Callie about him. Semenov has been known to go after journalists who come too close to his business interests."

Well, damn. So much for warning him.

I said goodbye, ended the call, and sat back on the bench. It seemed like Callie knew more about this than I did. Worse, she wasn't sharing the information with me.

* * *

Francisca looked out the window as the van pulled in front of a block building behind the church. She was helped out of the vehicle and escorted through a door with an electronic lock into a hallway with offices. A smiling woman greeted her outside the first office.

"¡Hola! Mucho gusto. ¿Cómo te llamas?"

She was relieved to be spoken to in her own language and continued in Spanish. "My name is Francisca."

"Welcome, Francisca, my name is Mariana. We'll help you however we can. How did you get to our country?"

"My family paid a coyote to smuggle me across the border in a truck. When I was coming out of the hiding place a boy came running towards me and attacked the man who had brought me there. He told me that I was to be sold into slavery. We ran, and he has been helping me to find shelter."

"Is this young man with you here?"

"No, Pablo said he was searching for his sisters, he wouldn't come."

A voice from the hallway gasped. Carmelina stepped through the doorway.

"You saw my brother?"

Chapter Eleven

Carmelina stared at the new arrival. "You saw Pablo?"

Francisca looked at her. "The boy who helped me was named Pablo, yes. He said he was searching for his sisters."

Tears poured down Carmelina's cheeks. "Thank God he is all right. Did he tell you how he escaped? I saw him taken away in a tomato picker's truck."

"He said he was being kept captive and forced to pick the fruit twelve hours a day in the heat. When he couldn't take it anymore, he struck the foreman with a rock and ran away."

Mariana looked alarmed. "Did he kill the man?"

"He didn't think so, but he didn't wait to find out. He ran for his life."

Carmelina said, "My brother had a right to defend himself, they made him a slave!"

"Calm down, little one, I only meant that if the man died, the police might be searching for Pablo. We should have your reporter friends check police reports to see if anything like that was called in."

Carmelina grabbed Francisca's arm. "Did he say where he was going?"

"Yes, back to the truck depot where he found me. He wanted to make them tell where his sisters had been sent."

Carmelina looked alarmed. "Mariana, call Will Harper and tell him what's happened. Francisca, do you know the name of the truck depot?"

"Florida East Coast Trucking. Pablo told me to be sure to remember it."

Carmelina looked at Mariana. "Tell Will, maybe he can stop Pablo from getting caught again. He needs to know I'm safe, and then we can help find Leilani."

"I'll do it right now. Would you take Francisca and show her around and introduce her to the other girls?"

"Yes, but please, let me know what Mr. Harper says."

* * *

Jimmy Wilkins finally caught up to the rusty pickup truck with the big red tomato on the side as it pulled into a field where pickers toiled under the sun.

The driver got out, removed his hat and wiped sweat from his forehead. Jimmy noticed a bloodstained bandage at the back of his head. The man put his hat back on, turned and looked at Jimmy through the open window.

"This is private land. You need to get out of here."

Jimmy got out of his Camaro and said, "Just a quick question, sir. I'm looking for an illegal alien that was believed to be in this area." He pulled out a printed picture. "This is his photo. Have you seen him?"

The man squinted at him with suspicion. "What'd he do?"

Jimmy decided on the fly to make up a story. "He's wanted for questioning in a missing persons case."

"You a cop?"

"No. I'm working for the missing person's family." It was mostly true, anyway.

"He looks a lot like the ungrateful little bastard that hit me in the head with a rock and took off."

"Ungrateful?"

"Yeah, we give them damn spics a roof over their heads and a job, and then he clobbers me and runs off still owing the company money. Let me know if you catch him, okay? I'll make him sorry he hit me."

Pay dirt. "Sure thing. Let me have your name and a phone number to contact you, and I'll let you know when we find him."

"You can call the office. Here's the number. Ask for me, Boss John."

The man wrote down the number on a scrap of paper, handed it to Jimmy through the window, and drove off. Wilkins got back in the Camaro and voice-dialed Will's number as he left the tomato field. "Will, it's Jimmy. I finally found the pickup truck we've been looking for."

"That's great! Did you get any leads on Pablo?"

"Good news there. Pablo escaped after hitting the crew boss of the pickers with a rock. The boss was the guy driving the truck, and he's pissed. Would you believe he said Pablo was ungrateful?"

"For what? Being sold into slavery?"

"Nope. He said they gave him a job and a place to live, and that he left owing money to the company."

"That's ridiculous. Slavery is not a job. What they do is tell the captives they can buy their way to freedom but charge them so much for food and housing they can never get out."

"Well, at least he's free for now."

"Yes, but for how long? We need to find him."

"What do you want me to do next, Will? I'm way out in the tomato fields. Should I head back to Bradenton?"

"Hold on, I'm getting a call from the shelter where Carmelina is staying. I'll call you right back."

Jimmy found a parking lot for an old gas station, and he pulled into the edge of the drive to wait. It didn't take long for the call back.

"Jimmy, you're not going to believe this. I just heard most of the story you told me from Carmelina. Pablo went to the trucking company where he was sold to the tomato picker and hid outside the fence for a couple of days.

"When he saw a girl getting pulled out of a box in a truck, he knew she was going to get the same treatment as his sisters. He ran in there, knocked out the guy holding her and ran off with the girl. It took him a while to convince her that she was going to be sold, but she finally understood, and they went searching for shelter for her. Her name is Francisca."

"Don't tell me she ended up in the same shelter as Pablo's sister?"

"Yep. Sure did."

"Damn. So, is he there too?"

"No, that's the bad news. It's a women's shelter, and he didn't come with her. She said he was going back to the trucking company to try and find where they sent his sisters."

"Crap. He's liable to get caught and sold again."

"Or worse."

"We'd better find him fast. Any leads on the trucking company?"

"Even better. Pablo told Francisca the name."

"Text me directions and I'll head that way now."

✳ ✳ ✳

Alvarez was getting impatient. He picked up the phone and dialed direct. "Carson! Why don't I have any news on finding the girl who robbed me?"

"Sir, it takes time for the girls to get admitted to the shelter and then to find out if Carmelina is there or has been there. They've only made it through two shelters each so far, and they have three more to go."

"Dammit, tell them to get going faster! I'm tired of waiting."

"Well, the problem, sir, is that they can't just leave. They need a plausible cover story so the other shelters don't get warned off. We have to give them a new identity every time, and then a believable story about why they are leaving so fast."

"Screw cover stories, I want results! If you want to keep your job, you'd better deliver them, and fast, understand?"

"Yes sir, I'm doing my best." He realized as he finished speaking that he was listening to dead air.

* * *

It was early evening when Callie returned to the *Wanderlust*. She walked into the cabin, tossed down her bag and laptop case, and flopped on the cushions.

"God, what a day! I spent hours searching databases for boats owned by a bunch of Russians. All those long names ran together until my eyes started to cross."

"Callie, did Alvaro tell you I spoke with him today?"

"Yes. He said we're switching the focus of the search for Leilani from looking for the boat to looking for a sign of her being advertised online. That was fun to hear after all those hours searching for boats."

"The goal is to find her, not to use any particular method."

"I *know* that, Will. It's not much fun to find out I've been wasting my time, though."

She sounded irritable, but I needed to press forward. "Did he give you the warning about the Russians?"

"Yes, he did, okay? Don't be overprotective."

"Callie, this Semenov guy has *murdered* journalists! Cut one informant's head off and dumped his body in the bay. Don't you think that deserves a little caution?"

"Don't be dramatic. After all, I'm not really a journalist, right? Not much more than a research assistant."

"Where's this coming from? You sure haven't been assisting me."

"Oh, so now I should be by your side all day, taking notes for you, I suppose?"

I shook my head. "You know I've never asked you to do that. Hell, lately I don't know where you are most of the time." *I'll bet Alvaro knows, though.*

She got up, grabbed her bag and headed for the door. I put a hand on her arm to stop her.

"Wait. Please don't go. I bought a couple of steaks for dinner. Can't we spend the evening together?"

She stared at me. "Is that really what you want?"

"Yes. Let's have a glass of wine and you can tell me how your day was."

The fight seemed to go out of her. "Okay. I'm sorry I've been so on edge lately. When I started working on this story, it felt like an opportunity to do something good, something that mattered. Now it feels like I stare at a screen all day. That's not my idea of being a journalist."

I couldn't help but smile. "That's not all it is, but it's unfortunately a big part of the job. Lawyers, cops, private investigators, writers, none of them are as exciting in real life as they look on TV. A lot of the work is methodical research. It's exciting when you find what you look for and get that 'aha' moment, but it takes a long time to get there."

She looked grim. "Great."

I pulled her to me for a hug. "Nothing worth doing is ever easy."

She sighed. "Yeah, my dad told me the same thing."

"He was a wise man."

"Yes, he was. But I didn't like it when he told me that, either." Sighing, she said, "So where's my glass of wine?"

I poured, and soon we were deep in a wide-ranging conversation that reminded me of when we first met. Wine led to dinner, which led to dessert and then to bed together.

It was a start. Maybe there was still a chance for us.

* * *

Carmelina and Francisca sat together on the couch at St. Mary's shelter for immigrants, talking of their shared experience.

Carmelina said, "I crossed the border in a box on a refrigerated truck, much like you said you did, but they took my brother away at gunpoint. I suppose he told you that."

"Yes, he's been frantic to find you and your younger sister."

"They sold Leilani to a man on a boat. I fear they wanted her for sex."

Francisca took her hand. "Pablo seemed very determined. I think he will find her."

"I only hope they don't catch him again. I'm afraid they wouldn't just sell him this time. They might hurt him instead."

"Pablo was very brave to save me from that man at the trucking company. Especially since he did not even know me. Have faith."

* * *

Another young girl watched them from across the room. She couldn't hear everything, but she heard enough. This was the girl the lawyer told her to look for.

Chapter Twelve

J immy drove past the truck depot without stopping, then looked for a spot to pull off the road. He found an abandoned driveway a few blocks away and pulled into the clearing in the weeds.

He walked the road until he was in sight of the depot fence, looking for the most likely place to hide. With brush grown up all around the fence, he had plenty of choices. Calling on his Ranger training, he moved silently through the undergrowth, staying farther back from the fence than he would if he was doing surveillance on the property.

This was a different approach, because he was watching for the watcher. Within twenty minutes, less than halfway around the perimeter fence, he spotted him. Pablo was seated, leaning on a tree and drinking from a water bottle. A baseball cap shaded his eyes.

He was staring intently at the empty space in front of the depot warehouses, waiting for the man who sold him to the tomato grower.

Jimmy had no idea if he might have a weapon, so he approached him on cat feet, careful not to step on any brush that might make a sound. When he was right behind him, he whispered, "Carmelina sent me."

Pablo jumped to his feet, confused but ready to defend himself. He said, "Who...?"

"Shhh! We don't want to be overheard in the truck depot. Carmelina is free, and she is safe. Follow me away from the fence where we can talk." Jimmy turned his back on Pablo and walked softly towards the surrounding woods.

Pablo followed, not sure what he was getting himself into. But the man knew Carmelina.

Jimmy stopped when they were far enough away and turned and spoke to Pablo.

"English?"

"A little." The weeks on the run had taught him enough to communicate. "You've seen Carmelina?"

"No, but I have friends who are helping her. She is at a church shelter where she is protected. She's been very worried about you since she saw you led away at gunpoint by the tomato picker."

Pablo spat. "That bastard. I hope I killed him."

Jimmy laughed. "Well you didn't, but he said similar things about you."

Pablo's eyes got big. "You talked to him?"

"Yeah, he's still wearing a bloody bandage on his head where you hit him with a rock. He says you owe the company money."

"That son of a puta!"

"Hey, I didn't believe him. I know they made you a slave. Right after I spoke to him I got the call that Carmelina was safe. She's anxious to see you."

His eyes lit up. "She is near?"

"It will take us about forty-five minutes to get there."

"What about Leilani?"

Jimmy said, "My friend Will is searching for her. If anyone can find her, he can."

A tear ran down Pablo's cheek. "Take me to my sister. Please."

* * *

Jimmy called Will from his car. "Hey, I have Pablo with me and we're on the way to the shelter. The drive should take less than an hour. Can you call them and let them know that I'm bringing Carmelina's brother to see her? I don't want to have them locking us out."

"Sure, that's great news. Is he okay?"

"Yes, he's fine. He was a little surprised when I appeared behind him, but we got through it without any bruises."

"Thanks, Jimmy, I can always count on you."

"Since that's a women's shelter, he can't stay there. Where should I take him after he sees his sister?"

"Hmmm, I hadn't thought about that. Let me makes some calls and see if there's a men's immigrant shelter with room for him. I'll meet you at the church and let you know."

Jimmy ended the call and turned to Pablo.

"It's all set. Let's go see your sister."

For the first time, Pablo smiled. "Gracias."

* * *

A nervous Cristy made a call on her burner phone to the attorney who had sent her to this place. "Hallo? It is Cristy. She is here."

"Excellent."

"What should I do?"

"Start a fight with her. Try to avoid witnesses, then tell the staff that she started it."

"What if they don't believe me?"

"Scratch your own face if you have to. Better yet, put some bruises on yourself where they won't show before you start the fight."

"Bruises?"

"You know, squeeze your arm under the sleeve where it will look like she grabbed you. Hit your thigh with a book or

92

something where you can say she kicked you. Then when the fight starts, scratch your own face."

"But, sir..., hurt myself?"

"Trust me, it will be worth it to you if they believe it and kick her out."

"But I was told I was only to help find this girl, not attack her!"

"Cristy. Do you want to be sent back?"

She took a deep breath. "Okay. I'll try."

"No, you'll do it. Start the fight in half an hour." He hung up the phone.

She was alone in her room, and she looked for something to hit herself with. The books on the shelves were paperbacks, but there were bookends with horse heads on them. She picked one up. It was very heavy. She closed her eyes and slammed it into her thigh.

✳ ✳ ✳

I drove over to the shelter to meet Jimmy and Pablo, making calls along the way. All of the men's shelters were full. The wave of immigrants into Florida had overwhelmed most facilities set up to help them, and Bradenton was no exception.

Damn. I may need to put Pablo in a hotel until we can find something else.

When I got to the shelter, I was surprised to see Jimmy standing outside, nose to nose in an argument with a large Hispanic woman.

"I told her we weren't having any of that crap in my shelter! I'm sorry her brother is here to see her, but violence or drugs will get you kicked out immediately."

Pablo pleaded with her. "Please, señora, my sister is an angel, she would never strike another person! There has to be some mistake."

She waved a finger in his face. "The girl she attacked has a bloody scratch on her face! I sent for a doctor because she may need stitches. She's got bruises on her arm where Carmelina grabbed her and threw her on the floor, and a massive bruise on her thigh where she kicked her. There is no mistake."

Pablo shook his head. "This cannot be."

"Well it is. She is no longer welcome here. She's lucky we didn't turn her over to the police for an assault charge."

Jimmy pulled Pablo back and spoke to the woman. "Can you at least tell us where she went?"

"I have no idea. Once we send someone out the door, they're on their own."

I overheard most of the conversation. "Jimmy, I assume this is Pablo?"

"Yes. We don't know where Carmelina went."

Pablo shook his head. "I cannot believe she did this."

I said, "Don't worry about that now. We need to find her."

* * *

Carmelina walked on the sidewalk, tears streaming down her cheeks. She couldn't believe this was happening to her. She'd thought she was safe, and Pablo was on his way to her. Then the crazy girl jumped at her and screamed.

Now she was on the street again, lost and alone. A long Mercedes pulled up next to her, and the window rolled down.

"Hey, honey, can you use a lift?"

She knew better than to get into a car with men. She said, "No," and walked faster down the sidewalk. She heard the car door open, and the rush of footsteps behind her. A powerful hand gripped her arm.

"Come with me. Someone wants to have a chat with you."

He shoved her in the back of the car and got in beside her, then looked at the driver. "Get moving. Mr. Alvarez is eager to see her."

Jimmy and I had both driven all of the streets in the surrounding area, but there was no sign of Carmelina. We met back at the church parking lot.

"I looked everywhere I could think of that she could have gotten in a half hour."

He said, "So did we. I even drove through parking lots and alleyways, but she seems to have vanished."

"Maybe she got a ride with someone."

Pablo said, "She would never get in a car. I warned her about the things that happen to girls in this country."

I said, "I don't know what to do next. I can't think of anywhere else to look."

Pablo was distraught. "She should have been safe in the church. Now both of my sisters are gone again."

There wasn't anything to say to that.

* * *

Jimmy and I took Pablo out for a decent meal, then Jimmy took him back to his houseboat for the night. I went home to the *WanderLust*, where I found a somber looking Callie looking at her laptop as she sat on the settee. She was wearing a t-shirt, and I noticed she was also wearing panties for a change.

"Hey, Will."

"Hi. I hope your day was better than mine."

"I doubt it. I spent the day looking at escort sites, trying to find Leilani. At least looking at boats and marinas wasn't this depressing. What about you?"

I opened a Red Stripe and sat down across from her. "We lost Carmelina."

She sat up in a rush. "Lost her? What do you mean?"

"They kicked her out of the shelter for fighting and she vanished. Jimmy and I drove the area looking for her just a half hour after she left, but she was gone."

"That doesn't make sense! She's so soft-spoken and sweet, I can't believe she'd get in a fight. The other girl must have started it."

"That's what Pablo said too, but the other girl is the one with cuts and bruises. The house-mother said Carmelina didn't have a mark on her."

"What did she say happened?"

"She said she didn't do anything, but it looked bad for her."

"Where's Pablo?"

"He's sleeping on Jimmy's houseboat tonight. We couldn't find a shelter that could take him."

"God, what a mess. We're going backwards instead of forward." She looked over at me. "What are we gonna do?"

"The only thing we *can* do. Keep looking."

✳ ✳ ✳

Mariana approached the doorway. The medic who had come to look at Cristy's injuries followed behind her. As she neared the opening to the room, she heard a quiet voice, stopped, and held up her hand to signal the medic to wait as she listened.

"I did it, okay? I got her thrown out. Now can I get what you promised me?"

She stepped into the room and saw Cristy, cell phone to her ear.

"Uh, listen, I have to go. You'd better come get me now!" She ended the call.

Mariana said, "Who were you speaking to?"

"No one. Just a friend. It's no big deal."

"I think it is a big deal. I think you lied to get Carmelina thrown out. Tell me why."

"No! It's nothing like that. You saw what she did to me."

"Cristy. Tell me now who put you up to this, or I'm calling the police."

"No! They will turn me over to ICE."

"Then you'd better talk fast."

"Please, you don't understand. He'll hurt me. He did before."

"Who?"

"Eduardo Alvarez. He's a rich sugar company executive. I worked in his house when I first came to America. He kept me locked in a room."

"I need to call the police."

"Please, *please*, don't. I'll do whatever I can to help."

Mariana shook her head. "You'd better be telling the truth. Give me your phone."

Cristy reluctantly handed it over, then watched as the house-mother paged the front desk. "Send a security guard to 12B. I need him to watch someone." She waited while the medic cleaned and bandaged Cristy's self-inflicted wounds. When the guard arrived, she said, "Keep her here. No phone calls, and don't let her out of your sight."

She left the room, walked down the hall and turned up the corridor. She needed to call Will Harper.

Chapter Thirteen

Leilani wasn't sure how much more she could take. There had been a steady stream of sweaty men, pawing at her body, barely speaking to her as they used her. Her only refuge was Leo. When he brought her food, and in the brief moments she was allowed on deck, they talked.

"Sometimes I think of jumping into the sea."

"Please, Leilani, don't say such things. I'm working to get you off this boat, but not that way. Please have faith."

Quiet tears ran down her face. "I want to. But when? I cannot stand this much longer."

He leaned in to whisper to her. "The next time we go to the dock for fuel and supplies, I'm going to create a diversion."

"A diversion? What's that?"

"Something that will make everyone look somewhere else while I get you off the boat."

"But, Leo, they lock me in the cabin."

He reached in his pocket and pulled out a brass key. The light from the deck reflected off of it. "I stole a key."

"But, won't they know it's gone?"

"No. I got it copied and put the original back the last time we docked. No one but you knows I have it."

"What is this distraction you have planned?"

"It's better if you don't know. Just trust me, okay?"

She had no other choice.

* * *

The phone call from Isabella Calderon was a surprise.

"Will, this is Isabella. I have news."

"What's up?"

"Could you meet me at the office at five? I'd rather tell you in person."

"Yes, I suppose I can. Why the secrecy?"

"I'll tell you at five. See you then."

She ended the call before I could ask anything else. *Guess I'll find out at five.*

The next phone call almost made me cancel our meeting.

"Will? This is Mariana, the house mother at St. Mary's immigrant shelter?"

"Oh, I remember you." I knew I sounded snotty, but I wasn't pleased that she'd tossed Carmelina out of the shelter without at least calling us first.

"Listen, I'm really sorry, okay. I was wrong. Cristy, the girl who was injured in the fight? She confessed. She was trying to get Carmelina thrown out."

"But, why?"

"The man she worked for wanted Carmelina out so he could get to her. Cristy was too scared of him to refuse."

I didn't get it. "Who did she work for?"

"Eduardo Alvarez."

Crap. Now I understood.

I told her we were searching for Carmelina, and after she apologized again, we ended the call. I immediately phoned Jimmy.

"Hey, Will, what's up?"

"I think I know where Carmelina is. Eduardo Alvarez has her."

"Dammit! How'd he get his hands on her again?"

"The fight at the shelter was staged to get Carmelina thrown out. Alvarez probably had goons close by ready to grab her."

"What can we do?"

"I can't call the cops without proof he has her. Could you do a little surveillance, see if you can get a photo to show she's there?" I knew Jimmy had a long-lens for his Nikon.

"Okay. Text me his address. What should I do with Pablo?"

"Crap, I forgot he was staying with you."

"If you can meet me near Alvarez's house, I'll hand him off to you. Okay, Will?"

"No, that won't work. I have to meet Isabella at her office. She says she has news about Leilani."

I could almost see his eye roll. "Better watch out. I think that woman has the hots for you."

"This is a business meeting, nothing else, Jimmy."

"Riiiiiight."

"Just keep Pablo with you, please?"

Why is it everyone thinks women are after me?

* * *

It was a few minutes after five when I got to the offices of Worldwide Rescue. Isabella met me in the lobby.

"Will, so good to see you!" She leaned in and kissed me on the cheek as she held both my hands.

"Sorry I'm running late. I hit an open bridge and had to wait."

"No worries, let me just grab my purse and we can go."

"Go?" Sometimes I can be slow on the uptake.

"Yes, there's a nice cafe' a block away, and I thought we could talk over a glass of wine.

Uh oh. "I don't have a lot of time. Couldn't we just talk in your office?"

"Nonsense! There's always time for wine. It won't take any longer than meeting in my stuffy office would."

I sputtered my objections, but she was in her office and back with her purse in a flash. She grabbed my hand, said, "Let's go," and pulled me out the door.

We walked down the sidewalk, and she still didn't relinquish her grip on my hand. "It's so good to see you, Will? How have you been?"

"Um, fine. I've been pretty busy with the search for the three immigrants."

She smiled. "So, I wondered why I hadn't heard from you. Here is the cafe´. Would you rather sit inside or at the sidewalk tables?"

"Better make it indoors." I wouldn't be pleased if Callie drove by and saw us together.

We were soon seated, and Isabella ordered a bottle of Merlot over my objections.

"Maybe just one glass. I don't have a lot of time."

"Don't be in such a rush. Relax." The wine arrived, the waiter poured us each a glass, and discreetly left us alone. Isabella held her glass up in a toast. "To new friends."

I didn't want to be rude, so I clinked glasses. "You said you have news?"

"You get right to business, don't you?" She looked annoyed, but continued.

"We got a lead on Leilani. One of our researchers found a listing for her online through the facial recognition software."

Now, I was excited. "Did you get the name of the boat?"

"No, it doesn't say on the webpage. You have to make a date, pay a deposit on your credit card, and only then do they tell you where to meet."

"I was afraid it wouldn't be that easy."

"The researcher didn't want to use his credit card just to try and get the boat name. I have the page marked for you." She handed me her phone, and on it was a photo of a sultry-looking Leilani. I couldn't believe she was the same fresh-faced fifteen-year-old whose photo I'd been carrying.

"I guess I'd better make a date."

Isabella perked right up at that. "Wonderful! Where shall we go?"

I could feel the heat on my face. "Um, I mean with Leilani."

She recovered quickly. "Oh, right. Of course, that makes sense," She still wasn't through with me, though. "And after, maybe you'll have time to spend with me?"

"Isabella, I'm sure I told you. I have a girlfriend."

She peered at me over her wine glass. "A little birdy told me that the two of you weren't getting along. Maybe it's time to try something new?"

I was annoyed by the gossip. "Who said that?"

"Oh, you know, just girl talk. I'm not sure who told me."

"Sorry, but I'm not looking for another relationship. I don't know what will happen with me and Callie, but unless something changes, I'm spoken for."

She sighed. "Callie is a lucky woman. In the meantime, if you get lonely some night and want company..."

I tossed back the glass of wine. "I'll keep it in mind. Do you have the listing for the boat Leilani is on?"

She pouted, then reached in her purse, pulled out a business card, wrote on it and tossed it across the table to me. "Here's the information on the listing. Her name on the site is Desire."

"I'll let you know what I find out. Thanks for the tip." I stood up.

"Won't you at least stay and help me finish this bottle?"

"Sorry, but I can't. I don't want to make those rumors come true."

I tossed a twenty on the table and waved. She glared at me as I started out the door.

I don't need any more enemies. Maybe I should have stayed a few minutes.

I turned around to speak to Isabella, but she was busy flirting with the waiter. She'd be fine without me.

* * *

Jimmy had taken the long route to Eduardo Alvarez's Palm Beach home. After he crossed the bridge, he drove to a vacant lot two miles from the mansion and parked. He and Pablo began the long walk up the beach. At least all he was carrying was his camera. *This is a piece of cake compared to those hikes with a fifty-pound pack.*

Not that he missed those days. He did miss his Army buddies, but there was a lot to be said for being a civilian.

It didn't take long to get to the house, and after a quick scout of the perimeter, Jimmy found a spot beside the pool house where there was good cover. *This is perfect. We could stay here all night and not get spotted.* He hoped they wouldn't have to wait that long.

"Jimmy, is this grand house where Carmelina was taken?"

"Shhhh. Keep your voice down. We don't want anyone to know we're out here."

He mouthed, "Sorry." He turned to Jimmy and whispered. "Is my sister here?"

"We'll watch and find out."

There weren't a lot of lights on in the house. The flickering light coming from windows on the lower level told him that must be the TV room. Only one upstairs room had lights.

Wonder if that could be where Carmelina is? Nah, that would be too easy.

The light in the room went dark. Jimmy stared into the darkness, waiting as his eyes adjusted. He saw a hand push back the curtain and look out. All he could see was a silhouette. But it was a slender shape with long hair.

* * *

Carmelina stared out the window into the darkness. She could see the lights on the mansion's grounds and the moon reflecting off the ocean. She couldn't believe she was a prisoner here again.

When she'd been brought to Eduardo Alvarez's house by the men who grabbed her, she'd been led to his study and made to stand before his chair.

"So, Carmelina, you have returned."

"I'm being held here against my will. People will be looking for me."

He laughed. "No one cares where you are. Once they kicked you out of that shelter, you weren't their problem. You seem to forget, you came here illegally. In this country, you don't exist."

She shook her head in anger. "Lies! My brother is looking for me. When he finds out you took me, you will be sorry."

He glared at her. "You are the one who is going to be sorry. You've stolen from me, and I want to be paid back."

"I have no money. All I took was a small amount, much less than you owe me for all of the unpaid work I have done for you."

He roared in her face. "I owe you nothing! I put a roof over your head and food on your plate. And how did you thank me? By stealing from me and sneaking out of my house. But you will pay me back, starting right now."

He turned to one of the men who brought her to him. "Take this girl to the room next to mine. Make sure there is nothing that can be used as a weapon in there, and lock her in."

"Yes sir, Mr. Alvarez." He grabbed Carmelina by the arm. "Come with me."

She squealed as he squeezed her upper arm. "You're hurting me!"

Alvarez said, "Hey, no bruises!" Then he grinned. "The only marks on her body will be the ones I put there."

Chapter Fourteen

The man dragged Carmelina up the stairs, past the doorway to Alvarez's private quarters, and into a room with a small bed and minimal furnishings. The second man searched the room while the other one continued to grip her arm.

"Everything's clear. No weapons."

The first man gave her arm a shake. "If you know what's good for you, you'd better be nice to Mr. Alvarez. If you please him, he might keep you around a while. Otherwise..."

She yanked her arm free. "I'd rather die first."

He smirked at her. "I'm sure that can be arranged."

The men locked the door when they left.

Carmelina went to the window and stared at the ocean. *Maybe I will find a way out and just run into the water, let it take me. It would be better.*

She had no way of knowing help was nearby. She sat and cried.

* * *

I returned to the *WanderLust,* feeling like I'd escaped a trap with Isabella Calderon. She had an interest in me that was not mutual, and I sure didn't need the complication it would bring to my relationship with Callie.

After opening a beer, I sat at my laptop and called up the website with the listing for Leilani as "Desire." The web designer had certainly made her look sexy and willing to party, but I knew that was an illusion.

After reading through the process for booking a session with her on the party boat, I picked up my cell phone. I was about to dial the contact number when I felt my boat rock in the slip. I looked expectantly at the cabin door as Callie walked in.

"Hey, Will, I'm glad you're here. I have big news." She looked like she was about to bust keeping it in.

"So, tell me your news."

"We found Leilani." She waited expectantly for my response.

"Where?"

"She's still on the party boat, and Alvaro found a listing for her. You need to make a date online so we can get the name and location of the boat."

Then I did something stupid. I showed her my laptop. "You mean this listing?"

Her eyes grew wide. "How did you find that?"

"Isabella Calderon gave the information to me."

"That bitch! She knows you and I are working together. Alvaro was keeping her informed of our progress, but I can't believe he already told her about the web listing."

"Sorry. She called me and said she had information. I had no way of knowing you had the same info." I paused. "When did you find the listing?"

"Alvaro and I were up late last night searching possible websites when we came across it."

I said, "Last night? And you're just telling me the following afternoon?"

She had the grace to look embarrassed. "We were working at his apartment, and we got so excited about finding Leilani that we opened a bottle of wine to celebrate. I fell asleep on the couch."

"I wondered where you were."

"You have no right to question me. You were with *Isabella*."

"That's ridiculous. I met her at her office. *Not*, I might add, at her apartment."

She looked doubtful. "Was there anyone else at the office? Were you alone?"

"I don't think anyone else was there, but we went to a cafe´ down the street and several people were there, including the server."

Her look hardened. "So, you had lunch with Isabella?"

"No, she wanted to talk over a bottle of wine. I only agreed to one glass, and then I left."

She sniffed. "I'm not sure how I feel about that."

I couldn't believe her attitude. "Callie. I had a glass of wine with a woman in a public place. You drank a bottle of wine with your friend, *Alvaro*, and spent the night! I think I'm the one who should be doing the complaining here."

"At least he wants to work with me. All you do is meet with your sources without even telling me. You have no right to be mad at me."

"Callie, this is absurd. The whole argument started because you didn't like me having a glass of wine with a woman in a public place. You're just being defensive because you feel guilty for passing out at Alvaro's place."

She glared at me, then stomped down the steps to the master cabin. I followed, and said, "What are you doing?" She had the dresser drawer open and was stuffing shirts, pants and undies into a small suitcase she'd pulled from under the bed.

"I'm going to Alvaro's. He'll let me stay at his place so you can be free to drink with however many women you want to."

"Oh, come on, this is crazy."

"So now I'm crazy, is that it?"

"No, that's not what I meant at all! I just meant it makes no sense to leave over a silly argument. Are you going to sleep on his couch forever?"

"He said if I needed a place to stay, he has a guest room, and I'm welcome to use it any time I wish. So there."

Now I was confused. "Then why did you sleep on the couch last night?"

She blushed. "We both passed out from the wine and fatigue, that's why."

"On the same couch?"

"Um, he was on one end, and I was on the other."

"That's just great. Passed out with your boyfriend at his apartment. And *you're* mad at *me*?"

"Will Harper, don't you try to turn this around on me. You're the one with the girlfriend."

"Apparently not the one I thought I had."

Her mouth dropped open, and I stormed out of the cabin before she could respond. I grabbed a Red Stripe from the fridge, climbed the ladder to the flybridge and sat in the twilight, trying to calm down.

What the hell just happened? Our relationship had started with such promise. Now it seemed like all we did was fight. I didn't understand what had changed.

After a few minutes, Callie followed me up to the top deck. She sat across from me in the gathering darkness. "I'm sorry that happened."

"Me too."

"I thought you'd be so excited that we found out where Leilani is. When I heard you'd already gotten the news from that Calderon woman, it set me off."

"How do you think I feel? I was looking forward to telling you the same news, but you've known it since last night. A night that you spent drinking wine and sleeping over at Alvaro's."

She put her face in her hands, then lifted her chin and looked at me. "This isn't working anymore."

I wasn't shocked by her statement. I'd been anticipating it for a while.

"No, it's not."

She sighed. "I'll take one bag for tonight. Let me know when it's a good time to come get the rest of my stuff."

"You have a key. Come anytime you want."

She stood, then put a hand on my shoulder. "Thanks, Will. I'm sorry things turned out this way."

"So am I." She began walking away, and I said, "Callie?"

She turned back to me. "Yes?"

"I'll miss you."

A tear ran down her cheek. "Me too. Bye."

She returned to the salon, picked up her bag, and stepped off the boat to the dock. I sat and watched as she walked up the boards to the parking lot.

Another one gone.

*** *** ***

Carmelina stood and stared out the window at the water as the sun disappeared. With the high ceilings in the mansion, her window was close to twenty-eight feet off the ground. *Will I survive if I jump? Would it even matter if I died?*

She was willing to risk her life to escape, and she was prepared to run to the ocean and end her life rather than be recaptured. Carmelina stared into the darkness and got a glimpse of something below her window. The low light made it difficult to see what it was, but she saw stripes on fabric.

An awning. I wonder if it's strong enough to hold me if I jump?

There was only one way to find out. She unlocked the window and slid it open. She hadn't noticed the electrical contact at the bottom of the window frame.

A siren went off as the window went up. Panicked, she leaned out the window. The awning was offset from her window, but she thought it looked close enough to reach. She heard footsteps thundering up the stairs.

No time! She slid onto the window ledge. Then she jumped.

* * *

Pablo stood up as the siren went off. "What is that?"

Jimmy grabbed him and pulled him back. "Stay down. It sounds like a burglar alarm. Maybe we'll get a chance to get in the house in the confusion and look for your sister. We'll have to see who comes out."

They watched the back of the house as lights came on in the yard, and through the glare saw something fall from the upstairs window that had been lit. It fell, bounced on an awning, and fell again.

Pablo said, "There! I think it's Carmelina." She lay still on the ground.

A man leaned from the window and shouted, "There she is. Go get her."

Jimmy leapt up and sprinted to where she lay. She was stunned, but conscious. "Carmelina, are you all right?"

She sat up. "I... I think so. It just knocked the wind out of me." Her eyes widened as she spotted her brother behind Jimmy.

"Pablo!" She tried to get up and hug him, but her legs were shaky.

Jimmy picked her up and ran for their hiding place. He turned and said to Pablo, "Come on! They'll be out here after her any second."

They made it to the shadows as two large men rushed out the door under the awning. Both were in black pants and black shirts. The men looked around at the empty grass.

The taller one said, "Where the hell did she go? She looked unconscious."

The short one said, "She can't have gotten far after that big a fall. I'll grab a couple of flashlights, and we'll search the grounds."

In the shadows of the pool house, Carmelina had her arms around Pablo. She whispered, "I'm so glad you are safe."

Jimmy said quietly, "They'll search the pool house for sure, we need to get out of here." He stood, helped Carmelina to her feet, and said, "Come on."

They made their way to the beach, then started down the waterline towards the adjoining property. When they were about a hundred yards down the beach, they heard splashing in the surf.

"Footprints! A lot of them. Looks like she has help. Let's get em'."

Jimmy recognized the tall guy's voice. They were going to run them down for sure. "Pablo, take your sister back to my car and wait there. I'm going to slow these guys down."

"Do you want me to help?"

"No, you need to get Carmelina out of here. I'll be fine by myself. Now *go*."

As they left him and ran down the beach, Jimmy stepped into the shadow of a tree.

He waited, the only sounds being feet hitting sand as the two thugs ran towards him. When they got close, he peeked around the edge of the tree, then as the tall one tried to sprint past him, Jimmy stuck out a foot and tripped him.

With a howl of pain, the big man hit the sand hard, then rolled, holding his knee. The short guy skidded to a halt behind him, saying, "What happened, Raul? Are you okay?"

"What do you think happened, you idiot? I tripped over something in the dark. I think I wrenched my knee." He looked around on the sand. "I don't know what the hell I tripped on. I don't see anything."

Shorty said, "What should I do? Do you want me to get help?"

"No! Chase her down. If she gets away again, Mr. Alvarez is gonna be pissed, and he's gonna blame *us*."

The short guy took off down the beach, stubby legs pumping as fast as he could go. The tall guy sat in the sand, moaning and holding his knee.

Jimmy reached in his pocket, pulled out a long athletic sock, then knelt behind the palm tree and quietly filled it a third of the way with sand. When the tall guy turned towards the water, Jimmy stepped behind him, and took a swing towards his skull just above his ear.

Raul crumpled to the ground silently.

Perfect. Much easier than busting a knuckle on his skull. He turned and ran down the beach towards his car. In less than five minutes, he saw the car with Pablo and Carmelina standing by the passenger door. Shorty stood with a pistol pointed at them.

There was no time for subtlety. He hit Shorty on the run, shoving his gun arm in the air as he did. A shot rang out and Carmelina screamed. Jimmy punched Shorty, who collapsed on the sand.

He turned to Carmelina. "Are you hurt?"

"No, I'm okay."

"Both of you get in the car and let's get out of here. They'll be looking for these two guys."

They wasted no time leaving Palm Beach and headed back to the safety of Jimmy's boat.

Carmelina looked at Jimmy as he drove and said, "I'm sorry I screamed. I hate guns. Too many nights at home we heard gunshots." She turned in the passenger seat and took Pablo's hand. "I am so glad you're safe."

He grinned, and said, "Hey, you're the one who needed rescuing." His grin faded. "Now we must find Leilani. *Then* we'll be a family again."

Chapter Fifteen

E duardo Alvarez was in a rage. "What the *hell* do you mean she's gone? That bitch was supposed to be locked in the damned room!"

Carson was regretting his decision to stop by the mansion. "I'm sorry, sir. She appears to have jumped out a window onto an awning."

"I heard the alarm go off. Didn't Raul and Luis chase her?"

"Yes sir, but she seems to have had help getting away. Someone tripped Raul when he ran after her, and now his knee is messed up. Luis caught up to her, but there were two men with her. Luis was knocked out and they took his gun."

The deep red that suffused Alvarez's face was frightening.

"Imbeciles! Can no one catch this young girl? I want her found. Now!"

There was no point in arguing. "Yes, sir." He was hoping she wouldn't be caught. He wasn't sure what Alvarez might do to her.

* * *

When I got a phone call from Jimmy, I hoped he could confirm Carmelina's presence at Alvarez's mansion. The news was considerably better than that.

"Will, we got her!"

"Got who?"

"Carmelina. She jumped out a window onto an awning while we were watching the house. Me and Pablo slowed down the search party chasing her, then I got all of us out of there in my car."

"That's terrific, Jimmy. Nice work."

"I wish I could say I deserve the credit. Carmelina jumping is what got the ball rolling."

"Did she know you were waiting outside?"

"No, that's the funny thing. She had no idea we were there. She just couldn't stand being held prisoner one more minute, so she jumped out the second floor window. With the high ceilings in that place, she'd have broken bones for sure if she hadn't spotted that awning and aimed for it."

I shook my head. "Looks like our guardian angel is working overtime on this one. Are you taking them back to your houseboat?"

"Yes, I didn't know what else to do with them. I'm afraid Alvarez would find them at a hotel."

"You're probably right. We can't risk it. I'll bet Eduardo gets madder and madder every time Carmelina gets away from him."

"Guess I'll have houseguests for a while."

"Thanks, Jimmy. I'll chip in on the food costs for them so you won't be out of pocket."

He laughed. "No worries, Will. I'm already running up a bill for you."

"I'll gladly pay it. You did a good job on this. Now let's keep Pablo and Carmelina out of sight until we can rescue Leilani."

✳ ✳ ✳

The next day, I woke with the knowledge that two of the three siblings were safe, and that we had a good lead on the third. I made coffee, got a bowl of vanilla ice cream from the freezer, poured blueberries on it, and sat on the stern deck watching the boat traffic.

There are some advantages to living alone. There's no one to tell me ice cream is not a healthy breakfast.

That good feeling of freedom didn't last long. My cell phone rang. It was my editor, Ben Carlson.

"Hi, Ben."

"Morning, Will. Listen, how are you coming with the stories on the three immigrant kids?"

"Doing great. Jimmy and Pablo rescued Carmelina from Eduardo Alvarez's mansion last night."

"That's terrific! When are you going to have a story on it for the *Journal*?"

"Uh, Ben, I thought I'd need more documentation before we print an accusation about somebody as well-connected as Alvarez."

"No problem. Just call him a 'wealthy Palm Beach resident.' It will drive everyone crazy wondering who it is."

"Okay, I planned on using fake names for the three siblings to protect them from immigration authorities. I guess one more mystery won't matter."

"Keep em' guessing, Will. It sells papers."

"You sound like my editor in Atlanta. The paper there was hanging on by a thread. He was always looking for a bombshell story to sell papers."

Ben laughed. "At least we don't have to worry about the money anymore."

When billionaire Dillon Haverhill bought the *Journal*, their money woes came to an end. Putting me on a retainer had been a bonus to the deal.

"I'll get to work on it. You want it for tomorrow?"

"If you can get it done, that would be great."

"I'll email a draft when it's finished."

"Great." He paused. "Will? What's going on with you and Callie?"

"Why do you ask?"

"She's here anytime Alvaro is at the office, and today they came in together."

I didn't feel like talking about it. "Ask her. I need to get busy writing."

"Sorry, Will, I didn't mean to upset you."

"I'm not upset. I just don't want to talk about it, all right, Ben?"

"Okay, sorry again. I'll watch for the story. Bye."

I ended the call, now in a sour mood. *Callie sure moved on in a hurry.* I got out my laptop, sat at the table and started writing.

Two hours later, I had the first draft completed. I emailed it to Ben Carlson, then opened a cold Red Stripe to reward myself. Immersing myself in work had helped to take my mind off Callie's departure. Unfortunately, it wouldn't last.

"Yo, Will! Permission to come aboard?"

Great. "Come on in, Rick." I knew he wouldn't be put off the same way as Ben. Rick asked questions like he was prosecuting me.

He glanced at my beer. "Got one of those for me?"

"Sure, help yourself."

He opened the fridge, got a bottle and used my opener to pop the cap. He sat across from me, took a long pull on the bottle, set it on the table and stared at me.

"What?"

"When were you planning on telling me?"

"Telling you what?"

"Don't give me that crap. When you were going to tell me that Callie dumped you?"

"Rick, it just happened last night, and I haven't told anyone. How did you even know?"

"I saw Callie carrying an empty box down the dock this morning. She saw me and asked if you were on the boat. I told her I thought you were, and she turned around and left."

"Why would that make you think she dumped me?"

"Because she obviously didn't want to see you, and she looked prepared to get her stuff off the boat. Am I right?"

I hung my head. "Yeah."

"Sorry to hear that, Will. I really thought she might last."

"So did I."

"Was it still the career stuff?"

"Yes. We've been heading towards this for a while. She wanted a career more than she wanted a boyfriend."

He shook his head. "I don't get it. You saved her life *twice*. Seems like that would be worth something."

I laughed bitterly. "I thought it would. Guess the laugh is on me."

He put a hand on my shoulder. "I really hate this, Will. She was a good one. You sure have rotten luck with women."

"You don't need to remind me. I'm swearing off relationships for now."

Rick grinned. "Seems like I've heard *that* before."

"Trust me. I'm through giving my heart to a woman. Dating is more fun. No entanglements."

Rick rolled his eyes. "Face it, Will. You're a romantic. That will only last until you meet someone special, and you always do."

"If I do, punch me and tell me to snap out of it. I need a break from women."

He sat there and smiled at me as we finished our beers in silence.

Guess I'd better get used to things being quieter onboard. I might be alone for a long time.

* * *

By the next day I had myself composed enough to start trying to arrange a "date" with Desire. I hated that making a date and paying for it was necessary, but it seemed to be the only way I'd find out where they were keeping Leilani.

As I made the call to the escort service, I worried about acting suspicious, but I needn't have. Plenty of inexperienced men have likely sounded as nervous as I did when I called.

"Uh, hi, I'd like to make a date with the girl named 'Desire.'"

"Have you been with Desire before?"

"No. I've, um, never done anything like this before."

The man on the phone laughed. "Well, you picked the right girl. Desire can teach you a few lessons you won't forget."

"That sounds fun. Where do I come to?"

"Not so fast. I need your name and credit card number. We'll run a deposit on the card, and if it clears, then I'll call you with a meeting place. Got it?"

"Yes, I've got it." I gave him a fake name with a credit card number that had been set up for me to use. "How long do I need to wait for the call?"

"You wait until you hear my voice on the phone."

"Okay. Then what?" I waited for an answer, but he'd ended the call.

Hope that wasn't a waste of money.

It only took him a half hour to call back, but the news wasn't all good.

"Your card cleared for the deposit."

"Great. When can I meet Desire?"

"Sorry, she's booked solid for the next three days. You want someone else?"

Damn! "No, I really want her. Where do we meet in three days?"

"Be ready in four days, not three. I'll call you with a place to meet. Wear boat shoes."

"Can you at least tell me where on the coast so I can be close by?"

"No. Four days. Be ready." He was gone.

I hate the thought of her spending another day being abused. Maybe I should call Isabella Calderon and see if she has any leads

118

on the boat Leilani is being held on. At least I don't have to worry about Callie being pissed about it.

I looked up her number in my contacts and pressed send.

"Hello, this is Isabella."

"Hi, it's Will Harper. Is there any progress on finding the boat?"

"Well, you get right down to business, don't you?"

"Sorry. How are you doing?"

"Better than I was when you ditched me at the cafe´ the other day. That wasn't very gentlemanly of you."

"Listen, I'm sorry about that, Isabella. I'd been having some trouble with my girlfriend, and I was worried about her reaction to us being together."

"Ah, the jealous type, eh?"

"You could say that."

"Will she not be angry that you are calling me?"

I wasn't sure it was a good idea, but I didn't know how else to answer. "We broke up."

"Will, I am so *sad* for you."

She didn't sound very sad. "It's okay, it had been coming for a while."

"If you need someone to turn to..."

I cut her off. "Right now I need to concentrate on finding Leilani. Have you had any luck?"

She sounded annoyed. "I'm not feeling very lucky right now." She paused, then added, "But we did get a tip. A sixty-foot cruiser named *PlayTime* has been docking at several different marinas around Fort Myers. It's moved around enough to raise suspicions."

"What's unusual about visiting other marinas?"

"The odd part is that none of the marinas are more than forty miles apart. Paying for daily dockage is a lot more expensive than a monthly rate. Some of the dockmasters have wondered why they don't seem to have a home base."

"Have they noticed any young girls on board?"

"No, no girls at all. It always seems to have a couple of crew on board, but no one sees any passengers."

"That is strange for a boat that big. Passengers usually like to watch the docking."

"Unless, they're being kept out of sight."

"Exactly. Could you email me a list of the marinas it's been visiting?"

"Are you sure you wouldn't like to come by and get them in person? We could visit the cafe´ down the street, order some wine and pick up where we left off last time?"

Her voice was seductive and I was tempted, but the last thing I needed right now was another entanglement with a woman. "Email will be faster. Thanks, Isabella."

"Your loss." Then the line was dead.

Chapter Sixteen

It had only been two days since Carmelina's escape from Alvarez, but things weren't going well at Jimmy's houseboat when he called.

"Will? Listen, we've got a problem here."

"What's going on?"

"This boat wasn't built for three people to live on it, especially when one is a female. Pablo hasn't complained about sleeping on an air bed and I'm sleeping on the couch, but Carmelina feels bad about taking my bed, and the three of us sharing the one tiny head is an issue.

"Pablo and I end up sitting on the dock when Carmelina is in the shower, because there's no way for her to get in and out of there with any privacy. She's a good sport about it. She's even been cooking for us, but there's no room in the galley either.

"I was wondering. Do you think Pastor Marlee might let Carmelina stay with her in the motorhome until we can find them a permanent place?"

"I'll be glad to ask her. She knows Carmelina from the shelter, so they aren't strangers. Let me give her a call and get back to you."

"Thanks for understanding, Will. Have you had any luck with finding Leilani?"

"I have a lead on a boat that could be the one. I'm thinking about taking the *WanderLust* down to Fort Myers to be close to the area where the boat has been spotted."

"Is Callie planning to go with you, or to stay here to work on the story at the *Journal*?"

I didn't answer right away.

"Will?"

"Yeah?"

"Uh, was that a bad question to ask?"

"Callie moved out."

"Oh, wow, I'm sorry about that, Will. Do you think she's gone for good?"

"She hasn't left Bradenton, she just left me."

Jimmy wisely changed the subject. "Want me to help take the boat to Fort Myers?"

"I'd feel better with you here keeping an eye on Pablo and Carmelina. I'll see if Captain Rick can make the trip with me."

"Okay, that makes sense. Let me know what Pastor Marlee says when you've talked to her. I think Carmelina will be happier sharing a space with another woman."

"Right. I'll call you when I have an answer."

I ended the call and hit send on Marlee's number. "Pastor Marlee? It's Will Harper."

"How are you, Will? I heard about your rescue of Carmelina, that was such great news."

"Thanks, but I can't take any credit for it. She jumped out of a window onto an awning, and Jimmy and Pablo were there to carry her away from the house to Jimmy's car."

"Goodness, that sounds like quite an adventure. Is Carmelina okay?"

"That's why I'm calling. She's fine, but she and Pablo have been bunking on Jimmy's houseboat, and it's feeling a little crowded."

"Well, then you just bring her over here! I'll be glad to keep her until we can find those three kids a permanent home."

"Thanks, Marlee. I know she'll appreciate it, and Jimmy will too. He's been sleeping on the couch."

"Oh my, that's not fun. I hate giving up my bed, but that won't be necessary anyway. I have a foldout couch that will be just fine for her." She laughed and said, "Zoe will be thrilled. She loves having someone to jump all over."

Her ten-pound Shi Tzu bounces off the walls with pent-up energy. "I'm sure you're right about that. Is it okay if I have Jimmy bring Carmelina over this afternoon?"

"That's fine, just make it after five so I can get to the store. I don't eat all that much, and I know how teenagers can clean out a pantry."

"I'll be happy to reimburse any expenses."

"Nonsense. You've done plenty for those kids already. I don't mind a modest contribution of my own."

"That's really nice of you, Pastor Marlee."

"Please, just call me Marlee. It's okay to call me pastor at church or in the office, but no need for it on personal conversations."

"Okay, Marlee it is. I'll call and tell Jimmy to bring Carmelina after five."

"Marvelous. I'll give Zoe a bath and then go for groceries."

I knew better than to argue again. "Thanks, Marlee. You're a good friend."

I realized as I ended the call that I hadn't mentioned Callie. I knew that Marlee would be disappointed at our split, but I doubted that she'd be surprised. I hadn't been.

* * *

When Isabella emailed me the marinas where the *PlayPen* had been spotted, I saw why it looked odd to the dockmasters. The boat was rotating between three marinas within a twenty-five-mile radius, not a very cost-effective approach. She had a list of the dates the boat docked at the various marinas, and there seemed to be no schedule to it. The order was random, and there was a small enough period between dockings that they must have a home base somewhere within the area. Even a big boat can't stay out indefinitely without fuel, water and provisions, and the Gulf was too rough to anchor in open water offshore.

Maybe they have a cove they tuck the boat into where it won't be spotted. I looked at the charts, but there were too many possibilities to consider along the shoreline and the barrier islands. *I don't even know that she's on this boat.* The name and the strange behavior of the boat's refueling and provisioning stops made it a likely candidate, but nothing I could report to the Coast Guard.

I picked the marina in the middle of the target area, Moss Marina, on Fort Myers Beach. I called and arranged a slip for the *WanderLust* in two days, with an unspecified length of stay. Good thing they had the space.

Then I headed out to the dock and walked up to Captain Rick's boat, the *Waxing Gibbous*. Rick had seemed disappointed by my breakup with Callie, but I knew a trip on my big Grand Banks would brighten his mood.

He was on deck, sanding the port-side railings in preparation for another coat of varnish. It's a never-ending job on a boat that has as much wood trim as a Grand Banks trawler does.

"Hey, Rick, permission to come aboard?"

"Sure. Just give me a minute to sweep the dust from this sanding overboard, and I'll meet you on the flybridge. Grab us a couple of beers on the way up, would you?"

I stopped and grabbed a couple of Yuenglings from his fridge in the galley, then headed upstairs. He was seated and wiping his face with a cloth when I got there. He took the bottle gratefully.

"Thanks." He took a deep drink of the frosty beer. "Ahh, perfect. Sanding is a sweaty, dusty job. This makes it all better."

I said, "I'm glad to see your taste in beer has improved."

"What can I say, it was on sale at Publix. I'd drink Red Stripe every day like you do if it didn't cost so damn much. It's the cheap, local beer in a lot of the Caribbean, but here they treat it like it's a German import."

"Supply and demand, I guess. Yuengling is good for the price."

Rick grinned. "Any time it's on sale." He took another drink, and said, "Any progress on finding Leilani?"

"That's why I'm here. There's a boat named *PlayTime* that's cruising several different marina's around Fort Myers Beach. It never stays more than one night, and no passengers ever show their faces while it's docked."

"That does sound suspicious. Do you have any proof that Leilani is on board?"

"Not yet. But I called and made a date through an escort website for a woman named 'Desire.' The photo is of Leilani."

"Great! When is the date? Are you sure it's on that boat?"

"Slow down, Rick. That's why I'm here. The guy on the phone from the website said she's booked for three days, and that he'd call me on the fourth day and tell me where to meet them."

"Well, hell, that's no good. Waiting sucks. We need to get that girl off the boat."

"I don't even know for sure that it's the right boat. I plan to cruise the *WanderLust* down to Moss Marina and keep it docked there while I wait for the call back. You interested in making the trip with me?"

"Damn right I am. You know I'm always up for a boat trip, especially on that big hunk of teak and mahogany you call home."

"That's great. I'll get everything stocked and ready for us to leave in the morning at eight, if that works for you."

"Perfect. You think you can get up that early, Will?"

"Just because I don't prefer mornings doesn't mean I can't do it when I need to."

He hesitated, then said, "Are you going to let Callie know you're going? I'd hate for her to come here looking to patch things up and find your slip empty."

I shook my head. "Sorry, Rick, but she's not coming back. We're both over it."

"I hate that for you, Will." Then he grinned. "Plus, she's a lot better to look at than you are."

I smiled back. "Sorry I'm not your type."

That startled him. "Damn, Will, you'd better find another woman!"

All I could do was roll my eyes. I finished my beer, stood and said, "See you at eight."

As I started up the dock, I heard him yell, "I'm locking my door tonight!"

Everybody's a comedian.

* * *

Jimmy arrived at the RV park at 5:30 and made his way past the rows of giant motorhomes to Marlee's spot. Carmelina was impressed.

"These rolling homes are bigger than our farmhouse in Guatemala!" she said.

Jimmy said, "Some of these rigs go for more than a half a million dollars."

Carmelina said, "Holy mother of God! I will be living like a princess."

Jimmy laughed, and said, "Easy there, your highness. Pastor Marlee's motorhome is a bit older than some of these luxury models. It will certainly be more comfortable than my houseboat, though."

Carmelina blushed. "I know it will be grand, *Jeemy*. I'm so grateful to have a place to stay."

"Here we are. Let's go say hello to Marlee, then we'll get your things out of the car."

They made their way to the small steps, and Jimmy knocked. Marlee answered with Zoe wiggling in her arms.

"Jimmy, it's good to see you again. You too, Carmelina." They stepped inside, and Zoe jumped down and launched herself through the air, leaping up to be petted by the two visitors.

When Carmelina reached down to pet her, Zoe flipped over on her back, paws in the air. The young girl laughed at her antics. "Oh my gosh, she is so cute!" She stroked the dog's little pink belly for a moment. When she stopped, Zoe flipped back onto her feet and resumed jumping on the girl's legs, begging for more attention.

"Is she always this friendly?"

"She sure is. She loves people. I should warn you, Carmelina, you'll be sleeping on the fold out couch, and that's Zoe's trampoline."

"Trampoline? I don't know that word."

"It's a springy surface to help people jump. Zoe uses the couch as her launching pad. If you're sitting on it, you're liable to get jumped on."

The big smile on the young girl's face told Marlee it wouldn't be a problem.

* * *

While she chatted with Marlee, Jimmy retrieved Carmelina's small duffle bag of clothes and toiletries from his car. The bag was one of his army issue duffles, and he'd taken her shopping for the essentials to fill it.

"Thank you for letting me stay on your houseboat. It was most generous of you."

"No problem, but I think you'll be happier here, with Pastor Marlee and her dog."

"I'll miss Pablo. Could you bring him to visit me?"

"Sure, I can do that."

She looked at Jimmy. "And you will find Leilani soon?"

"Yes, we will." He hoped it was the truth.

Chapter Seventeen

Early the next morning, I cranked the engines on the *WanderLust*, the low rumble of the twin diesels disturbing the quiet of the dock. A group of seagulls who'd been scavenging by the fish-cleaning station took to the air at the noise.

"Cast off the lines, would you, Rick?"

"Aye aye, Captain." Rick grinned as he said it, happy to take to the water.

He stowed the lines and climbed to the flybridge as the big boat cleared the dock and made a turn towards the channel.

I said, "It feels good to head out on the water again. I spend too much time at the dock."

Rick chuckled. "Can't argue with you there. The first year you were at the marina I was starting to wonder if this thing even had engines."

"What can I say, I got caught up with helping Sandy with her marina problems."

"That's one way to put it. More like you got caught up with Sandy, period."

"Hey, now, I helped her before we ever got romantically involved."

"Calm down, Will, I'm just ragging on you a little. You're too touchy about your reputation as a lady's man."

I was about to snap at him that, "I'm not touchy," when I realized how stupid that sounded. I laughed instead. "Okay, I suppose I am a little sensitive about the label. It's not like I go around looking for women to get myself in trouble with."

"That's part of the problem, Will. Both women *and* trouble seem to find you all on their own."

"Too true. At least right now, while I can avoid the trouble part, since I'm out of the dating pool. A little solitude sounds pretty appealing."

Rick said, "I know what you mean. When my first wife took off, I couldn't decide whether to cry or celebrate."

Rick didn't talk much about his personal life, and I was surprised by his revelation.

"Did you ever remarry?"

"Yep. Four more times." He grinned as he said it.

I was shocked. "You've been married *five* times?"

"What can I say, I'm a slow learner. Kind of like someone else on this boat."

"Hey, I've only been married once."

"Yeah, they don't stay around long enough for you to marry them."

Ouch. "I'm not interested in getting married again, Rick."

"Neither was I. Not one of those five wives did I meet with a plan to get married. They had other ideas."

"Well, it's off the table for me. Like I said, no entanglements." I desperately wanted to change the subject. "How long do you think it will take us to get to Fort Myers?"

"It's about seventy-five nautical miles, but the ICW has more No Wake Zones than it has manatees. Depending on the traffic we should make it by mid-afternoon."

"That's not too bad. At least we can get docked and checked in at the marina well before dark."

"No problem there. We'll be at the bar by five."

We made the turn from the Manatee River towards the ICW in the Anna Maria Sound. It was a fine day to be out on the water.

"Thanks for making the trip with me, Rick."

"Are you kidding me? I'm happy to go out on the boat any time you need a hand. I'd always rather be at sea, and I can't afford to take the *Gibbous* out much. Not the way she sucks fuel."

My friends at SailFin Pointe all knew that money wasn't a problem for me and were discreet enough not to mention it. They also knew I was generous when someone needed help.

"I hear you. The twin diesels on *WanderLust* aren't exactly fuel efficient."

He laughed. "Will, nothing that looks this good is economical." He winked at me. "You might want to keep that in mind."

I gave him a mock salute and turned my attention to the waterway. A big Viking cruiser blasted around us, ignoring the No Wake signs. I blew the horn, but he just signaled back with his, waving as he went by, the bikinied girl at his side waving along with him.

We were caught in the wave as he went by, rocking the boat heavily from side to side. "Dammit, what's wrong with that idiot! Would you go below and check for damage? I think I heard something crash down there."

He watched the speeding boat pull away. "That's *Good Time Charlie*. He's been reported numerous times to the Coast Guard for damage caused by the wakes he creates."

"They should get that maniac off the water."

Rick climbed down the ladder and was back in a few minutes.

"Nothing too bad. Your fancy coffee maker took a dive off the counter, but that's it."

"Crap. I can't do without my morning coffee."

"No worries," Rick said. "The metal carafe has a dent, but it looks like it will still work."

"I guess it could be worse."

"You aren't kidding. More than one boat lost a television back when they had big glass tubes. What a damn mess that is to clean up."

"Isn't there any way to stop that guy?"

"You know there's no license needed to drive a boat. It's crazy. You need a permit to drive one of those little-bitty mopeds, but you can get behind the wheel of a million-dollar yacht without the first bit of training and take off. Stupid."

"I'll say."

The rest of the cruise was thankfully uneventful, and we had the *WanderLust* tied up at Moss Marine in plenty of time to make happy hour. We made the short walk to Nervous Nellies and grabbed a table on the crowded deck just as another group paid their check and left.

The view of the water was hard to beat, and as I looked over the menu, I was tempted to enjoy the vacationer's environment with a Pain Killer. The name sounded good, but the mixture of Pusser's Rum, pineapple juice, orange juice, and cream of coconut was likely a bit too sweet for me.

We were in the mood for Nellie's Drunken Wings, and I like them hot. That made a Yuengling draft a better choice of drink.

Rick said, "I can't believe you're going for the hot sauce on those. Even the medium is plenty hot for me."

"That's what the beer is for, to cool things down between wings. Hey, did you see the coconut-crusted onion rings?"

"Sounds a little weird to me."

"I love coconut shrimp; I think I'll give them a try."

"Tell the waitress, not me."

I looked up from the menu and saw a curvy girl with dark hair to her shoulders headed our way. She got to the table, and said, "Welcome to Nervous Nellies. Can I get you guys an appetizer or something from the bar?"

"Are the coconut onion rings any good?" I asked.

"They've been really popular so far. They've only been on the menu for a couple of months."

"Okay, I'll try an order of those and a Yuengling draft."

Rick said, "Just the beer for me."

"No appetizer today?"

"Nope. Gotta save room for the wings."

"Okay, let me get your beers, and I'll be back to get your order."

She was back shortly with icy mugs of beer. Soon she had our dinner choices on her pad and left us alone.

Rick picked up his mug and said, "Here's to good hunting."

I clinked mugs. "I'll drink to that."

"What's the plan for tomorrow?"

"The first thing this evening is to walk the docks and see if the *PlayTime* happens to be docked here. We're not liable to be that lucky, so tomorrow we'll rent a small fishing boat and cruise the other marinas to see if we can spot it."

"Why not just take the *WanderLust*?" Rick asked.

"The gas we'll save in a smaller boat will pay for the rental. Plus, we don't want to attract too much attention."

"Good point. The *WanderLust* is definitely an attention-getter with all that teak and mahogany trim."

We were interrupted by a food runner bringing my coconut crusted onion rings. I took a bite of one, and said, "Mmmm, these are as good as advertised. Sure you don't want one?"

"No thanks. At my age I know what I like already."

"How do you know if you never try them?"

He gave me a sour look. "I just know I won't."

"Okay, your loss. Just means more for me."

"Whatever."

I decided to change the subject before Rick got cranky on me. "Anyway, I'm due to get a call from the escort website in two more days to find out where to meet them. We can move the *WanderLust* to whatever marina they're in, and I'll see if I can find a way to get Leilani off the boat."

"What if there's no safe way to free her?"

"Then I'll report the boat to the Coast Guard and tell them women are being held prisoner. That should get things happening."

"Sounds like a good plan."

Just then the wings arrived. The waitress said, "Here you go, hot for you," then she turned to Rick, "and medium for you, honey. Enjoy."

We said thanks and she was on to the next table. Rick said, "Notice that she called me 'honey'? Some women appreciate an older man."

I laughed, and said, "More like saying 'Bless your heart.' It doesn't always mean what it sounds like."

His nose went in the air. "Hmph. You're just jealous."

I didn't want to start trouble with Rick. He could be a little moody. So I dropped it. His attitude had improved considerably by the end of his plate of wings.

"Ahh, that hit the spot. Maybe one more beer, since you're buying."

I just smiled. Rick was a lot easier to be around after a couple of beers.

* * *

We finished dinner and I paid the bill, then we walked back to the marina.

"Shall we walk off dinner with a stroll on the docks? Maybe we'll get lucky and spot the *PlayTime*."

Rick said, "We're on your dime, so whatever you think works. I'm not expecting to find it that easy, though."

"Neither am I, but we'd feel pretty stupid if we search the area by boat and find out it's been docked a few slips away the whole time."

"You have a point. Lead the way."

We took close to forty-five minutes walking up and down the many docks, stopping occasionally to check the name painted on boats that were close to the right size and type. We weren't surprised not to find the *PlayTime*.

Rick said, "That was a waste of time."

"It's never a waste of time to walk the dock and look at boats. It sure beats watching some mindless TV show."

"Can't argue with that. Shall we head back to the *WanderLust* and have another beer?"

"That makes four beers for you. Good thing we aren't driving anywhere."

"Who are you, my mother?"

"No, I just know that more than three beers and you fall asleep."

He grinned. "I'll try to stay close to my bed so I'm ready when that happens."

"Always good to plan ahead."

We returned to my boat and sat on the covered stern deck, watching the boat traffic. Watching cars go by is boring as hell, but there's something about watching boats pass on the water that's endlessly entertaining.

Our conversation was sparse after the beers and the big dinner, and I wasn't surprised when I saw Rick nodding off in his chair. I finished my beer, then shook him awake.

"Um, what?"

"Time to turn in. You were supposed to be close to your bed when that happened."

He yawned, stretched, and said, "I think I can make it that far. Good night."

"Let's get breakfast at 8, then I'll find us a boat rental. We should be out on the water by 9 or 9:30."

"I'll be up by then. See you in the morning."

I checked the lines once more, then closed up the boat and turned out the lights. When I crawled into the big bed, I couldn't help but think how empty it looked without Callie in it, waiting for me.

Chapter Eighteen

W hen Jimmy drove up to Pastor Marlee's motorhome, Pablo was impressed.

"Wow, this is as big as a bus! I thought it would be like a small trailer."

Jimmy smiled. "Wait until you see the inside. This thing makes my houseboat look like a shack."

"What is a shack?"

"It's not a very nice place to live. I saw a lot of shacks when I was oversea in the Army."

They knocked, and Marlee opened the door. "Welcome, come on inside and get acquainted with Zoe."

The two of them made their way up the steps and through the narrow door, and Pablo embraced his sister as soon as he saw her. "I've missed you, Carmelina." He looked at Marlee. "It's nice to meet you, Pastor."

"Please, when we're home just call me Marlee. Zoe makes sure I don't take myself too seriously around here."

Zoe jumped up in Carmelina's lap as they sat on the leather couch.

Jimmy said, "Looks like you've got a new friend."

Marlee smiled. "She loves everybody, especially if you rub her belly."

As Carmelina reached for Zoe, she flipped on her back, presenting her little pink belly. "She sure is friendly. She spends all day in my lap."

Marlee said, " Only until bedtime. She likes to take over the bed."

Pablo said, "Back in Guatemala we weren't allowed to have animals in the house at all. They slept in the barn."

Carmelina said, "You're right. Mama would, how do you say it? 'Have a cow' if she knew I was sleeping with a dog in the bed."

Marlee said, "Well, I won't tell her if you won't."

They caught up on news of the search for a while, then Jimmy stood up. "Pablo and I are going to take off. Call me if you need anything, okay Marlee?"

"I'm sure we'll be fine. Maybe you could bring Pablo to visit her again soon?"

"Sure, I can do that."

Pablo said, "I want to help look for Leilani."

Jimmy put a hand on his arm. "I know, but right now it's more important to keep you out of sight. We don't want ICE or any of the traffickers spotting you."

He sighed. "Yes, that is true."

Marlee said, "We won't leave the RV park, and they sure aren't liable to be looking for Carmelina here."

Jimmy said, "Once we find Leilani we'll need to see if they can all get refugee status. Between the danger in their home country and the abuse they've suffered at the hands of traffickers, surely the public can put pressure on the government to let them in the program."

"Maybe," Marlee said. "The current administration has been very anti-immigrant, and they don't seem to respond much to public opinion."

Jimmy said, "I'll bet Will can write their story where it will be unthinkable to turn our backs on them."

Pablo sat with his hand in his sister's. "Gracias," is all he said.

* * *

The next morning, Captain Rick and I found an older Boston Whaler center console for rent, and took to the water to search for signs of the *PlayTime*.

Rick wanted to drive, and I was happy to have him behind the wheel while I kicked back and drank my morning coffee from my Yeti mug.

We'd picked up charts for the area at the marina store, and the plan was to go to the two nearest marinas north and south of Moss Marine, checking every cove in between if it was deep enough for the *PlayTime*.

It took us a half hour to get to Pink Shell Beach Marina, and maybe ten minutes to cruise the long single dock that parallels the shore. No sign of the *PlayTime*.

We turned south, back past Moss Marine to Salty Sams. The trip took an hour with all of the "Slow, No Wake" zones, but it was a smallish marina and it didn't take long to see that the boat we were seeking wasn't there.

Rick looked at the chart and said, "How about Snook Bight Marina? It's not that far, and it's close to Estero Bay State Park. That would have a bunch of places to hide, I'll bet."

"That's fine with me, but I'm kind of hungry. Why don't we dock here and try the Parrot Key Caribbean Grill? I'll bet they have jerk chicken."

Rick gave me a big grin. "Now you're talking." He looked at his watch. "It's close to noon, sounds like beer-thirty to me."

I agreed, and we docked at the transient dock near the restaurant. We tied up, made the short walk to the entrance, and took a seat on the deck with a view of the water.

Rick said, "This is perfect. We can keep an eye out for the *PlayTime* while we eat, so I'm still on the clock."

I laughed. "Don't worry, Rick, I'm buying."

The waitress came, and we ordered a pair of Red Stripes. By the time she returned with them, we'd made up our minds.

I said, "I'll have the fried grouper sandwich with kettle chips."

Brenda, the youngish waitress, said, "That's our most popular dish." She turned to Rick. "And you, sir?"

He said, "I'm more adventurous than he is. I'll have the Chicken Tostones."

I rolled my eyes at his comment.

"Excellent choice. It's popular with the locals. We'll have it out shortly." She took the menus and walked towards the kitchen.

"What's in that? Sounds kind of Mexican."

He said, "Nope, it's jerk chicken, with tomatoes and onions on toasted plantains. It doesn't get any more Caribbean than that."

"Maybe I'll try I bite."

He bristled. "Depends on how big the portion is. I don't want to go hungry."

I could only roll my eyes at that. He could tell I was mildly annoyed, and when the food arrived, his plate was loaded with food.

He was chagrinned. "Want to try a bite, Will?"

"You sure you can spare it?"

He cut a healthy chunk off his tostones, and put it on an appetizer plate. "Here you go."

We both tried it at the same time. "Man, that is good. Maybe I should have gotten that instead of the fried grouper."

"You want half?"

Wow, I must have really guilted him.

"No, thanks. I really was in the mood for fried fish."

He laughed. "Will, you like anything if it's fried."

"Not true. I don't like fried oysters or calamari. Both are too chewy."

The conversation dropped off as we got serious about eating. We had one more Red Stripe to wash it all down, then sat back in our chairs to digest.

Rick said, "That definitely lived up to the description. It was more than I could finish. Sure you don't want some?"

"No thanks, I'm pretty full, myself. If I eat anything else I'll need a nap, and we need to get back to our search."

He sat up, and said, "You're right. I guess we'd better get going." He surprised me when he signaled the waitress for the check, then surprised me again when she brought it to the table and handed it to him.

"Hope you gentlemen enjoyed your lunch. Thanks for coming in."

He smiled, said, "My friend here gets the bill. I'm just along for the ride."

I got out my wallet and reached for the bill. I said, "I thought for a minute there you were offering to pay."

"What, and spoil a perfect record?"

We left the restaurant, took the short walk back to the boat and soon were on our way again.

It was a longer ride down to Snook Bight Marina, and we ducked into several inlets along the way to see if the *PlayTime* might be anchored there. No luck. It was late afternoon by the time we reached the marina, and a quick search revealed no sign of the *PlayTime*.

We were hot, sweaty, and tired, and I'd had enough. "It looks like we struck out on this trip. Let's head back."

Rick said, "At least it was a day out on the water. Any day afloat is better than a day on land."

"I think I'd rather get back to the *WanderLust* and have a cold beer on the covered deck."

He grinned. "Now, *that* might even be better than another boat ride."

It was dusk by the time we made it back to Moss Marina. As we approached the rental slips we passed the gas dock.

Rick said, "Look at that big boat at the gas dock. Could that be the *PlayTime*?"

I raised my binoculars. "It's hard to be sure in this light, but I think it is. Take the wheel."

He stepped around me to the helm station.

I said, "Come up behind it slow, so we can see the name on the stern. If it's the right boat, drift by it close, then get me under the bow flair. Just don't bump the boat. If anybody spots us, act like a couple of drunk fishermen."

He smiled. "I think I can manage that."

As we came closer, I saw the name *PlayTime* painted on the stern. There seemed to be no activity on the boat, but I did see someone handing cash to the dock boy who pumped the fuel.

Rick got me in perfect position, and I reached in my pocket and pulled out a pair of GPS trackers, one painted silver and one painted white. The silver one was magnetic, and the white-painted tracker had a strong adhesive with a peel-off covering.

It looked like the best option would be the white one, and I returned the other tracker to my pocket. I peeled the cover off the adhesive, and as we drifted under the bow I reached up and attached it at the top of the flare of the hull. It would be hard to spot there.

"Hey! What are you guys doing? Get away from the boat."

I pushed off and Rick put on his best drunk fisherman act. "Sorry there, bud. We just drifted a little coming in. Don't get your shorts in a bunch, we didn't hit nothin."

I kept my cap low on my head as the man stood on the dock and glared at Rick. I didn't want to be recognized.

"Get out of here, this boat is private property. If I see you do that again, I'll shoot a hole in the bottom of your boat."

Rick hit the gas to pull away, rocking the *PlayTime* against the pilings with our wake. He muttered, "Asshole," and we slowed back down as we moved first into the marina basin and then cruised to the end before heading back to the rental slips.

I didn't want the guy on the gas dock to know where we came from.

Rick turned and high-fived me. "We got 'em."

I said, "Now let's just hope that tracker works."

Chapter Nineteen

Alexei Semenov was quietly angry. "Boris, what is this I hear of a 'party boat' that is trafficking women for sex in Fort Myers?"

"I heard rumors about it, boss, but I figure it's just one boat. Can't be but a few girls at a time on it. Shouldn't be no threat to us."

Semonov's voice got lower. "There is no 'us.' There is just *me*, and people like you who work *for* me. I don't want any competition. If we let them continue, more people will try it. I want them gone."

His deadly tone made Boris stand at attention. "Yes, sir. I'll get rid of them quietly to avoid attracting the authorities."

"No! I want them to leave my territory in a way that everyone will see the price of trying to go against me. Understood?"

He gulped. "Yes, sir. I'll make sure it's a big explosion."

"If you wish to continue working for me, make it soon."

Boris nodded, said, "Yes, boss, I'll get right on it," then left the office, closing the door quietly behind him. He knew he'd better make it a really big blast.

* * *

Captain Rick and I turned in the rental boat just before closing time, then made our way back to the *WanderLust* for a beer. It had been a long, but productive, day.

I said, "Rick, how about getting us a couple of Red Stripes while I boot up my MacBook Air and see if we're linked to the tracking device?"

"Sounds great. I'm looking forward to seeing how that gizmo works, right after I wet my whistle."

He was back on the rear deck with two beers as the laptop chimed it's startup tone. It's all solid-state, and the startup process is quick. I started the tracking program, and there it was, the flashing X nearly on top of us on the map.

"Got it. They're so close that you can hardly tell us apart on here."

Rick said, "They haven't moved off the gas dock?"

"It doesn't look like it."

"Think they're going to go back to some cove and hide?"

"Maybe, but since it's almost closing time the dockmaster might be letting them stay on the gas dock until morning. Most marinas are pretty good about that."

"Do we need to keep an eye on them tonight, or do you think it'd be okay to go grab some dinner?" Rick doesn't like to miss any meals, especially if I'm buying.

"We don't have to stay close. That tracker will tell us where they've gone up to fifty miles."

"Got anything in mind?"

"Let me Google it, see what's close by." It took me a few minutes of looking at what was walking distance, but one jumped out at me. "Hot damn, Doc Ford's Rum Bar and Grill is only a few blocks across the Matanzas Pass Bridge."

"A few blocks? Have you seen how long that damn bridge is?"

I laughed. "Relax, Rick. A little walking will do you good. Besides, they have oysters on the half shell, and I'm buying."

"Well," he grumbled, "I guess I could walk a little ways for oysters."

"You mean for free oysters."

Rick tried to look mad but couldn't hide his grin.

* * *

Leo looked both ways, saw no one, and went down the corridor to Leilani's cabin. When he opened the door, he found her curled in a ball on the bed.

"Mi amor! Are you all right?"

She raised her head and looked at him, eyes red and streaming tears. "I cannot bear this anymore. Please, kill me so I can be free from this torment."

He sat next to her on the bed and took her in his arms. She felt nearly lifeless to him. "Darling, have you not noticed we are at the dock? I will spring my distraction soon, and I'll get you off this boat. Just hold on a little longer."

She said, "I swear, the next man they send to me, I will bite his ear off! Then he will strangle me, and this nightmare will end."

"Hush, no more of such talk. They will send no one while we are docked, and we will escape tonight. I promise you."

She finally returned his embrace. "Please, Leo, take me away from this cursed boat."

"Yes. Tonight."

* * *

We were just about done with dinner when I noticed an alert from the tracker app that I had open on my phone. "Finish up, Rick, it looks like the boat is on the move."

"I thought you said we could just track them on the GPS?"

"I did, but something weird is going on. The tracker shows them moving into the mooring basin, but now they're stopped. They shouldn't be anywhere near all these sailboats."

146

I dropped a pile of cash on the table more than enough to cover the bill, finished my beer in a long pull, and we were out the door.

* * *

Leo rushed into her cabin. "Leilani, come, we must get off the boat quickly!"

"You said we would escape while at the dock, and I felt the boat moving. Why?"

He rubbed a hand across his sweaty face. "I don't know what's happening. We moved away from the dock, but the engines are not running. I think we are adrift."

"What about your diversion?"

"It won't work while we are away from the dock. I'm hoping the boat being loose will distract the crew. Come with me."

She looked terrified. "What if they see us? They'll kill me."

He looked torn. "Something strange is going on. I'm afraid that we'll be in worse danger if we stay aboard. Now come!"

They made their way on deck, staying out of sight from the crowd on the flybridge and at the bow rails. Crewmembers were using boat hooks to push them away from the numerous sailboats. They had already made contact with a few of them, and at least one liveaboard was yelling at them over damage to his boat.

"What the hell is wrong with you people? Get that damn boat out of here! What are you doing floating out here without lights? I'm calling the dockmaster to report you. You're going to pay for every boat you hit."

The captain of the *PlayTime* was just as unhappy. "Calm down! Someone cut our lines and pushed us out into the water. Now the engines won't start, and the running lights are out. We're doing our best to fix it, okay?" The last thing he wanted was the attention this fiasco would attract.

The big boat drifted back into the open water of the marina, propelled by the motion of the boathooks pushing away from the sailboats. The captain hit the intercom to the engine room. "What's going on down there? Why aren't the engines running yet?"

"I'm working on it, captain. It looks like somebody yanked a bunch of wires loose. I'm trying to reattach the right ones as fast as I can."

His anger boiled over. "Bastards! If I find out who did this, he's a dead man."

The engineer returned to his task. He knew that every minute that it took to repair the wires the greater the chance of crashing into another vessel.

Up on deck, Leo and Leilani made their move. They slipped from under an awning onto the stern, opening the door to the swim platform. They were preparing to jump when a long arm reached out and grabbed Leilani.

"Oh, no you don't. You're not going anywhere." Leo turned and saw one of the crew's enforcers pointing a pistol at him while pulling Leilani closer.

He froze. "We're only trying to save ourselves. We were afraid the boat was going to hit something and sink."

"Bullshit. You're probably the one who cut the dock lines."

"No! I wouldn't do that."

"I've seen how you look at this *chica*. I'm not stupid. Your little trick has failed. As soon as we drift into the clear, the captain will drop the anchor and wait for a tow back. We might even get the engines started by then. My guess is that we'll take you out into the ocean and let you both have your little night swim."

* * *

Rick was out of breath as we ran down the dock towards where the *PlayTime* had been berthed. "Damn, Will, I knew we shouldn't have walked that far for dinner."

"That's what you get for eating the whole dozen oysters by yourself."

"You just wanted to go there because that author fellow owns the restaurant."

"Yup. We writers have to support each other."

We arrived at the empty slip and looked out over the dark water. "I don't see it in the mooring field."

Rick said, "There, to the right in the turning basin. I see it. His lights are off."

I said, "I don't hear the engines. I think he's without power. Look, he just dropped the anchor."

"Well, at least he won't be a danger to anyone that way."

* * *

When the anchor hit the water with a splash, the enforcer turned his head at the noise. Leo saw his chance, and grabbed the man's gun hand, shoving it in the air. The man fired a shot into the air, and before they could react, the three of them felt a rumble as the engines caught on the *PlayTime*. The enforcer was much stronger than Leo, and forced the gun down, aiming it at Leo.

Then the world turned white.

Chapter Twenty

"Oh my God, it exploded!" We watched, stunned, as pieces of the destroyed boat rained down, the water sizzling as the blazing hulk sank lower. "We've got to see if anyone is alive in the water."

We took off running. I'd noticed a skiff on our dock with keys in it. "There's a boat we can use on the next dock," I gasped out as I ran. "We'll look for survivors."

Rick huffed as he ran, and said, "I'll get the boat started, you grab that big battery light you keep on the *WanderLust*."

"Good idea. I'm right behind you." I hopped on my boat as he ran past, got the battery light, turned it on to make sure it was working, then hurried to catch up with Rick. As I passed the dock box I grabbed a boat hook leaning against it. Time would be critical if anyone was still alive after the blast.

He had the skiff running with all but one line cast off, and I handed him the light and jumped in beside him. I released the final dock line, and we were off.

I said, "Go slow once we get close. No telling how far someone could have been thrown by the blast."

Rick looked irritated by the advice but said nothing. As we approached, he slowed, and I began shining the light on anything floating in the water. There was a lot of debris, along with seat cushions, chunks of fiberglass, and pieces of clothing that were likely in cabinets when the boat exploded.

I saw a shirt that seemed like it was not empty. "Rick! On the right, that might be a body."

He nodded, and slowly pulled the boat closer. Hands were sticking out of the sleeves. I took the boat hook and pull the form closer. It was a man, and as I dragged him towards us, I realized his legs and lower torso were gone.

"This one's dead. Keep looking." I let the body drift away.

Then I saw a female form, badly burned. Rick said, "Damn, I hope that's not her." There was no way to tell. We kept going.

We saw several more bodies, but no survivors. We made a second circuit of the burning hulk, and were on the verge of abandoning the search when I heard a weak voice.

"Help me."

Rick steered us towards the sound. "Do you see anything?"

I said, "Not yet." Then I heard it again. "There! On the left towards the channel marker."

He drove the boat slowly to the marker, and I shone the light on two figures holding on to the wooden post.

"How badly are you hurt?" I didn't want to make any injuries worse dragging them from the water."

The male said, "I'm okay, but I think her arm may be broken."

We got as close as we could, then he pushed the girl towards us. "It's her left arm. Please don't hurt her."

She groaned as Rick and I lifted her into the boat. We laid her across one of the benches, and he shined the light on her. *Leilani!* I said, "Thank God."

Rick said, "Let's get the other one into the boat so we can get back to the dock and call an ambulance."

We helped him into the skiff, then slowly headed back to the dock.

He said, "I'm Leo, and this is Leilani. Thank you for saving us."

"How did you manage to survive the explosion? It looks like everyone else is dead." Rick turned towards us as I asked the question. I know he was thinking the same thing I was. Were they the ones who blew up the boat?

"We were standing on the swim platform, about to jump into the water when the boat blew up. It threw us in the air, and when we landed in the water the wave pushed us into the marker post. I was holding Leilani in the water, and she hit the post first. I think it broke her arm."

I asked the obvious question. "How did you know the boat was going to explode?"

Leo looked startled. "I didn't. We planned to escape while we were docked. I was going to trip a fire alarm and take Leilani off the boat in the rush. When the boat drifted away from the dock, I knew we were out of time, so we tried to jump in the water, but Rocky, one of the crew, caught us and held us at gunpoint. I don't know what happened to him. He was on the other side of the stern rail when it exploded. He had Leilani by the arm, so it's lucky he let go."

I looked at Rick. "That must have been the first body we saw. The stern rail must have shielded these two from most of the blast." I turned to Leo. "You two are very lucky."

Rick said, "We'll get her taken care of. I'm sure someone has called 911 already. I heard sirens."

Leilani's eyes shot open. "No! Please don't call the authorities. They will send me back."

Leo said, "She is illegal, but she was a prisoner on that damn boat. It's not her fault."

"Easy there, we're on your side. Rick and I were here looking for Leilani."

She looked stunned. "But, how?"

"Carmelina told us about you and Pablo. They are both safe, and they know we've been searching for you."

"Madre De Dios! Gracias, señor." Tears rolled down her cheeks.

I said, "We'll do our best to keep you away from ICE and get you into a safe house. Trust us." They didn't have a lot of choice.

* * *

We got the two survivors of the explosion back to the dock, where EMS personnel were waiting. With quick thinking on the trip back, Leo had a way to keep her out of custody. He filled us in, so we were all three ready for it.

EMS put Leilani on a stretcher and carried her to the waiting ambulance.

Leo said, "Please sir, my wife is in pain, can't you give her something?"

It wasn't hard to see from the swelling on her arm that it was likely broken, and the paramedics knew she couldn't fake the pain she was in.

After a quick check with Leo about any allergies or illnesses, which he confirmed with Leilani speaking only in Spanish, they gave her a shot of morphine. She was soon out cold.

The local sheriff's department wanted to get a statement from her about what happened but was told they'd have to see her at the hospital when she woke up. The deputy intending to question her was annoyed but decided to settle for getting Leo's statement. They stepped from the parking area back onto the dock to give the paramedics room to work.

The deputy said, "Tell me what happened."

"Sir, my wife had never been on a boat before, and the motion made her sick. She was losing her dinner at the stern rail when it went boom. We were thrown into the water, and she hit the marker post. That's the whole story."

The deputy said, "So this was a charter boat?"

"I don't think so. She was talking to a man about the boats in the marina, and he offered to take us for a short ride."

The deputy looked skeptical. "He was going to give you a ride for free?"

Leo winked at him. "Sir, my wife is very beautiful, and she is used to men offering to do things for her."

"I'll need to get your ID so we can contact you and your wife if we need more information."

Leo looked chagrinned as he pointed to the boxer shorts that he was wearing.

"I'm sorry, officer. My trousers were dragging me down in the water from the weight of my keys and wallet, so I took them off and they sank."

That earned him another look. "You're telling me you lost your ID and your keys?"

Leo drew himself up straight. "Sir, my wife was in great pain, and she was struggling to stay above water. I can always replace my ID, credit cards and keys, but nothing would replace my Leilani!"

"Okay, okay. I got your phone number. I'll call if we need additional details."

I'd been listening in and could only shake my head after the deputy left.

"Damn, Leo, that was quite a performance."

He grinned. "I learned the art of telling stories from my papa."

"It looks like EMS is ready to transport Leilani to the hospital. We'll call an Uber and meet you there." Then I leaned in and said quietly, "Make sure she stays asleep, even when the morphine wears off. There are likely Spanish speakers on the staff."

He nodded that he understood and walked up the dock to the ambulance. Rick stood close by holding a bundle.

"What'cha got there, Captain Rick?"

He looked sour. "A soggy pair of pants. Can't he just put them back on?"

I laughed. "Not just yet. I'll explain later."

We called an Uber, and I directed them to Gulf Coast Medical Center, where the paramedics said we'd find the closest ER. On the short drive I called Jimmy to fill him in.

"Jimmy, it's Will. We have Leilani."

"Is she okay?"

"She was on the *PartyTime,* like we thought. The boat exploded, but she was thrown clear. She's got a broken arm, plus cuts and bruises, but nothing life-threatening."

"Damn! At least I'm glad she's okay. Want me to call Marlee and tell her and Carmelina?"

"Why don't you take Pablo with you and tell them in person? That way I can call you after we get to the hospital and let her talk to her brother and sister at the same time."

"Good idea. I can't wait to hear the details myself."

I didn't argue with Jimmy, but I had a feeling there were some details we'd rather not know about Leilani's ordeal. I'd leave it up to her to decide how much to share.

* * *

Chad Carson was dreading this meeting. When Eduardo Alvarez had summoned him, he knew why. He'd had no luck finding Carmelina Saucedo. Carson had some of Alvarez's men watching the immigrant shelter and Will Harper's boat, with no luck.

He'd even put teenage girls in the other local shelters to watch for Carmelina, but there'd been no sign of her. Even worse, now Harper's boat was gone. He could be anywhere, and the girl might be with him.

Alvarez had been getting increasingly frustrated that Carmelina had not been found, and Carson expected to receive the brunt of that anger. But this time, he had a plan.

He knocked on the study door.

"Come in."

"Yes, sir, you asked for me?"

Alvarez stared at him. Then he spoke. "Have you found that damned girl?"

Carson knew he'd have to speak fast before he was fired. He knew Alvarez never took back an order. "No, sir, she seems to have vanished. But I do have a plan, Mr. Alvarez."

"Let's hear it."

He cleared his throat and began. "I think Will Harper is hiding her. Now his boat is gone from the dock, and I think he may have her on board. My thought is to grab Harper's girlfriend, Callie. She's been working out of the *Bradenton Journal*, and we can grab her when she leaves at night.

"What good does that do us?"

Carson restrained his urge to roll his eyes. *Being wealthy doesn't always make you smart.*

"Sir, he'll come running when he finds out she's been grabbed."

Alvarez was slow to understand. "How does that get us closer to finding Carmelina?"

"We'll be watching when he returns in his boat. If she's on it, we'll grab her as soon as he leaves. If she's not there, we'll send Harper an anonymous message that if he doesn't hand over Carmelina, bad things will happen to his girlfriend."

Alvarez finally smiled. "What kind of bad things did you have in mind, Carson?"

"Uh, sir, it's really a bluff. I don't believe Harper will take a chance on her being hurt."

Alvarez stared at him with dark eyes. "I don't bluff. If he doesn't hand over Carmelina, make this girl Callie pay the price for his failure."

Oh crap. "Yes, sir." He wasn't going to ask what Alvarez meant by "Pay the price." He was afraid he might tell him.

Chapter Twenty-One

Leilani got her broken arm set and in a cast and her scrapes cleaned up and disinfected. Between that and the bruises, she looked worse than she said she felt.

"Are you sure you're up to traveling?" I asked her.

"Si, señor, I want to see my brother and sister. We have been apart for too long."

"We can rent a car and drive you up there, or we can all go in my boat. It will take longer, but it's a pretty ride from the flybridge."

She smiled, and from Leo's reaction, it had been a long time coming.

"I thought I would never want to see a boat again. But, riding on the rooftop would be very different from being locked in my cabin all day and night. Let's take your boat."

Leilani was soon released from the ER, and I called us an Uber for the ride back to Moss Marina. Leilani and Leo were delighted when they saw the *WanderLust*.

She said, "Mr. Will, your boat, she is beautiful! All of this wood, so warm and cozy. Nothing like the soul-less plastic on the horrible boat I was locked up on."

Leo said, "Yes, this is truly a fine vessel. Might I steer for a bit when we get into open water?"

It was heartening to see their excitement after all they'd
been through. I said, "Certainly you may. Have you piloted
large boats before?"

"I have. I've been saving much of my pay for months so that
I can take the commercial captains course. I hope to have my
own boat someday."

"Good for you. Owning and living on a boat are a great way
of life. What type of boat are you saving for?"

Leo said, "I'm afraid all I'm saving for is the captains license
right now. I'd like to have a small passenger cruiser, to take
tourists around to the islands."

Leilani's eyes lit up at that. "I could be your mate!"

She didn't get her own double entendre, but Leo blushed
bright red. "I would like that very much."

Rick couldn't resist. "Hold those thoughts for later, Leo.
Where do you plan for the four of us to sleep tonight, Will?"

"Why don't we put our guests in the two front cabins. I
guess you can sleep in the king-sized bed in my cabin."

Dead-pan, he said, "But where will you sleep?"

"Very funny. I meant you could share my bed. It's big
enough to give us plenty of room."

"I might not have come on this trip if I'd known I'd have to
bunk with you," he grumbled.

I laughed. "We can take the bolsters off the settee and build
a wall down the middle of the bed if you'll feel safer."

Rick scowled. "That's not necessary. If I feel crowded, I'll
just give you a kick."

I ignored his remark. "We'll leave early, so everybody
should do their best to get some sleep."

I had a feeling it was going to be a long night.

* * *

We were up a little after dawn, and by the time Leilani and Leo
emerged from their cabins, I was on my second cup of coffee
and ready to shove off. Rick had walked to the marina store

and picked up a bag of donuts, so we wouldn't need to stop for breakfast.

I poured them each a cup of coffee, and said, "We're going to get going, but you two sit and enjoy your donuts. No rush."

Leilani said, "Can I bring my coffee up to the top and watch while we go?"

"Sure, just don't fill the mug too full, Rick might be driving the boat and he manages to hit all the wakes."

Rick said, "Ignore him. I've been piloting boats since he was still in diapers."

I rolled my eyes and earned a giggle from Leilani. She said, "Leo, come up there with me. Maybe you can learn something from watching Captain Rick."

Rick scowled at me. "See? *Somebody* knows who has the real experience on this boat!"

Joking aside, Rick knew how much I trusted him at the helm of the *WanderLust*. I cranked the big diesels from the lower helm station, then went on deck to cast off the lines. Rick had already unhooked the power and water connections.

I called up to the flybridge. "Captain Rick, you've got the helm. I'll single the lines, and you tell me when to cast off."

He was grinning, and I didn't have to see him to know it. I unhooked the port side dock lines, flaked them on the deck, (which means lay them down in neat spirals), then called up, "Ready when you are, Cap."

He replied, "Cast off when ready," and I removed first the stern line, then the bow line.

I called, "Lines aboard," and Rick put her in gear, slowly backing out of the slip. I climbed the ladder and joined the three of them on the flybridge.

Leo said, "You guys look like you've done that a time or two."

Rick laughed and said, "Will was just showing off. Get him to tell you how many times he's tried to leave with a dock line still attached."

"Hey, I only did that once!"

"Oh, right, it was the water hose you had to replace twice when you forgot to unhook it."

He had me there. "At least I'm learning, right?"

Rick looked over at Leo and used a stage whisper. "I wouldn't take any boating lessons from Will, okay?"

"Very funny. I've come a long way since I first bought this boat. And I *did* take lessons."

He said, "Good thing, too."

I was glad our back and forth was keeping Leilani entertained, and keeping her mind off her recent ordeal. It was a good sign that she wanted to go for a boat ride. I wouldn't have blamed her if she never wanted to set foot on a boat again.

Somehow, I thought her willingness to try had something to do with her rescuer, Leo.

It was an uneventful trip up the Gulf Intracoastal Waterway, and Leilani was delighted when a pod of dolphins began playing in our bow wave, leaping in the air as they surfed along with us.

By the afternoon we were nearing Bradenton, past Anna Maria Island, making the turn into the Manatee River. The peaceful trip was interrupted by the VHF radio. We monitored channel sixteen, the hailing channel, and heard *WanderLust, WanderLust*, this is SailFin Pointe Marina."

"Marina, this is *WanderLust*. How can I help you?"

"*WanderLust*, please go to channel 68."

I made the channel switch, and heard "You there, *WanderLust*?"

"Reading you fine, Henry. What can I do for you?" I recognized the voice as Henry, who ran the marina store.

"Sorry to bug you when you're out cruising, but a Ben Carlson has been calling here all day trying to reach you. I told him your boat was out of the slip and had been gone a few days, but he was pretty insistent. I tried earlier on the VHF, but I couldn't get you."

Uh oh. I'll bet Ben wants another story on the traffickers. "Okay, I'm almost back to the marina. I'll give him a call as soon as we tie up."

"Don't take too long. He said it was urgent. Do you want his number?"

"Nope, I've got it. Thanks, Henry."

"No problem. Glad you're heading home. SailFin Pointe out."

"*WanderLust* out."

Rick said, "What do you think that's about?"

"Probably pushing for another installment on the trafficking series. I haven't written anything this week."

"He'll love the exploding boat story."

Just then I noticed the distress on Leilani's face. I motioned to Rick. "Um, Rick, maybe we'd better not talk about that now."

"Oh, sorry. I wasn't thinking."

Leilani said, "Please do not worry about me. The bastards who took me and tormented me are dead. I will survive this."

Leo took her hand and squeezed it.

Within a half hour we had the boat back at the slip. I tied the lines as Rick shut down the engines. When I began hooking up the power and water, I saw Henry running down the dock. He was holding a phone.

"Will! It's that guy Ben, he just called again. Says it's life and death."

He handed me the phone. "What's so urgent, Ben?" I asked.

"Will, they have Callie!"

"They who?"

"I don't know. Alvaro and Callie were coming back to the paper last night after dinner, and they got jumped by two big guys. They knocked Alvaro out, and when he came to, Callie was gone."

"Damn! Does he have any idea who took her?"

"He's in the hospital with a concussion, and still kind of confused. Where the hell have you been? I've been trying to call you since last night."

"Sorry, we rescued Leilani last night, and brought her back on the boat today."

"Hey, that's great news, Will! What happened?"

I barely managed not to snap at him. "Ben, right now we need to find out what happened to Callie. What hospital is Alvaro in?"

"Manatee Memorial. Sounds like they plan to keep him a couple of days."

"Meet me there in the lobby in twenty minutes."

He'd barely said "Okay" when I cut off the call. I grabbed my car keys and wallet, gave Rick a quick explanation, and ran for my car.

I couldn't believe this was happening again. This was the third time Callie had gone missing in the year I'd known her, and now we had broken off our relationship. That didn't mean I could turn my back on her.

It was a short drive to the hospital, and by the time I got parked Ben was waiting for me.

"Will, good to see you. Sorry it's under these circumstances."

"So am I. Maybe Alvaro will be alert enough today to give us some direction on where to look for Callie."

"We can hope. Do you have his room number?"

"Yes, I came to see him last night. Follow me."

We got on the elevator to his floor and walked to the room without checking in at the nurses station. I didn't want to get told to come back later. The door to his room was closed, but we went in quietly without knocking. It was dark, with the curtains drawn. I approached the side of his bed.

"Alvaro?" He appeared to be sleeping. I touched his arm and startled him awake.

"Uh, um, who is it? Nurse?"

"No, it's Will Harper. Can you wake up enough to talk?"

He struggled to sit up, and I took the remote and raised the head of the bed for him. He croaked out, "Water."

I picked up the cup of water from the bed table and directed the straw towards his lips. He sucked down a few sips, cleared his throat, and took another sip.

"That's better, thanks."

"Sure. What can you tell us about what happened last night?"

He glanced over at Ben, who nodded. "Will is here to help us, Alvaro."

"There's not much I can tell you. We were just walking from the parking lot to the newspaper office after we got back from dinner, and these two guys jumped me and grabbed Callie. The big one punched me, and when I went down I must have hit my head. I don't remember anything after that."

"Did they say anything?" I asked him.

"The shorter one had Callie by the arm, and she screamed. He said 'Quiet' and put his hand over her mouth. Sorry, but that's the only thing I heard either of them say. Then I was out cold."

"I know it's only one word, but did you hear any kind of accent?"

"Accent? Not that I noticed. Why do you ask?"

"I'm just trying to get a read on who could be behind this, that's all."

Ben stepped in. "Get some rest, Alvaro. We need you back at the paper."

"I feel terrible that I couldn't stop them from taking Callie. Is there any news about her? Do you think she's okay?"

Ben said, "We haven't been contacted by anyone. I'm hoping that they'll reach out to us, or to Will, soon."

"I hope so too. Let me know if you hear anything."

We said our goodbyes and walked out into the hallway. Ben said, "Are you thinking Russians are behind this?"

"I don't know, but they seem to be the only ones with a motive. I warned Callie not to get their attention with her investigating."

He shook his head. "That's the thing. The *Journal* hasn't run a story with her byline that mentions Russians in connection with human trafficking. I suppose her interviewing people about it could get back to them, but I was doing my best to keep her out of their sights."

I patted him on the shoulder. "It's not your fault, Ben. Whatever happens."

"Let's hope she all right."

Right now, I just hope she's alive.

Chapter Twenty-Two

I 'd barely left the hospital when I got a call from Captain Rick.

"Will, it's Rick. I was inside the boat talking to Leo and Leilani, and we heard a noise on the deck. When I went to check on it, I found a rock laying on the bow with a note wrapped around it. It said, 'You know what we want. Give her back to us and we'll give your girl back.' There's no contact name or number though."

Oh, God. "I can't believe this is happening to Callie again."

"We can't call the cops. Whoever has her is liable to kill her if we do."

"They must not have known Leilani was on my boat, or they might have grabbed her right then."

"Hey, now, Will, she was inside with two guys to protect her."

"You have a point." I wasn't about to say that a young deckhand and a much older boat bum weren't much protection against Russian mobsters.

"What can we do?"

"I'm going to call Ben. Maybe he can somehow arrange a meeting for me with Alexi Semenov through his contacts. If I can make him understand that we had nothing to do with his party boat blowing up, maybe he'll be willing to let Callie go."

Rick said, "Sounds like a long shot to me."

"I know, but I'm out of ideas. We don't even have a way to contact these guys."

"I suppose it doesn't hurt to try. Unless Semenov decides to just kill you, that is."

"I have to do something."

"I know, Will, I know. Let me know what Ben says."

I ended the call, and dialed Ben's cell phone. He didn't like my request.

"Meet with Semenov! Have you lost your mind? Don't you remember the story about the guy who lost his head by pissing the guy off?"

"Do you have a better idea?"

He was silent for a moment. "No, but this idea is terrible, Will."

"I know, but it's all we've got."

Ben hesitated, then said, "Let me call the boss, Mr. Haverhill. He has a lot more pull than I do. He may not be able to guarantee your safety, but Semenov may not want a billionaire as an enemy."

I had to smile at that. "Never thought I'd see a newspaper with a sugar daddy owner."

Ben said, "It's just too bad that's what it takes for a newspaper to survive these days."

"Let me know what he says, okay?"

"I will. Cross your fingers that Haverhill's not out of the country somewhere that I can't reach him."

"Thanks, Ben."

All I could do now was wait.

* * *

Pastor Marlee's call caught me off guard.

"Will, wonderful news! Donations to the immigrant shelter have been pouring in since you and Callie started writing stories about our three siblings. Now that all three of them are safe, this might be a good time to appeal to the governor for a special asylum ruling."

I hated to burst her bubble. "Marlee, we have a problem. Alvaro was attacked last night, and the attackers took Callie. I think it's the Russians."

"Oh my Lord, that's awful! What can I do?"

"Ben Carlson is trying to set up a meeting for me with the local leader of the Russian mob. It's a long shot."

"That sounds dangerous. Are you sure it's wise?"

"No, but I can't just turn my back on her. Callie and I may have broken up, but she is still important to me."

"Please be careful. Have they said what they want?"

"Not directly, but they left a note on my dock with no names. It sounds like they want to trade Callie for Leilani."

"Will, you can't do that!"

"Don't worry, I won't. But we've got to find a way to get Callie back."

"I understand, but don't get yourself killed. That won't help anyone."

"Believe me, I have a healthy sense of self-preservation."

"How is Leilani handling this?"

"I haven't been back to the *WanderLust* to check on her. Rick is with Leilani and Leo on the boat."

"Who's Leo?"

"Didn't Leilani call you?"

"No, I'm sorry, I've been at the shelter getting updates about all the donations. I left my phone at home in a case Carmelina needed something, but told her not to answer it unless it was me calling from the shelter."

"Okay. Anyway, Leo worked on the boat and helped Leilani escape. He's hiding out with her in case the gang behind the trafficking is after him. They may blame him for the boat explosion."

"But, surely he didn't have anything to do with that!"

"No, but they'll want to blame someone, and he's an easy target."

"I suppose that makes sense. You'll keep them both safe, won't you, Will?"

"That's the plan." *If the Russians don't kill me first.*

There didn't seem to be much else to do, so I stopped by Publix to pick up supplies. I keep some food onboard, but not enough to feed three people. After stocking up, I drove back to the marina.

When I arrived, I parked my Z4 in its covered spot, loaded the food and supplies into a dock cart, and rolled it all down to the *WanderLust*. My reception was mixed.

Captain Rick said, "I see you went shopping. Did you buy any beer? We're running low."

We weren't running low when I left. Rick must have been busy drinking it.

"I did, but only one case. This boat doesn't exactly have tons of cold storage."

He smiled. "No problem! I can keep some of it on my boat, if it will help out."

"No thanks, I'll manage. Is Leilani doing all right?"

"Not great. She feels responsible for Callie's kidnapping."

I started handing the groceries from the cart up to Rick on the boat. "There's no reason for her to blame herself. She doesn't even know Callie."

"Yeah, we both know it's not her fault, but you can't tell her that. I mean you *can*, but she won't listen."

Sigh. "The last thing I need right now is a boat full of people with problems."

Unfortunately, Rick chose that moment to open the door to the cabin, and my words reached Leo. He stepped out the door to the side deck.

168

"Hey, Will, we don't want to be a problem, okay? I have a little money. Leilani and I can find a cheap hotel somewhere and get out of your hair."

Crap. "Leo, I'm just having a bad day. It's not your fault. I'm glad you and Leilani are here, and we need to keep you out of sight. It's easier to do at the marina."

"Just let me know if you get tired of us being here. We'll figure out something."

"Don't give it another thought. Right now I'm just focused on finding Callie."

"Sure, let me know if there's anything I can do to help."

We put away the groceries without any more discussion, then Rick said, "Guess I'll head back to my boat. Call me if you need anything."

"Thanks for your help, Rick."

"No problem."

Leilani waved as he walked up the dock, then turned to me. "Is there anything I can do to help here, Mr. Will?"

She must have picked the 'Mister' up from Leo. "You could help me cook dinner later."

Her smile told me it was the right answer. "That would be wonderful! My mama taught me much about cooking. Where do you grow the vegetables?"

Her English had improved since she'd been on the party boat, but her knowledge of the way things work in the U.S. was still lacking.

"We buy meat and vegetables from Publix."

"Is that like a marketplace?"

"Exactly. I'll take you there some time." It seemed that she would have some adjusting to do in her new country. Maybe Leo could help her. For tonight, I just hoped for a quiet evening, but it was not to be.

* * *

Dinner had been a bit of an adventure. I grilled pork chops, and Leilani was amazed that they came in a shrink-wrapped package. To keep it simple I cooked corn on the cob in the microwave, which seemed like magic trick to the young Guatemalan girl.

"Mr. Will, it has been in your oven for such a short time, how can it be cooked?"

"This oven doesn't have a heat source. It cooks by bombarding microwaves onto the food."

"It works like a television then?"

I laughed. "No, it's only for heating things up. TV signals are very different."

"We didn't have a television at our home in San Antonio Las Nubes, but when I traveled to the town at the bottom of the mountain I saw one. It was magic, but it did not seem to have much purpose. This magic box cooks food!"

"I guess that does make it sort of magical."

When I served up dinner, the two young people ate it with gusto. We'd finished eating and were cleaning the dishes when my phone rang. I saw it was Ben calling.

"Hi, Ben, what's up?"

"Mr. Haverhill set up the meeting you asked for. Can you be at the *Journal* by nine?"

"In the morning? Sure."

"No, nine tonight."

"It's kind of late, but I can do it. Are we meeting in your office?"

"Not exactly. Semenov wants you to be on the sidewalk at 9:15, and he'll pick you up."

"I can't say I like that idea, Ben."

"Neither do I, but he dictated the terms of the meeting. I don't believe even someone like Semenov would drive off with a reporter in front of the newspaper just to kill you."

"Gee, that's comforting."

"Will, you're the one who asked for this, remember?"

"I know, I know. Doesn't mean I like it."

"So, you'll be here at nine?"

"Yes. Where do I meet you?"

"In the lobby."

I ended the call, then buzzed Rick. "Can you come over and keep an eye on Leo and Leilani tonight? I'm going to meet Semenov at nine."

'Damn, Will, I was hoping you weren't going to go through with that."

"It should be okay. Ben set it up, and he doesn't think Semenov will do anything to me."

"Let's hope he's right."

Chapter Twenty-Three

T he drive to the *Journal's* office didn't take nearly long enough. It felt like I was headed to the gallows.

You asked for this, Will Harper. I couldn't believe I was risking my life again to rescue Callie, my now ex-girlfriend. *It's time to go back to playing the field. No entanglements, remember?*

It was too late for second thoughts. I parked my Z4 and patted it affectionately as I walked away. *Maybe the next owner will take good care of it.* I shook my head. Gotta stop these morbid thoughts. *It won't help to meet Semenov if I looked terrified.*

On entering the newspaper's lobby, I spotted Ben Carlson pacing by the elevators.

"Will! Glad you made it on time."

"I'm actually a little early."

"Let's sit down and talk for a few minutes before Semenov arrives."

"Sure. Got any tips for meeting with pissed off Russian mobsters?"

'Yes. Don't try to be funny. I hear he doesn't have much of a sense of humor."

"Glad you warned me."

"What's your plan, Will? If he really wants Leilani, you can't hand her over. Why do you think he'd be willing to send Callie back?"

"I'm hoping that I can convince him that Leilani had nothing to do with that boat exploding. All she did was escape. Kidnapping a reporter won't bring his party boat back."

He shook his head. "That sounds like a heck of a long shot, Will."

"If you have a better idea, I'm all ears."

He was quiet for a moment. "No, I don't." He looked out the window as a limousine drove up. "He's here. You'd better get outside."

I walked out the door to the sidewalk.

A large man got out of the front of the limo, walked to the rear door, and motioned me over. He patted me down thoroughly, then unbuttoned my shirt to check for a wire.

I said, "I have no weapons, and I'm not wearing a wire."

He continued his search without a word. When he was satisfied that I had nothing, he opened the door to the limo and directed me inside. I saw a smallish man in a sport coat and open shirt sitting on the back seat. He pointed to a bench seat along the side.

"Sit."

I did. "Mr. Semenov?"

"What is it you want, Harper?" His English was good, but the strong Russian accent was evident.

"I think you know, sir. I want Callie back."

He looked annoyed. "And who is this Callie?"

"Uh, she's a reporter at the *Journal*, and we used to be in a relationship."

"What the hell does that have to do with me?"

I was really confused. "Two men took her from in front of the paper yesterday. I had reason to believe they work for you."

"What reason is that?"

"I had just rescued a young girl who was aboard the vessel *PlayTime* when it blew up. A note I received indicated that Callie would be returned in exchange for the girl from the boat."

His eyes glittered. "So. You are confused."

He was right about that. "Sir?"

"That boat has nothing to do with me. It was run by someone who thought he might compete with me in providing, shall we say, entertainment. Now he is no more."

Oh boy. "So, you don't have Callie?"

The annoyed look returned. "I have no interest in anyone you saved from that boat. Therefore, I have no interest in your Callie."

"Then who...?" The words were out of my mouth before I could stop them.

"Our meeting is over. Do not bother me with foolish questions again. People who waste my time this way find it... unhealthy."

The door opened, and the driver said, "Harper. Out. Now."

I almost said, "Thank you," to Semenov, but I thought it might not be appreciated. I got out, and stood on the sidewalk as the limo sped away. My hands were shaking.

Ben walked up beside me. "Well, what happened? You're at least still breathing."

"That was very strange, Ben. He says he didn't have anything to do with Callie's disappearance, and I believe him."

"Really? Why do you trust what he says?"

"Because he said the *PlayTime* was run by a group attempting to compete with his business. It sounds like he had the boat blown up."

"He told you that?"

"Not in so many words. He said they wanted to take business from him 'And now they are no more.' It seemed pretty clear."

"So, Will, who has Callie?"

That was the big question.

* * *

I stayed and talked to Ben a few more minutes, but the encounter with Semenov left me exhausted. I walked to my car, got in, and drove slowly back to the marina, deep in thought. *Where is Callie?*

The note made no sense to me. If Semenov didn't have Callie, who was it that wanted Leilani back?

Then it hit me. Leilani wasn't the target. *Eduardo Alvarez.*

Carmelina had escaped from him twice. Maybe he hadn't given up on getting her back. I picked up my cell phone and called Jimmy.

"Jimmy, it's Will."

"Hey, Will, why are you calling so late? Is something wrong?"

"Yeah. I just met with Alexei Semenov, and he doesn't have Callie."

"Whoa, you met with him? Are you nuts?"

"I had to know if he took Callie. He seemed irritated by the question. Seems the *PlayTime* was run by a bunch of rogue competitors. I think he had it blown up."

"Damn. What are you going to do now?"

"Can you meet me at the hospital first thing? Say about eight in the morning, in the lobby."

"Yeah, I can do that. Is this about Alvaro?"

"Yes. I have a couple of questions for him, and I want you to hear the answers."

"Okay, sounds mysterious, but I'll be there."

"Thanks." I ended the call. I didn't tell him what I was thinking. I wanted to see if he came to the same conclusion.

When I arrived at the *WanderLust*, Rick was sitting on the stern deck in a lounger with one of my Red Stripes in his hand.

"Hey, Will, good to see you survived the meeting. Any luck?"

"Sort of. The Russians don't have Callie."

He sat up. "Then who does?"

"It's still a guess, but I think Eduardo Alvarez might have grabbed her."

"Alvarez? Then why didn't the note say they wanted Carmelina back?"

"He had no way of knowing we'd rescued Leilani. Because it had just happened, I assumed that was who the note was referring to."

"Well, crap. You can't just call him and ask if he has Callie. What are you going to do?"

"I don't know. She could be anywhere. He's got all of those sugar cane fields. Remember how long it took me to search the sheds in those damned fields when Jasper Thornton's son, Bart, took Hanna and Karla?"

"Boy, do I. Feels like I can still smell the smoke. So, what do we do?"

I rolled my eyes in the dark. Captain Rick had been safely on his boat when Jimmy, Callie and I were out searching the fields.

"Jimmy and I are going to see Alvaro at the hospital in the morning. I'm hoping he might be able to confirm my suspicions."

"Then what?"

"We start searching."

* * *

At eight I was already sitting in the hospital lobby. Jimmy walked in right on time.

"Thanks for coming."

"Glad to, Will. Do I need to know anything before we talk to Alvaro?"

"No. I want to hear your take on it without influence from me."

"Okay, let's go on up, then."

We walked to the elevator, entered when it arrived, and rode to the floor where Alvaro's room was located. The door to his room was shut, and I knocked lightly, then entered. He was eating breakfast from a tray across his bed.

"Hi, Will."

"How are you feeling?"

"I still have a headache, but the pain is less than it was. I think they might let me go today. If not, tomorrow for sure."

"Alvaro, have you met Jimmy Wilkins?"

He nodded at him. "Not in person, but Callie spoke of him often."

I didn't like him using the past tense to refer to her. "He's helping me look for her."

"Let me know if there's anything I can do to help."

"We want to talk to you about the night you were attacked."

"I told you everything I could remember."

"Humor me. Describe the two men who hit you and who took Callie."

"Like I said, the big one hit me, and the shorter one grabbed Callie by the arm. I was out after that."

"Did you notice anything odd about the guy who hit you?"

"Well, he did walk kind of funny. Sort of stiff, like if he was wearing a brace."

"Did he have a brace or a cast on?"

"Not that I could see. He did have kind of baggy pants, though. He could have had a brace underneath his pants. It was hard to tell in the dark."

"What color were the pants?" Jimmy asked.

"Black. They were both dressed in black pants and black shirts."

Jimmy turned to me. "Could we step out in the hall a minute, Will?"

We did, and Jimmy spoke quickly. "Are you thinking the same thing I am?"

"That the guys who snatched Callie could be the same two who chased Carmelina when she ran from Alvarez's mansion? Yes."

"So that's who has Callie, not the Russians."

"It sure looks that way to me." I stepped back into the room long enough to thank Alvaro, then left without answering any questions. There was no time.

I said, "Alvarez didn't use Callie's name in the note because he didn't think he had to. He had no way to know about Leilani being rescued. He thought we'd assume it was Carmelina he wanted."

"I'm with you on this, Will. So what do we do now?"

"Without some evidence that he's holding her, I can't get the police to search his mansion."

He said, "I know, but we can't just wait. How about if you ask for proof that he has her and she's alive? That could at least give us a clue."

I swallowed hard. I wasn't ready to accept that she could be dead. "It's worth a try. I'll call him now."

We went out to the parking lot, and I dialed Alvarez's number. A staffer answered. "Alvarez residence."

"I need to speak to Mr. Alvarez."

"Mr. Alvarez is not available at the moment."

"Tell him Will Harper is calling. I need to speak with him if he wants his missing item returned."

"I'll give him the message, sir. Does he have your number?"

I read it to her, and she ended the call. We waited, and ten minutes later the phone rang. "Mr. Harper? This is Chadwick Carson, Mr. Alvarez's personal attorney. Is there something I can help you with?"

I knew he'd watch his words carefully, so I did the same. "Yes. I understand that Mr. Alvarez believes I have something of interest to him."

"And?"

"I need assurance that the item is still in good condition."

"I can assure you that it is in excellent shape."

"Mr. Carson, while I'm sure you're a man of your word, I need more than that. I'd like a picture of the item with a newspaper bearing today's date, so I know that it's current."

"I'll relay your request. If you are satisfied with its condition, are you prepared to return Mr. Alvarez's property to him in exchange?"

I ground my teeth at his description of Carmelina. "Yes, if her safety can be assured."

He scolded me. "Mr. Harper, do not refer to his property as *her*. I realize that many people harbor affection for jewelry and antiques, but my employer does not believe in such fanciful anthropomorphic terms."

Spoken like an attorney. He didn't want anything incriminating to be recorded.

"Just be sure he knows the rules."

He sniffed audibly. "I shall pass along your request." He hung up.

I turned to Jimmy. "Now we wait."

Chapter Twenty-Four

It seemed wise to drop by Pastor Marlee's motorhome and give Carmelina a heads up that Alvarez was after her again. I called to make sure they were home and told them we were on the way.

I got my usual enthusiastic greeting from her little dog, Zoe.

The door opened, and as I stepped inside I could see a whirlwind of gray fur running around my legs and leaping in the air as she tried to get my attention.

"Hi, Zoe! Are you glad to see me?"

Marlee laughed. "Can't you tell?" Then she got serious. "So, what brings you by, Will?"

I sat on the couch, where Zoe immediately occupied my lap and licked my face. "I wanted to talk to you and Carmelina about the search for Callie."

Carmelina came out of her bedroom and joined us. "Is there news? Have you found her?"

"No, but we know who has her now. Eduardo Alvarez."

She looked stricken. "Oh my God! This is because of me."

Marlee put an arm around her shoulder. "Don't blame yourself for the actions of an evil man. This is not your fault."

"But he took Callie because he could not find me. He wants to trade for me, doesn't he?"

Oh, boy. "Yes, but we're not going to let that happen, don't worry."

"Mr. Will, Callie should not suffer because of me. Trade me for her freedom. I will survive."

"Listen, Carmelina, I'm not sure you would. Alvarez is anything but honorable, and I'm afraid he is capable of harming or even killing you. A trade is out of the question."

She said, "Then what can we do? He might kill Callie!"

Marlee said, "Yes, Will, what *is* the plan?"

"For now, we're letting Alvarez think we're open to a trade. That buys us time. I've asked for proof that Callie is alive and well, and I've got Jimmy headed to the county records office to see what properties Alvarez owns. Callie is likely to be hidden in one of them."

Tears ran down Carmelina's cheeks. "I should never have left Guatemala."

Pastor Marlee said, "You left because you felt you had no choice."

"Yes, but I did not know it would be like this!"

I said, "You've been mistreated by evil men. You had no way to know that would happen."

The young girl looked at me with sadness in her eyes. "We trusted them. America beckoned to us with a promise of a better life. Instead, we became slaves, all three of us."

"Our country has its share of people who will do anything for money. Everyone is not that way."

"Oh, I know that. You and Pastor Marlee have been most kind. Callie was so nice to me. I don't want to be the cause of something bad happening to her."

"We *will* rescue her. Trust me."

I hoped I could deliver on that promise.

* * *

After driving back to SailFin Pointe, I filled Captain Rick in on what was happening.

"What can I do to help, Will?"

"For now, the best help is for you to continue to stay with Leilani and Leo when I have to be away from the boat."

He looked frustrated. "That's nothing more than babysitting. I want to be of some real help."

"Rick, it *is* real help. You are protecting them in case someone comes here after them, and you're preventing one or both of them from leaving and putting themselves in worse danger. Sounds pretty damn important to me."

"Okay, I get it. I just feel useless doing nothing but waiting while you and Jimmy try to solve this thing and find Callie."

"You're keeping us free to do that by watching over the two lovebirds for us. No telling what scheme they might come up with on their own. Carmelina was all ready to trade herself for Callie, remember? I sure don't need Leo running to the rescue and Leilani running after him. I need you here to keep them contained and safe."

He grumbled, but said, "Okay, I'll do it."

I sent Rick up to the RiverHouse Restaurant to pick up food for the four of us for a late lunch while I Googled Eduardo Alvarez to see if any of his holdings showed up. There were lots of stories about the sugar company, the cane fields and the pollution problems, but nothing about any property purchases.

Jimmy was more likely to find something in the county records office than I was online, but I needed to feel like I was doing something.

Guess this is what Rick feels like with nothing to do.

He returned shortly with the food, and I called up to the flybridge to Leilani and Leo. "Lunch is here! Come down to the galley and get a plate."

Leo said, "Be right there." I wondered what we might have been interrupting on the roof of the *WanderLust*. The two lovebirds were doing their best to be alone with each other in a cramped space.

"This looks great, Rick. Thanks for picking it up."

He muttered, "Sure. You paid for it though."

I patted him on the shoulder. "Got to keep the bodyguard's strength up, you know?"

That at least earned me a small grin.

Leilani and Leo came through the cabin door, and he said, "I'm starving! What do you have?"

Rick said, "Sandwiches, salads, chicken strips, chips, a little bit of everything."

Leilani was quiet, but I noticed that she filled her plate with a substantial pile of food. I took that as a good sign that she was recovering from her ordeal.

When their plates were full, Leo said, "Mind if we take ours back to the flybridge? We won't spill anything."

I laughed. "There's nothing up there that can be hurt by a little spill. I just hose it off."

He blushed, and they took their plates and two plastic mugs of iced tea up the ladder outside.

Rick said, "Those two sure seem to have hit it off."

"I'll say. I hope she's not rushing into anything because he came to her rescue."

He looked startled. "Oh, come on! This coming from the man who rescues women and then invites them to move aboard with him?"

"Hey, I only did that once, with Callie."

"Yeah, but you seem to get involved with all of the women you save."

"That's not true!"

Rick just laughed.

"Well, not *all* of them. I didn't rescue Bonnie. More like the other way around."

"You've got me there, Will. Maybe that should tell you something. Stick to the ones who don't always need saving."

"Easier said than done. The ones who need saving seem to just land in my lap."

Rick roared with laughter. "In more ways than one!"

"Okay, okay, I get your point. Anyway, Callie and I aren't a couple anymore, but that doesn't keep her from needing to be rescued, does it?"

He got serious. "No, it doesn't. She should be glad you're the one looking for her."

"Now I just have to find her."

* * *

I felt strange. We'd rescued all three young immigrants, but their safety and their future in the United States were very much in doubt. Callie and I were through, but now I felt responsible for her safety. Watching Leilani and Leo in the beginnings of young love on my boat didn't make things any easier.

Having things that needed to be done for everyone but me kicked in my selfish side.

Why am I losing sleep over Callie? She not only dumped me, she left for a younger reporter. I'm the reason she got into journalism, now she doesn't need me anymore. She only needs to be rescued. Again.

I shook my head to clear it. This wasn't doing me any good. I needed to get away from the love birds on my boat.

"Rick, do you mind staying here for a while? I need to get with Jimmy and see what he's found on Alvarez's properties. There's plenty of beer in the fridge for you."

"Well, when you put it that way..."

"Thanks, Rick. I'll have my phone on if anything happens here."

"Are you okay? You look kind of gloomy, Will."

"Yeah, I'm all right. I just want to find Callie and get this chapter over with."

He said, "This ain't no magazine article, you know. This is her *life* we're talking about."

"I know. And my life too. I'm ready to move on with it."

Deadly Traffic

He didn't have an answer for that. "I'll be here."

I walked out of the cabin, stepped onto the dock, and walked towards my car. On the way I phoned Jimmy. "Hey, it's Will. Where are you?"

"I just got back to the houseboat. Want to come by and I'll fill you in on what I found?"

"On my way now." I ended the call and got into the Z4. Maybe there was an end in sight.

It was a short drive to Jimmy's place. I parked, and found him on the front deck, drinking a beer as he pored over documents spread out on the low table.

He pointed to the cooler. "Hey, Will, grab a beer and join me."

I pulled a Yuengling from the ice, twisted off the cap, and sat down. He looked at me.

"Are you okay?"

"Yeah, I'm just frustrated with how things are going, that's all."

"But, I haven't told you what I found yet."

I perked up. "Anything promising?"

"Yes, but there's a lot of papers to sort through. Alvarez has bought and sold a bunch of properties in the last few years. I'm having a tough time getting a lead on where he might have Callie."

"My suggestion would be to start with his house and work outward from there. Alvarez is a control freak. I can't see him sending her away to be held prisoner. He's the type that wants to gloat in your face."

"What do you mean by start at his house? He's owned that for a long time. I thought we were assuming that since she'd escaped from there before that he'd try something different."

"But Jimmy, he could have built a guest house, a garage, a pool house, something like that. Did you look for building permits?"

He hung his head. "I never thought of that. There are so many properties he's bought, I got wrapped up in searching those."

"Grab your laptop and we'll look in the county building permit database."

It wasn't the fast answer I was hoping for. Jimmy scrolled through page after page of listings. "Man, this guy has something being built or renovated on that mansion practically every month. Plumbing, electrical upgrades, paving, you name it. It will take me a while to sort through these application forms."

I felt like crying. "We can't quit on it. Callie's life depends on it. Want me to look through them while you go through the property search papers you've already got?"

He handed the laptop to me. I leaned back in the deck chair and got to work. Forty-five minutes later I was no closer to finding a likely hiding place. I stood up to stretch, and when I did, I heard a text tone.

Jimmy said, "Was that your phone? I don't see anything on mine."

I took it out of my pocket and looked. It was an anonymous number. I clicked on the text, and the photo popped up. It was Callie, taped to a chair. A pair of hands held a *Palm Beach Post* with today's headline. At least for now, she was alive.

Chapter Twenty-Five

I breathed a sigh of relief. "She's alive, and she looks okay." When I handed the phone to Jimmy, he looked and said, "She looks pissed off."

I had to smile. "That's better than looking scared."

He stared closely at the photo. "I can't see what the background is." He clicked on the photo and enlarged it, then scrolled around the edges. "The wall behind her is metal, and the chair looks like it's sitting on a concrete pad. That doesn't tell me anything." He handed the phone back to me.

I looked at the enlarged photo. "Look at all the sand on the floor. Did he have any beachfront properties where there might be an outbuilding?"

"Not that I've found so far. How about in the building permits?"

Sitting back down, I paged through them, scanning as I went. Ten minutes later, I spotted it.

"Here's a permit to repair a beach tunnel."

He said, "I thought those weren't allowed in Palm Beach?"

"Maybe it's grandfathered in as an existing structure. Besides, if you have enough money you can get anything done." I scanned the details of the permit application. "Looks like the project was to replace old support walls with a new metal shell." I looked at the diagram. "There are doors at each end. I'm sure they'll be locked."

Jimmy grinned. "Did I tell you about the new lock-picking gun I bought with that last bonus check you gave me?"

I eyed him skeptically. "You're joking, right?"

"Nope. It's from Germany. Stick it in the lock, press the button and it vibrates the tumblers into place. It works fast, quiet, and doesn't damage the lock. No one can even tell you broke in."

"That sounds like quite a gadget. Have you tried it out yet?"

He blushed. "Um, yeah, but only on the locks to the storage and garage doors here on the owner's house. I didn't want to pick his house lock and set off an alarm."

I grinned at him. "I never would have pegged you as a cat-burglar type of guy."

"Well, last time I kicked in a door I bruised my foot. It hurt to walk on for a week. Picking the lock seemed a lot easier."

"Now that we know we can get past the lock, what about an alarm system? I can't believe somebody like Alvarez would leave an entrance to his home unprotected."

Jimmy borrowed my laptop to look at the diagram. "I don't think it goes into the house. This sketch makes it look like it ends in a stairwell by the pool. It might not have an alarm."

"Only one way to find out. Let's go see for ourselves."

"How sure are you that Callie is in there, Will?"

"I'm not, it's only a guess. But I have a feeling Alvarez wants her close by. We have to hope he hasn't hurt her."

"She looks okay in the photo."

"Let's find her while she's still healthy, Jimmy. I don't trust Alvarez a bit."

We decided to drive over to Palm Beach and rent a small boat to scout the tunnel opening on the beach. It would attract less attention than walking behind all of the mansions on the waterfront.

I called Captain Rick and asked him to stay the night on the *WanderLust* with Leilani and Leo while we were on the other coast. When I told him what we planned to do, he was not happy about it.

"Dammit, Will, I want to help! Who's gonna watch your back when you two go into that tunnel? If they catch you in there, his goons can block both ends of the tunnel. You'll be a sitting duck."

"Rick, if we leave Leilani and Leo unprotected, we risk losing two more instead of getting Callie back. I took you with me to Fort Myers, and left Jimmy behind, remember? Please don't argue with me about this."

He grumbled, "You treat me like an old man."

Sigh. "We need you where you are. It's important."

"Fine."

I could tell it wasn't, but there was nothing I could do about it. "I'll keep you posted."

He muttered, "Bye," and ended the call.

I'll need to do some fence-mending with Rick when this is over. I can't worry about that now, though. I've got to find Callie.

* * *

We decided to make the drive to Palm Beach in my Z4, since it would fit in well with all of the small sports cars that the area seems full of. We were wearing resort style clothes but took dark clothing to change into.

Jimmy said, "Won't the boat rental places all be closed by the time we get there?"

"Probably, but I'll bet with enough cash we can get someone to rent us a boat. I brought a good supply."

"That will call a lot of attention to us."

"Possibly, but all we're doing tonight is scouting. Anyway, if we find Callie and get her out of there, Alvarez will know who did it."

"I suppose you're right. I've always tried to stay off the radar, but it may not matter this time."

He was quiet for a while before speaking again. "Do you miss Callie, Will?"

Sigh. "Sure I do. But it doesn't mean I want her back. I mean, I want to save her from Alvarez, but not to be a couple again."

"Even if she's had a change of heart? Rescuing her could make you seem like a hero."

I laughed bitterly. "Have you forgotten that I saved her life *twice* already? Hell, when she was dangling from the Key West lighthouse, she almost took me over the side with her. If that didn't make her love me more than she loves Alvaro, nothing will."

"I guess. I don't pretend to understand women."

"Me neither. Of course, they don't understand us, either."

He shook his head. "So we blunder through our relationships, bumping into walls because neither of us knows what the other wants or understands what they say."

"Sad, but true, Jimmy."

"Hey, maybe they could write a couple of those 'learn a foreign language quickly' programs that will help us translate. You know, *Understanding Women for Dummies*!"

When we quit laughing, I said, "I think having them understand us might be even better."

He nodded. "You have a point. I hate being mis-understood."

"What's happening in your love life these days?"

"Nothing at the moment. I dated Hanna a couple of times and we had fun together, but when you told me she was looking for marriage and kids, I asked her about it. When she said yes, that was what she wanted from a relationship, I backed off."

"Not ready for the white picket fence and a few kids?"

He rolled his eyes. "Not any more than you were. When Hanna found out that wasn't what I wanted either, she didn't want to waste time on just dating. She seems to be hearing her biological clock ticking." He paused. "Did you ever want kids, Will?"

"When I was married, we thought about it. She even went off birth control, but nothing happened. In retrospect, I lucked out. If we'd had kids together, she'd have tortured me with them. She'd have used them to squeeze more money out of me, too. It's a good thing my Aunt Dotty didn't leave me money before the divorce. My wife would have done her best to get more than half."

"That sucks. I'm kind of surprised you trust women at all after being married to her."

"So am I. I keep thinking it's the last time I leave myself open like that, and then I meet some woman who needs rescuing. It's funny, when Callie and I met, she wasn't like that at all. Hell, she's the one who got us out of that burning cane field."

"Yeah, she was pretty badass that day."

"Yes, she was. I don't know, maybe needing to be saved turned her off on the relationship. It kind of changed things between us. She wanted independence, not to be rescued all the time."

"Not that you had a choice."

"Nope. And now we need to save her again."

* * *

We arrived at West Palm before sunset and found a small marina that rented skiffs for fishing. The owner was a little leery of us.

"It's late in the day to rent a boat. Sun will be going down in about a half hour. I'm waiting for the last boat to come in now."

I said, "We really wanted to get some photos of Palm Beach at sunset, with all the lights on in the big houses."

Jimmy had his camera with a long lens on it hanging from his shoulder. "The conditions should be perfect. Hate to waste the drive over here."

"I guess I can rent to you, but I'll have to charge you an extra thirty dollars for staying late to check you back in."

"That's fine, thanks." I pulled a hundred and two twenties from my wallet. "Does this cover it?"

Suddenly he was all smiles. "Yessir, that will do just fine. Let me show you where everything is on this boat."

He gave us a quick rundown on the safety gear, and we were soon heading over towards Palm Beach across the Intracoastal Waterway. I had printed off some Google Maps images to help identify the Alvarez mansion from the water, but it wasn't easy to spot in the fading daylight.

Jimmy said, "We're on the right stretch of beach front. Can you tell which one it is?"

"Looks on here like it should be the fifth house from the end. I think that's it, the one with the arched windows on the main floor."

"I think you're right. I recognize the striped awning over the patio. That's the one that Carmelina jumped onto. I don't see a tunnel opening on the beach, though."

"Let's beach the boat on the point, then we'll walk down to the house. There's a lot of landscaping close to the water. The entrance may be hidden by the bushes."

We took the boat slowly to the uninhabited space on the point and idled it up to the shore. There was nothing to tie it up to, so we dragged it above the waterline. We were at slack tide, and even though I didn't think it would go anywhere, I tossed a mushroom anchor onto the sand.

The sun was below the horizon and dark was fast approaching as we donned long sleeve black tees and black watch caps. I said to Jimmy, "You've been here before. Lead the way."

He nodded, and I followed behind as we walked down the beach behind the multi-million dollar homes. The display lighting on the palm trees and the house facades would make it hard for anyone to spot us in the shadows.

When we were behind the Alvarez mansion, Jimmy began poking around the tall shrubs and short palms. He spotted a small path, and we followed it into a mini-maze that concealed the tunnel entrance.

"Bingo."

I said, "Pretty ingenious. Nobody would know this door was even here unless they explore the bushes." I tried the door knob. "Locked. I suppose you brought your lock pick gun?"

"Yes, but before we bust in, let's scout the other end of the tunnel. If we have to get out of there in a hurry, I want to know where it comes out."

"Good idea." I followed him as we quietly made our way towards the rear of the house, staying clear of the landscaping lights. We crouched behind the edge of the pool house, the same place Jimmy and Pablo had been hiding when they saw Carmelina's escape. After a few minutes of staring at the silent house, a door opened, creating a pool of light on the patio, A man walked out, carrying a tray.

The man walked past the pool to what looked like a pool equipment shed and disappeared inside.

Jimmy said, "I'll bet the tunnel opening is in there."

"Listen, can you get down to the beach end of the tunnel fast? I need to know if that guy comes out the other end."

"I'm on it." He took off without wasted words.

I was betting the tray was for someone in that tunnel, but it wouldn't be a safe thing to just assume. Ten minutes later, the man returned and exited the pool shed, holding the empty tray under his arm. After he entered the house, I walked back to the beach and looked for Jimmy. I didn't see him, but that was no surprise given his military training.

"Pssst. Will. Over here." He rose from a wall of greenery. As I approached, he stepped out and said, "No man with a tray on this end."

"Yeah, he came back out the way he went in."

"That probably means Callie is in there."

I was ready. "So let's go find her."

Chapter Twenty-Six

J immy approached the hidden tunnel door and using a small pen-light he inserted his electric lock-pick into the keyhole. It vibrated for a few seconds, and we heard a "click." He turned the handle, and the door silently swung open.

I whispered, "That was easy."

He shined the penlight around the door frame. "I don't see any alarm sensors."

"There could be things further in the tunnel though," I said.

"Seems unlikely, when they don't bother to alarm the door."

Jimmy said, "Follow me." Using his light to illuminate the path forward, we entered the tunnel.

The walls were oval corrugated steel, rounded like the inside of a large drainage pipe. There was a wide layer of sand on the bottom that made walking easier. It also meant we'd leave tracks.

When we'd gone about halfway through the tunnel, I saw a door in the wall. It said "Electrical," with "Danger, Keep Out," printed underneath.

Jimmy said, "This could be the place." He shined the light on the sandy floor. "There are a lot of tracks leading to the house, almost none going to the beach. This door is getting a lot of use."

He tried the door. Locked. He reached for the lock-pick device, but before he could use it we heard a bang as a metal door shut at the house end of the tunnel, followed by voices.

"Shit! Come on, we've got to get out of here."

We raced to the beach doorway, got through it and quietly shut the door behind us. Jimmy took off towards the spot where we'd beached the skiff, with me trailing behind him. He didn't stop to talk until we got there.

I said, "That was close."

"Yeah, and I don't know why. There was at least two of them coming down the tunnel. I wonder if we tripped some sensor after all?"

"There sure wasn't anything we could see. Maybe when you tried the door on that electrical closet, it moved enough to trigger an alarm."

"I don't know, Will. Why leave the exterior doors without alarms, but put one on an electrical closet?"

"Maybe there's a lot of foot traffic to the beach that goes through the tunnel by day, but no one is allowed in the electrical closet."

He looked skeptical. "What do you want to do now?"

"We need to get Callie out of there."

He shook his head. "You don't even know that she's in there."

"I feel pretty sure."

"Sure enough to go up against two body guards, likely with guns?"

"There are two of us."

"Will, one of the first things we learned in Army Ranger training was not to rush into a dangerous situation without knowing what to expect. Good intelligence is crucial, and we don't have any idea what's inside that tunnel."

I wasn't going to be talked out of it. "Jimmy, if she's in there, we can't just leave her."

"Going in unprepared could get us all three killed. Let me round up a couple of former members of my Ranger team so we can at least improve the odds, okay?"

"How long will that take?"

"I keep in touch with a group of them in South Florida, maybe just a few hours."

It felt like I didn't have a choice. I couldn't force Jimmy to risk his own life. "Okay."

Reluctantly, I helped push the skiff back into the water, and we headed back to the rental dock.

It was later than we'd promised to return the boat, but a healthy tip and the promise of a return visit brought a smile to the owner's face.

I said, "We'll be back, probably tomorrow afternoon, and we'll need two boats. Same deal as today?"

"Absolutely my friend! I'll have them gassed up and ready when you arrive."

We walked back to my car and sat down to regroup. "What now?" I asked.

"My suggestion would be to check into a hotel and let me make some phone calls. Once I have help lined up, I'd like to go get some dinner. I'm starving."

My stomach growled at his words. "Guess I'm hungry too. I didn't even think about eating with all that's been happening."

He patted his tight belly and smiled. "Got to keep the machinery fueled up."

"I hear you." I started the Z4 to get the AC going. Even after dark the South Florida air was steamy. As it cooled down, I searched for a hotel on my iPhone, found one nearby and booked a room. I set the phone on the console and said, "Ready?"

Jimmy hooked his seatbelt. "Let's go."

We drove to the hotel, checked in, and went to the room.

Jimmy said, "Oh, good, you got two queens. I wasn't looking forward to sharing a bed, at least not with you. No offense, but you kick."

I winced. "Sorry, Nightmares do that to me."

"Hey, I'm just ragging on you, Will. No worries."

I sat on the edge of one of the beds. "I'll take this one."

"Fine with me." He got out his phone. "Time to round up some firepower for this gig."

"I'll check in with Ben at the *Journal* while you make your calls." I dialed his mobile number.

"Ben? It's Will. Any news on your end?"

"Hey, this *is* a newspaper, you know. News is our business."

Sigh. "You know what I mean. Anything new on Callie's disappearance or on the three siblings?"

"You sound grumpy. I guess that means no luck on finding Callie?"

"We have a good lead, but I don't want to say too much about it yet."

"Ah, thinking about breaking a few laws, are you, Will?"

"I wouldn't say that. More like shaking up a few lawbreakers."

"Anyone I know?"

"One of the usual suspects."

"You're being very cryptic tonight."

"Don't complain. I'm giving you deniability on anything that the police could question you about."

"Ooookay, I get the message. Listen, I know you're busy, but the *Journal* is going to run a story about the three immigrants to see if we can get the governor to back asylum for them. Could you do an update on their status now that Leilani is safe?"

"I can try. Right now my priority is getting Callie back."

"Hmm, interesting how you put that. Getting her back to safety, or getting her back with you?"

Groan. "Just getting her safe, okay?"

"Don't be touchy, I was just asking. You guys made a great couple."

"To remind you, Ben, *she* broke up with *me*, not the other way around."

"Yeah, but you're not one to give up easy."

"No, but I'm not interested in begging someone to love me, either. That ship has sailed."

"Sorry, sorry, I'll drop it."

"Thanks."

He was silent for a moment. "Bring her home, Will."

"I'll do my best." I ended the call, frustrated. *Why is it everyone thinks I send my romantic partners away? I may not be the easiest person to live with, but I'm loyal and dependable, and I like to think I'm a fun guy. I can't help it if they all leave!*

Jimmy was still on the phone, so I got out my laptop and started writing. The news deadline wouldn't wait.

* * *

I wrote for an hour and had at least the outline of a story update on Carmelina, Pablo and Leilani. What they had been through in their young lives read like an adventure novel, and I hoped it wouldn't be too much for the reading public to swallow. Somehow, when you use the word "slavery," people roll their eyes and think you're exaggerating. I don't know what else to call it when someone pays money to have control over another human life.

Jimmy was off the phone, so I shut my laptop. "How did it go finding backup?"

"I found two guys from my old squad who are free tomorrow, but I wouldn't call them 'backup.' One was my squad leader, and I'd suggest turning over the planning of this operation to him."

"Hey, he's not the one whose girlfriend is captive."

"Don't you mean 'ex' girlfriend?"

I could feel my face turn red. "I said that from habit. Anyway, just because she dumped me doesn't mean I don't still care what happens to her."

"Okay, I hear you. My point is, Diego is as sharp as they come, and he's used to getting a team in and out with minimal casualties. That's what we need."

"*Minimal* casualties? How about if we get everyone out in one piece?"

"That will be the goal, but when you're dealing with an armed resistance it's better to assume the worst. That's why I wanted to call in the cavalry. More people and more firepower make it less likely we'll be the casualties."

"You're not exactly filling me with confidence, Jimmy."

He bristled. "We can drop this plan right now and call the cops. Let them go knock on some doors and I'll sleep in tomorrow."

"Take it easy, I didn't mean it that way. You know I can't call the cops without any proof she's even in that tunnel. Besides, Alvarez would likely have someone on the police force who would tip him off that the cops were coming. There's always one cop who's willing to help out the rich guys. Then they ask for a cushy retirement job working security for them."

He rubbed a hand across his face. "Sorry. I did some arm-twisting to get Zack and Diego onboard, and I was hoping you'd be pleased."

"Hey, Jimmy, I am pleased. Forgive me. My nerves are a little strung out today."

He patted my shoulder. "It's okay. There's nothing we can do tonight. Shall we go find some dinner?"

"That's the best idea I've heard all night."

"Do you know any of the restaurants here in West Palm?"

"Nope. Would you rather drive around and look, or get a recommendation from the front desk?"

"I'd rather not waste time looking. You call the desk."

I picked up the phone and dialed zero. "Yes, this is Will Harper in 403. Can you suggest a good restaurant nearby?"

"Certainly, sir. What's your preference, seafood, steaks, sushi, Cuban, Italian…?"

"How about a good steak place."

"Yes, sir, that's an easy one. The Okeechobee Steak House is well-known in the area. It's a little old-fashioned and not cheap, but the steaks are terrific."

"Sounds perfect. Do we need reservations?"

"Actually, they can have up to a two-hour wait."

"Forget that one, we're hungry. What else can you suggest?"

"Before you give up, let me make a quick call Mr. Harper. I'll call you right back."

I barely said, "Okay," before the line was dead. "Well, he has a good place, but with a long wait likely."

Jimmy groaned. "I'm not up for waiting. If we wait that long in the bar, I'm liable to get bombed."

"Let's see what else he comes up with then."

In five minutes, the phone range. "Mr. Harper? This is Blake from the front desk. I have you a reservation at 8, will that do?"

I looked at the clock on the table. 7:25. "That's perfect. How did you get the reservation on short notice?"

"My brother is dating the hostess. She likes me."

I laughed. "Well, thank your brother for us."

"No problem. Enjoy your dinner, Mr. Harper."

I ended the call, and said to Jimmy, "How about the best steaks in town, table for us at 8 pm."

"That sounds perfect. Let me wash my face, change shirts, and I'll be ready to go."

Twenty minutes later, we were sitting in the bar at the steakhouse waiting for our table.

Jimmy said, "This is my kind of place. I'd rather eat at a good old-fashioned steak house than some fancy place with tiny portions any day."

"Yeah, judging by the crowd, it looks like the go-to spot for birthdays and anniversaries. That's usually a good sign."

We toasted with our drinks. "To a successful rescue."

He said, "I'll drink to that." We clinked glasses and drank. As we set down the empty glasses, the hostess came to take us to our table.

"Are you ready to be seated, sir?"

"That would be great. Lead the way." We followed her across the restaurant, and as we passed the door to a private room, a waiter exited. I heard a loud laugh, followed by a voice I knew.

"Never let business get in the way of my birthday, I always say."

The crowd said, "Happy Birthday, Boss!" I heard a round of cheers, and it felt like a punch to my gut.

The voice was Eduardo Alvarez.

Chapter Twenty-Seven

I raced to the table with Jimmy, then pulled him close after the hostess seated us and gave us menus. "Jimmy!" I whispered. "That's Alvarez in the private party room."

"Are you sure?"

"Yeah, he has a distinctive voice. Loud and obnoxious."

"So what do you want to do about it? Go in there and demand he hand over Callie?" He raised his eyebrows when he said it, and I could tell he was being facetious.

"No, of course not. But, he has a crowd of people in there for his birthday, and I heard one call him boss. There might be a short-handed crew guarding the house and the tunnel."

"And?"

"Maybe we should go get Callie out of there right now."

He shook his head. "Listen, Will, we have reinforcements coming tomorrow. Besides, the boat rental guy will be closed now. Do you propose pulling into Alvarez's driveway and busting her out?"

"Well, no..."

"We need to stick with the plan. Four men, heavily armed, two boats, and we go in through the beach side of the tunnel. Okay?"

I didn't like it, but I knew he was right. "I guess so."

"We've got a lot of work to do tomorrow, but for tonight, let's have a nice meal and get a good night's sleep so we'll be rested and ready."

We sat in silence and studied the menu. When the waitress came I ordered a bourbon on the rocks. Jimmy ordered a beer.

He said, "I've never seen you drink bourbon before, Will. It's usually beer or wine."

I wasn't in the mood to justify it. "Tonight, I feel like bourbon."

He could see I didn't want to talk. When the drinks arrived, we placed our order. The stress I was feeling hadn't diminished the hunger, and I ordered a Porterhouse steak, medium, with baked potato and Caesar salad.

Jimmy said, "The same for me, but medium rare with steak fries." The waitress left to take our order to the kitchen, and he said, "Man, I'm starving. This place looks like a good choice."

"Yeah, apparently lots of people think so."

"Don't let Alvarez being here spoil your meal. We'll deal with him tomorrow."

I took a deep breath and let it out. "I'll try. Let's not talk about him."

The salads arrived, and he dug into his with gusto while I picked at mine. It was really good, with shaved parmesan and a creamy dressing. When the steaks were brought to the table, they were as good as advertised. Before I knew it, I'd cleaned my plate.

Jimmy said, "Glad to see you found your appetite."

"I thought I wasn't hungry anymore until they set food in front of me. I have to admit, that was a great meal." The waitress came by to check on us, and I ordered a merlot while Jimmy ordered another beer as he finished off his steak.

"That was one of the best steaks I've had in a long time. Thanks for dinner, Will."

"My pleasure. Thanks for coming to help out with this rescue. At least, I hope that's what it turns into."

"Don't stress about it. We've managed to get Carmelina, Pablo and Leilani together again, and that's a big accomplishment. You had no way of knowing that Alvarez would grab Callie to use her as leverage."

"No, and besides, she wasn't listening to anything I had to say. The warnings I did give her were a waste of breath."

Jimmy shook his head. "Sometimes people have to learn from their own mistakes. You can't do it for them."

"I've made plenty of my own mistakes, especially where women are concerned."

He laughed at that. "If you're learning from experience, you ought to have a PhD in women by now."

I know he saw the humor in it, but it didn't feel funny to me. "Slow learner, I guess."

"Hey, I'm just ragging on you, Will. No offense."

"None taken. I'm just ready to get this chapter over with and move on with my life."

He raised his glass. "To getting Callie home."

I clinked glasses with him without comment. It was going to be hard to wait until tomorrow. I wanted this over now.

*** * ***

Eduardo Alvarez sat in the rear of his chauffeured limo, belly full from the sumptuous steak-house meal, along with several glasses of wine. The birthday cake, while delicious, had been too much, and he felt bloated.

It was a short drive back to his Palm Beach estate, but he still dozed off in the backseat. When his driver woke him, he was in the middle of a dream featuring a large-breasted woman and a birthday cake.

"Boss, we're home. Wake up."

He jerked upright in the seat. "What the hell did you wake me up for?"

"Sorry, boss, I didn't want to leave you asleep in the car, you know?"

Idiot. "Next time just sit here with the car on and wait until I wake up on my own. You screwed up a really nice dream."

The driver stood up at attention. "Sure thing, sorry, Mr. Alvarez."

Grumbling, Alvarez exited the car, and walked into the portico entry. The butler greeted him.

"Good evening, sir. Did you enjoy your dinner party?"

"Yeah, it was great. Get me a small scotch, will you? I'll be in my study." He still felt bloated but thought the scotch might help settle his stomach. He walked down the carpet-lined hallway to his study and opened one of the ten-foot tall doors. It always pleased him to see this room with its leather-covered furnishings and the walls lined with books.

The thousands of volumes were just for looks, as Alvarez's only reading pleasure was sugar production and cash-flow reports, with the occasional adult magazine thrown in for variety. Tonight, he had a different kind of entertainment in mind.

The butler entered the room, brought his scotch, and set it the table next to the padded leather wing chair Alvarez had sunken into. "Here you go, sir."

He nodded his approval, took a sip, and said, "Give me fifteen minutes to unwind, and then send Luis in here."

"Yes, sir." He knew better than to try to engage his employer in idle chat, and he turned and left the room.

Alvarez sipped his scotch and let his stomach settle as he awaited his employee's arrival. He wanted to be in the right frame of mind when he made his visit to the tunnel. Fifteen minutes exactly after he'd made the request, there was a knock on his study door.

"Enter."

Luis walked in. "You sent for me, sir?"

"Yes, Luis, I want to pay a visit to our 'guest' in the tunnel room. Is she presentable?"

"Uh, yes, sir, I mean, well, she's been locked in there for several days, you know, so she's not exactly happy. And she could use a bath, too. Do you want me to get her cleaned up for you?"

"That won't be necessary. I don't plan on getting that close to her. Not yet, anyway."

Alvarez drained his scotch, then stood up. "Take me to her now." He walked to the study door and entered the hallway as Luis scrambled to keep up. He trailed behind Alvarez but jumped ahead every time a door needed opening. When they exited the house onto the pool deck, Luis opened the door, then raced to the tunnel entrance.

He looked at Alvarez's velvet-topped lounge slippers, and said, "Sir, the sand down there is kind of damp."

His boss looked annoyed. "And so?"

"Well, your shoes..." he trailed off, afraid to continue.

"You let me worry about my shoes. Open the damn door."

Luis swallowed hard, then opened the door. Steps went down fifteen feet with a landing in the middle, then down to a concrete-floored alcove where a golf cart was plugged into a wall socket.

Alvarez sat in the passenger seat and waited as Luis unplugged the cart and coiled the charging cord before hanging it on a wall hook. Luis joined him in the cart, flipped the switch to forward, and drove down the gloomy tunnel.

After a very short ride, the cart stopped in front of the door marked *Electrical*. Luis hopped out, unlocked the door, and said, "Want me to go in and check things out, Mr. Alvarez?"

"No, I'll go in by myself. You wait out here." *I want to see the look on her face when she sees me.* He opened the door and entered.

Callie lay on a small cot, a blanket pulled over her against the dampness. She sat up in shock. "You! I should have known you were behind this."

He smiled. "No need to get nasty, Miss Lovett. You are uninjured, are you not?"

"No thanks to you." she spat at him. "You have me locked in this damp hole in the ground. I demand that you let me go."

"Now, Miss Lovett, you are hardly in a position to make demands, are you? As soon as your boyfriend returns my property to me, you will be free to go. Until then, you will remain my guest."

"Well, the joke's on you, Alvarez. Will and I broke up. He's not likely to worry too much about getting me back."

"Hmmm, that would be most unfortunate for you, I'm afraid. If my property is not returned to me soon, then you will have to take her place."

It suddenly dawned on Callie what he meant. "You think Carmelina is your *property*? You're a sick bastard."

He bristled in anger. "Miss Lovett, I'm going to let your rudeness slide for now, since I realize you're upset. But I warn you, should you take your friend's place in my household, I will tolerate no disrespect. And the penalties can be, shall we say, *quite* severe."

She crossed her arms in defiance. "If you so much as touch me, I will make you pay. Bet on it."

He laughed. "Thanks for the warning, Miss Lovett. If I decide that I require your services, I'll make sure you are in restraints beforehand." He was still laughing when he left and locked the door behind him.

Chapter Twenty-Eight

The next morning I woke a little hung-over but was functioning well enough to start writing again after getting my second cup of coffee. Jimmy had gone for an early morning run. He was much too energetic for my taste when he returned.

"Hey, Will, glad to see you're finally up and around! I was afraid I'd have to drag you out of bed this morning."

"I've already been up over a half hour, and I'm writing now. Could you hold the volume down a bit?"

"No problem. You finishing up the story on our three rescued siblings?"

"Yeah, Ben wanted an update. I think Pastor Marlee would like to get them some publicity too, see if she can get public sentiment behind a special asylum designation for them."

"Lord knows they've suffered enough since they got to this country. Seems like the least we could do is take them in now."

"I'm with you, Jimmy, but the political winds are not pro-immigrant at the moment."

He looked angry. "How about pro-humanity? These kids got sold into slavery in our state! That should not be allowed to happen in this day and age. I don't see how the governor could turn them away."

I gestured at my laptop. "Thus, the story. I'm hoping the publicity will help. When people know what those three have been through, they'd have to be pretty hard-hearted to send them back to Guatemala."

Jimmy said, "My two Ranger buddies are coming in around lunch time. I thought we'd give them a quick rundown on the situation here in the room where we can talk, then head out and get some lunch."

"That makes sense, I guess, since we can't do anything to bust into the tunnel until it's dark."

"Think stealth, Will. We're not planning on 'busting in.' I'm hoping we can get Callie out and be gone before Alvarez even knows we're there."

"I know, that was just a figure of speech, okay?"

"I want to make sure you understand the rules of engagement. We don't shoot at anyone unless we get shot at first. When weapons start firing, somebody might get killed, including us."

"Understood." I didn't like being lectured, but he was right to be concerned. A part of me wanted to go into that tunnel with guns blazing and take Alvarez and his men out. Fortunately, I had Jimmy to be the voice of reason.

He said, "I'm going to grab a shower while you're writing. Back in a few."

I took a deep breath and dove back into the story. I needed to think about something other than Callie, or about making Alvarez pay. Time enough for that later.

Within an hour, I was done. I emailed it to my editor, closed the program, then shut the laptop. I looked up and saw Jimmy on the couch, feet up on the coffee table.

"You finally done, Will? I've been sitting here for more than a half hour, and I swear, you didn't even know I was in the room."

I grinned at him. "So? I get into my work."

"I'll say. More like it sucked you in, and just now spit you back out." He put his feet on the floor and sat up. "Zack and Diego texted me that they're about a half hour out. Anything we should talk about before they get here?"

"Yeah. The first priority is getting Callie out of there safely. After that, I'm not too worried about Alvarez or anyone on his team getting hurt."

He rolled his eyes. "We don't shoot first, got it?"

"Got it." *Unless I have to.*

"I called the front desk to arrange a room for my buddies. Does that suit you, Will?"

"Good thinking. I don't know why that didn't occur to me."

"Probably because you're spending all of your time worrying about your ex-girlfriend."

He saw me wince.

"Sorry, man, I wasn't taking a shot at you. I just know how focused you've been on getting her back. I mean, getting her released."

"That's okay, Jimmy, no offense taken. I'm just not used to thinking of Callie as an *ex* yet."

There wasn't much else to say, so we waited quietly until his friends arrived. A short while later, I heard a knock on the door.

Jimmy opened it. "Hey, Zack, Diego, come on in."

They climbed the boarding steps amid back slapping and handshakes. "Will, this is two of the guys from my Ranger team, Zack and Diego."

Both men were built like Jimmy, tall, muscular, and fit. Zack had sandy hair and blue eyes, Diego with black hair to match his dark eyes.

"Nice to meet you guys. I appreciate your help with this."

Zack said, "No sweat. We're always there when an old Army bud needs us, especially if it sounds like fun."

I said, "I don't know how much fun it will be. We need to bust a friend of mine out of a locked room in a beach tunnel, and the guy who took her isn't likely to appreciate it."

"Jimmy filled us in on some of the details. This guy took your girlfriend to swap her for some chick he was keeping locked up to work for him, right?"

'Well, that's close. Callie was my girlfriend, but isn't anymore. Carmelina is a very young Guatemalan girl, and this rich asshole bought her from a smuggler."

Diego chimed in. "Still sounds fun to me, making some rich jerk sorry he messed with us. Fill us in on the plan, Jimmy."

He ran it down for them, then Diego said, "Hey, have we got time to get a bite before heading out on this gig? We got a fast-food lunch on the drive up, but it didn't exactly fill me up."

Jimmy laughed. "I should have warned you that Diego is a bottomless pit. He can eat a big meal and still be hungry, but never gains a pound."

Diego patted his flat stomach. "It's my fast metabolism, man. I burn it off."

I said, "Well, let's feed these guys then." We rode in Zack's Jeep and found a mom and pop diner that suited everyone. Watching Diego order was an adventure.

He told the waitress, "I'll have the fried chicken special with mashed potatoes, cornbread, a side of okra, and apple pie for dessert." He added, "That should hold me until dinner."

Jimmy said, "Man, if I ate that much, I'd be comatose. I don't burn it off the way I used to."

Zack slapped him on the back. "Getting soft, Sarge."

"What can I say? Working with Will has its benefits, but I struggle to keep up with my fitness program."

I jumped in. "Hey, what about the cycling and kayaking we've been doing? That was a great workout."

"Geez, Will, we haven't done that in a month! And they were short workouts to start with."

I bristled. "Not everyone is a trained soldier."

My comment was greeted with a trio of grins. The food came shortly, and I enjoyed a BLT as I watched the other three chow down on what would not be called "health food."

We made short work of our late lunch, then made the drive to the marina where we had reserved two skiffs. Jimmy and I picked up the two rental boats while Zack and Diego waited for us at our rendezvous point at a nearby abandoned commercial dock. We didn't want them to be recognized as the two men who loaded weapons into the boats that would likely be tied into the assault on Alvarez's beach tunnel.

The boat owner wasn't any happier than he'd been the first time that we were taking his boats out so late in the day, but the extra hundred I gave him eased his concern.

He said, "You boys remember now, I can't go home until you get back with my boats. I want them returned undamaged, you hear?"

I said, "Just like last time, no problems." I hoped I was telling the truth.

Jimmy and I steered the skiffs out into the waterway, then downstream towards the dock where Zack and Diego waited. It didn't hurt that the boat owner saw us leave in a direction opposite the Palm Beach mansion we were heading for.

When we pulled up to the dock, Diego said, "Damn, Will, is this the best you could find? I was expecting a pair of cabin cruisers. These things aren't much better than row boats."

"As long as they get us where we're going, they're all we need. Don't forget, we're going to beach these boats. Tough to do that with cabin cruisers."

He grinned. "Guess you've got a point there. Let's get the gear in these tubs. Hope it's not enough to sink 'em."

Jimmy said, "After that meal you ate, *you* might be enough to sink the boat."

I knew they were trying to lighten the mood, but my stomach was in knots. Callie's safety was all that mattered.

After everything was loaded, we made our way slowly up ICW to Palm Beach and the mansions that adorn the waterfront. The sun was just starting to set, so we had plenty of light to find the spot where I'd beached the skiff before. We'd brought a couple of fishing rods for cover, and we found a likely spot just offshore and did a few casts. I didn't think anyone would be suspicious, but it didn't hurt to be careful.

When the last rays bounced off the clouds and the light faded, we slowly ran the boats ashore. Everyone knew their parts in this operation, and we avoided talking, using hand signals. Jimmy led the way to the tunnel opening, and Diego went to the other end near the house. He'd be there to let us know if anyone entered from that direction.

Jimmy used his electric lock pick on the entry door, and then he checked in with Diego before opening the door. We were communicating using earwigs, tiny earplugs with built-in transmitters.

"Diego, still clear on your end?"

"All clear."

"We're entering the tunnel, let us know if that changes."

"Will do."

Jimmy said, "Here goes," and opened the door. Silence. He turned on his flashlight and pointed it at the sandy floor. "Follow me, but keep eight feet between us. We'll make a smaller target that way."

That's not encouraging. I was in the middle, so the two professionals could guard the front and the rear. I could almost feel the target on my chest. We moved slowly through the tunnel until we reached the door marker "Electrical, Danger! Keep Out". Jimmy listened with his ear against the door. Hearing nothing, he whispered a question to Diego at the other end.

"Still clear?"

"Yes."

"Okay, we're going in."

He gently inserted the key into the door lock, and pressed the button. It vibrated, then we heard the tumblers click into place. Jimmy opened the door.

Chapter Twenty-Nine

It was more of a cell than an electrical closet. There was a rack of breakers and wiring on the left wall, but it was behind a locked cage made of steel mesh. On the rear wall was a toilet and sink, and a cot hugged the right side wall. Under a thin blanket lay Callie, her eyes closed.

I rushed to her side, confirmed that she was breathing, then gently touched her shoulder. "Callie?"

Startled, she sat up quickly, bashing our heads together as she did. "Crap!"

I rubbed the knot on my head. "Are you okay?"

She groaned. "Oh my god, that hurts." She put her hand against her own lump. Then her eyes cleared, and she looked at me in surprise. "Will! How did you get here?"

"We've been searching for you. Are you all right?"

She said, "I think so. I've got a cold from being in this damp hole for days. Where the hell are we, anyway?"

"Don't you know?"

"They blindfolded me after they dragged me into the car and stuck something chemical smelling on my face. That's the last thing I remember before waking up in the cell."

"Callie, you're in a beach tunnel in Alvarez's back yard."

"What?! The nerve of that bastard."

I started to help her off of the cot, but she said, "Wait." She pulled the blanket off of her legs, exposing a metal cuff around one ankle. It was attached with a heavy chain to the bed frame, and the bed was bolted to the floor.

"Damn!" I looked at Jimmy, and said, "What now?"

He grinned. "No problem." He reached into a pocket on his black tactical pants and pulled out a loop of wire with ring handles attached to each end. It sparkled in the light from the bare overhead bulb. "It's a diamond wire saw."

He leaned over the pipe on the bed frame where the chain was attached and began quickly running the wire back and forth over the surface. I could smell hot metal as they saw started to bite. It was slow going.

Jimmy's head jerked up as he heard Diego's voice in in earwig.

"Three guys just came running out the back door of the house! One of them looks like Alvarez. Get out of there, now!"

Jimmy touched his ear and said, "We're trying to get Callie loose. Can you stall 'em?"

"I'll try," was the reply.

We heard a loud bang from above, and saw a bright flash bounce off the tunnel walls through the open doorway.

Zack said, "That's a flash-bang grenade, that should slow them down a little."

Sweat was pouring off Jimmy, his hands a blur as he whipped the wire blade back and forth through the metal pipe. Finally, it parted.

"Got it!" he said.

I grabbed a towel hanging on the wall and wrapped it around the shackle on her leg, then lifted Callie off the cot. "Let's get out of here."

Jimmy touched his earwig and said, "They're in the tunnel."

We rushed out the door, and I realized I was struggling with Callie's weight. She wasn't that heavy but holding her up in my arms still wasn't easy. Jimmy was getting ahead of me, and I stopped to hand Callie off to Zack, who could see I needed help. That's when I saw the golf cart racing towards us.

"Zack, behind you!"

He turned and jumped back into the open doorway as the cart slammed into the door. Alvarez was at the wheel, his face a mask of fury. The cart was knocked out of gear by the impact, and I started down the tunnel after Zack. I knew he couldn't slow Alvarez while carrying Callie. It was up to me.

Alvarez howled as he put the cart back in gear and raced after us. "Harper, you bastard! We had a deal!"

There was no time to argue the point. I tried to stay ahead of him, but he was almost on top of me when I threw myself against the wall. I reached out and yanked his arm off the wheel, causing him to veer into the tunnel wall. I never noticed the six-inch pipe running the length of the tunnel until the moment he hit it with that damn cart.

Water exploded from the pipe, and the cart flipped over with Alvarez behind the wheel. The narrow tunnel was filling up fast from the pulsing water main, and I found myself swept off my feet as a wave washed me down the sandy floor.

I struggled to stay upright, coughing as the water ran into my nose and mouth, and realized it was getting deeper. Jimmy was just ahead, trying to open the door, which had locked behind us. He'd placed a rock in the door frame to keep it ajar, but the water had washed it out, slamming the door on its powerful closing spring.

Zack was holding Callie high, out of the water, but there was nowhere to go.

Jimmy yelled, "The lock pick shorted out! Help me push on the door."

Zack stepped aside, and as I turned to help Jimmy, I saw the golf cart surging forward on the wave.

"Watch out!" I yelled. He jumped against the tunnel wall as the wave threw the cart into the door. There was no sign of

Alvarez. The cart bounced off the now dented door, but it still remained shut. The water continued to rise.

Jimmy said, "Will! Grab the side of the cart. We'll use it as a battering ram."

I got into position, and he said, "On three, one, two, three!" And we slammed the cart into the metal door. It bent but remained shut. At least some of the water began running out of the bent edges.

"Again! On three, one, two..." and we slammed the cart into the door. It flew open, carrying the cart and the four of us onto the beach in a wave of soaking wet humanity. Diego ran towards us as we lay sputtering in the sand.

"Is everyone okay?" he asked.

"I think so," I said. I looked over at Zack, whose body was wrapped around Callie. "Is she...?"

He unraveled himself and checked on her. She coughed and groaned. "She's still with us."

I saw a body that wasn't part of our group. I leaned over him, and saw sightless eyes staring at the sky. He had a bloody wound at the side of his head. "Looks like one of Alvarez's men didn't make it."

Jimmy crawled to his feet. "Let's get the hell out of here before reinforcements arrive."

Diego gave Zack a hand, and then he picked up Callie. "Meet you at the boats." They were soon ahead of us, with Jimmy lagging behind to make sure I kept up. We made it back to the boats, and Zack, Diego were already pushing off into the water, with Callie onboard.

I jumped into the other boat just before Jimmy gave it a shove towards the surf and jumped aboard. We could see the lights from Alverez's mansion from the water, but we didn't hear any sounds of activity. We pulled away from the shore, and I was relieved to see Callie sitting up in the other boat. She would be okay.

* * *

We had Callie checked out at an area hospital, and except for some bruises and dehydration, she was fine. I stood next to the ER gurney and talked to her.

"Kind of funny that you were dehydrated, after getting washed out of the tunnel like that."

She gave me a cross-eyed look. "Har har, still the comedian."

"Seriously, I'm glad you're okay."

She took my hand. "Thanks for rescuing me. Again."

"I kind of hope you won't need saving anymore. Three times is enough."

"How about if I promise to stay out of trouble?"

"You don't have to promise me anything, Callie. " I didn't mean it to sound harsh, but I could see the hurt look in her eyes. I didn't know what else to say.

"Sorry about how things turned out, Will. I mean, between us."

"Yeah, I'm sorry too."

She looked up at me. "Can we talk again when I'm not in a hospital bed?"

"Sure." I wasn't sure what else there was to talk about. I was glad she was safe, but that didn't change the fact that our relationship had ended.

I said, "Jimmy is going to take you over to Pastor Marlee's RV to spend the night. You shouldn't be alone right now. Carmelina is there, too. I know she'll be happy to see you."

"Will, I'm really glad the three siblings are free. I hope we can keep them in the country."

"Marlee's been working on that. She's running a publicity campaign to force the governor to support an asylum claim for them."

Just then Jimmy walked into the cubicle. "Hey, Callie, how are you feeling?"

"A little wrung out, but basically okay."

He smiled at her. "Nothing a good night's sleep won't fix, I bet."

She yawned. "That sounds great. That cot in the damp room wasn't easy to sleep on."

The doctor came in the room. "Miss Lovett? Everything checked out. No broken bones, blood work looks good, you're just a little run-down. Would you like to go home?"

"Yes, please." A tear ran down her cheek. "But, I need to figure out where that is."

***

There was fallout from our raid on Eduardo Alverez's little tunnel prison, but it didn't fall on me. Alvarez got a broken leg and a dislocated shoulder from his golf cart attack, and the police charged him with kidnapping and reckless endangerment. I could only hope that all his money wouldn't be enough to keep him out of jail.

Callie and Carmelina were becoming fast friends during their time together at Marlee's RV, Pablo was still on Jimmy's houseboat, and Leilani and Leo were still on the *WanderLust* with me. They're great kids, but watching them moon after each other in our close quarters was getting old.

A call from Ben Carlson at the *Bradenton Journal* brought relief.

"Will? It's Ben. I have some good news for you."

"I'm in the mood for good news. Shoot."

"Pastor Marlee's push for asylum is beginning to pay off. A bunch of groups, including the Chamber of Commerce, are pressing the governor to protect them because of what they've suffered in our state. He can't personally grant it, but he is a supporter of the president, and he can make the case that they deserve asylum."

"That's great news, Ben. Now I just need to find them a place to stay."

"That's the other news. Their story reached a family with a bed and breakfast in Fort Myers. The owners came to this country as immigrants and became citizens. They've offered all three siblings jobs and a place to stay while their immigration status is worked out."

"Wow, that is terrific. I'll be sorry to see them go, but it will be nice for them to all be together."

"Are you sure you'll be sorry, Will? With Leo and Leilani staying on your boat I'll bet it's close quarters."

I laughed. "You know me too well. I do treasure my alone time."

"You're not exactly a social butterfly, my friend."

"Yeah, Callie got me socializing more than I was used to."

After a pause, Ben said, "Have you talked to her since you got back?"

"No."

"She's still at Marlee's?

"Yes."

"Do you think..."

I cut him off. "I really don't want to talk about Callie, okay?"

"Got it, sorry."

"Do me a favor and email me the details on the housing and jobs for Carmelina, Pablo and Leilani. I'll make sure they're up to date on what's happening."

"Sure, Will. Talk to you later."

I couldn't tell him how I felt about Callie. I didn't know the answer myself.

Chapter Thirty

Leilani and Leo were ecstatic when I told them about the new living arrangements.

She said, "Thank you, Mr. Will!"

I said, "Hey, thank Pastor Marlee, not me. She's the one who got the ball rolling with her publicity efforts."

She looked confused. "What ball do you mean?"

Leo laughed. "It's just a phrase, sweetie. It means get things moving."

"Okay. I think English is not an easy language."

I said, "You're right about that. We have too many words that sound alike and mean different things."

Leo said, "Do Carmelina and Pablo know about our new home?"

"Um, no, but the B&B owners didn't mention a place for you, Leo. Just our Guatemalan friends. Sorry."

He looked disappointed. "I guess I couldn't expect them to take me in. I'm sure I can find some kind of job nearby." He put his arm around Leilani. "There's no way I'm being separated from her again."

I wished them both luck, then left them on the *Wanderlust*, and went to tell the others. When I told Pablo, he was overjoyed, and asked to go with me to tell Carmelina. I didn't have anything else going on, so we said goodbye to Jimmy, got in my Z4, and headed to Pastor Marlee's RV park. Pablo and I chatted on the drive, and I never noticed the old pickup truck two cars behind me.

When we got to Marlee's, Pablo wasted no time getting out of the car and rushing to the door. Carmelina opened it when he knocked, and they threw their arms around each other.

"I have missed you, little one. And now we can all be together."

She pulled out of the hug and looked at him. "How will we do that?"

I jumped in, trying to ignore the ten pounds of fur jumping on me for attention.

"Pastor Marlee's publicity blitz did the trick. A family who owns a bed and breakfast in Fort Myers has offered to give all three of you a place to stay and jobs as well."

Marlee picked up Zoe to keep her off of me. She said, "Will, that's amazing news! I can't believe they are willing to take all of them together."

"Well, it's not permanent, but it will give them housing while we wait on an asylum ruling. The governor has been getting a lot of pressure about it."

We were all standing, and she said, "Please, sit down. Would anyone like iced tea?"

I said, "Sure," and sat on the couch. Pablo was too busy talking to Carmelina to hear the question. When Marlee set Zoe back down to get the tea, the little bundle of fur and energy jumped towards the couch, straight at my face. It startled the hell out of me.

"Whoa! Didn't see that coming." Zoe was licking my cheek, her tail whipping back and forth as she did.

Marlee laughed. "Sorry, Will. She gets so excited when someone new comes over, you'd think she never been petted before. I promise you, Carmelina and I both spend hours every day playing with her. I call that her 'Supergirl' approach, flying straight at people, paws outstretched. I worry she going to give someone a heart attack doing that."

"No worries, I survived." Zoe settled in my lap as I petted her soft fur. Marlee brought the glass of tea and set it on a coaster next to me. "Thanks."

She sat in the chair across from me. "Shih Tzus are the best lap dogs. She always wants to be in someone's lap."

There was a knock on the door. Marlee said, "I wonder who that could be? I'm not expecting anyone." She walked to the door, opened it, and saw a man in coveralls and a dirty ball cap. He was pointing a gun at her.

The man pushed past her into the motorhome. He looked around, and his eyes lit up.

"Well, if it isn't Pablo."

Pablo swallowed hard. "Boss John."

I was confused. "Who the hell are you?"

He swung the gun towards me. I kept a grip on Zoe.

"I'm the man who owns Pablo."

Pablo said, "No one owns me! You kidnapped me and held me prisoner."

He snarled, "Shut up! I paid good money for you, and you're gonna pay for it one way or another." He squinted his eyes at Pablo. "After you hit me with that damn rock, the owner blamed me for letting you get away. Two weeks later two more ran away, and I got fired. Before I'm through with you, you'll wish you'd never run out on me."

Carmelina threw her arms around Pablo. "Leave my brother alone! We paid our way to this country. We did not owe you any money."

He turned his beady eyes on her. "Maybe I should take you along too." He licked his thin lips, then pointed the gun at Pablo. "Stand up."

Pablo stood, and he motioned him towards the corner of the room with the gun barrel. "Over there." Then the man sat next to Carmelina on the loveseat and ran his hand down her arm. "You look like you could be fun."

Just then, Callie emerged from the bedroom, rubbing her eyes. "What's going on?"

Boss John swung the gun towards her. Without warning Zoe jumped out of my lap, ran to the loveseat and launched herself at his face. Startled, he threw his arms up, and BANG! The gun went off.

Before he could recover, I grabbed his arm and fought him for control of the gun. As we struggled, Carmelina jumped up, grabbed a brass lamp from the end table and smashed it into the back of his head.

He dropped like a stone.

Callie stood there with eyes wide. "What the hell just happened?"

I ignored her and asked, "Is everyone okay?"

We all checked with each other. No one was bleeding except the man crumpled on the floor. He was bleeding from the back of his head.

Then Pastor Marlee said, "Oh my God, where's Zoe?"

We all scrambled, but there was no sign of her. The motorhome was filled with calls of "Zoe! Come here, Zoe girl," but we couldn't find her. At least there was no sign of blood anywhere, so I didn't think the bullet had hit the little dog.

Finally, Marlee thought to check under the sleeper sofa. We pulled the cushions off, folded the first section out and then the front, and there she was. Huddled in a corner under the bed frame and shaking like a leaf.

Pastor Marlee grabbed and held her tightly in her arms. "You're okay, baby, nobody's going to hurt you." She looked at us, and said, "She hates thunder and other loud noises. She panics when she hears gunshots, even at a distance."

I petted her furry head as she quivered. "That pistol went off right next to her. No wonder she's terrified." Then the obvious dawned on me. "That idiot could have shot one of us, and he was determined to take Pablo with him. Zoe saved us all."

We tied up the man who called himself "Boss John," then called 911. It made for a long afternoon, with the police requiring statements of everyone there after they hauled off our attacker. Callie was the only one who didn't see much, having been asleep in the bedroom when the gunman showed up.

I was concerned that the police might call immigration enforcement on Carmelina and Pablo, but the publicity surrounding their case seemed to have protected them for the moment.

When the cops were satisfied, they finally left us alone. We sat around the living room of Pastor Marlee's motorhome, exhausted by the ordeal. Zoe slept in her lap. I stood up.

"Pablo, we'd better get you back to the houseboat. I called Jimmy earlier to let him know what was happening here."

"Si, gracias." He put an arm around Carmelina's shoulders. "You and my sister saved us all."

I laughed. "I'm just glad she grabbed that lamp! I'm not sure he wasn't going to win our wrestling match for the gun."

Carmelina walked over and hugged me. "Thank you, Mr. Will. You have done so much to help us. You, Callie and Pastor Marlee."

I said, "And don't forget Zoe, She's the one who distracted that nutcase." I gave her a pat on the head. "Good job, Zoe."

Pablo followed me as I started out the door. Callie grabbed my arm.

"Wait! Could we talk for a minute before you go?"

I shook my head. "Can it wait? I'm pretty wrung out, and I imagine you are too. Let's save it for a day when we're all rested."

She looked disappointed, but said, "Okay."

As we drove away, I wondered what she would say. *Was it still goodbye, or had she changed her mind?*

I dropped Pablo off at Jimmy's, then drove back to my marina and the *WanderLust*. Captain Rick was waiting on the rear deck of my boat, drinking one of my Red Stripes.

"Hey, Will. Hope you don't mind that I helped myself. Jimmy called to let me know what happened at the RV park. Good thing, too, since *you* didn't call me."

Sigh. "Sorry, Rick. I kind of had my hands full. I headed back here shortly after the police left."

"No sweat, I'm not mad. I just like to be in the loop, okay?"

It had been a constant battle, trying not to hurt Rick's feelings when he felt left out.

He thought for a minute, then added, "How is Callie doing?"

"She seems to have recovered all right. She slept through a lot of the excitement."

"Has she changed her mind about you and her?"

"She didn't mention it."

He looked disappointed, so I threw him a bone. "She did say she wanted to talk, but I wasn't up to it. Not after wrestling that idiot for his gun. I told her we'd talk another day."

He brightened at that. "Hey, that's great, Will."

I don't want to give him false hopes. "Listen, I know you like Callie, but don't get your hopes up. She made it clear things were over between us, and I've made my peace with it."

He sniffed. "None of my business anyway."

I rolled my eyes, but he wasn't looking. I didn't bother to argue with him. "Where are Leilani and Leo?"

"I sent them for a walk. It was making me nuts watching them stare at each other. I thought the exercise would do them good. I told 'em not to leave the docks."

"Probably a good idea. I'll bet they're getting tired of being indoors, even on a boat."

"Hope it all works out for them. They're both awfully young."

Rick said, "Hey, nothing wrong with young love. My first wife was still in high school when I married her. I was shipping out on a Navy supply ship, and I wanted her to be there when I got back."

"Did she wait for you?"

"She didn't move away, if that's what you mean." He looked annoyed.

"No, I meant, how did the marriage work out?" I'll admit that I was picking on him a bit. He'd already mentioned being married five times.

"Not worth a damn. She wrote me these great letters for the first three months, really sexy stuff. Then they started getting newsy, what was going on around town. The letters got shorter and shorter. Then they stopped."

"What happened?"

"She found a longshoreman to move in with. Said I was gone too long. The Navy had us doing six-month cruises, and she was a young, horny girl. Hell, that's partly why I married her."

There didn't seem anything else to say about it.

Rick said, "Do you ever miss your ex-wife?"

"No. Well, not really. Sometimes I miss just having someone to come home to, to share a bed with."

He thought for a minute. "Callie is a lot more than that."

I didn't answer.

"Don't end up sorry you let her get away, Will."

Chapter Thirty-One

There had been plenty to do since we returned from our Palm Beach rescue. The reunited immigrant siblings had moved to their new home in Fort Myers, and they were learning their jobs, mostly by helping around the B&B. Pablo turned out to be quite the handyman, and his benefactors, the Wheelers, were thrilled. Carmelina was helping with cooking for the guests and Leilani was cleaning rooms.

Even better, Lottie Wheeler was a former English teacher, and she was giving all three siblings English lessons. She'd been surprised at how much of the language they'd already picked up from their experiences in Florida, and found them to be fast learners. Carmelina had given the letters she'd written in captivity to her sister and brother; and Lottie had her translate them to English for practice. Leo got a job working on a tour boat, and was spending every spare moment with Leilani.

Pastor Marlee's public relations efforts combined with the series in the *Bradenton Journal* increased the pressure on the governor, and he'd made a formal request to the president for asylum for the three siblings. The president campaigned against immigration, but we were hoping he'd see the publicity bonanza it could bring.

On the home front, I'll admit that I'd been avoiding the talk I'd told Callie I'd have with her. A part of me hoped she'd want to come back, and another part of me didn't want that at all. Since Leilani and Leo had moved to Fort Myers, I'd had the *WanderLust* to myself. I was enjoying the peace and quiet.

Yeah, the nights in bed alone weren't what I was used to, but there was no one to argue with or to complain about my habits. It wasn't all bad.

When she called and asked to meet me, I didn't think I could put it off any longer. We made plans for her to come by the *WanderLust* that afternoon. I was a wreck by the time she arrived, but I welcomed her into the cabin.

"Hi, Callie, how have you been?"

"Okay, I guess. Pastor Marlee has been nice to let me stay after Carmelina moved to Fort Myers."

"That is nice of her. The RV isn't all that big."

"It's a little crowded, but Marlee and I have talked a lot, and Zoe is a treasure. Any time I need some affection, she's right there."

There was an awkward silence. "Yeah, Zoe loves to be in your lap."

She looked wistfully around the salon. "I do miss living on the boat."

Ouch. She misses the boat, but not me. "You're the one who wanted to leave."

Now she looked miserable. "Will, please try to understand. I was excited to finally have a job that felt like the beginning of a career. And you were always worrying about me."

"Not without reason. I had to keep saving your life!"

"I know, I know, and I'm grateful, really."

She didn't sound grateful. It came out sounding like she resented it. "Wasn't I right to be worried?"

"Yes, but..."

"But what?"

"I felt smothered."

Now I was irritated. "So what should I have done? Let you fall off that lighthouse? Let the overdose kill you? Dammit, Callie, I *loved* you! Was I supposed to let you die to prove it?"

"Loved?" she said in a quiet voice.

I hadn't thought before I said it. But it was true. "Callie..."

"Please don't, Will. Just tell me. Is it over? Are *we* over?"

"You're the one who left, remember? *You* are the one who broke it off. What's different now?"

She struggled to explain herself. "I, I was excited to be doing something new. It felt like you were jealous of my independence."

"And I suppose Alvaro had nothing to do with it?"

She was squirming in her seat. "Not really, no."

"Callie, you slept in his apartment. After a night of drinking wine together."

"I know. I'm sorry."

"Did you sleep with him?"

"No! I swear I didn't"

"So nothing happened between you?"

She turned beet red. "Um, he kissed me."

"And that's all?"

She stared at the floor. "He touched my breasts."

"But he had nothing to do with us breaking up? Come on, Callie. I'm not stupid."

"I was just so confused about everything. I was a reporter, and he was helping me, and all you wanted was for me to stay home."

"That's not true. I wanted you to be safe, that's all."

She sat silent for a moment. "This is it, isn't it?"

"Yeah, I guess it is."

A tear rolled down her cheek. "A part of me will always love you."

"Me too." It was the best I could manage.

Callie stood up, walked over and kissed me on the cheek. "Tell Captain Rick and Jimmy I said goodbye."

I felt a lump in my throat. "I'll tell them."

And then she was gone.

* * *

The biggest difference between the time after Callie left and the post-breakup periods of past lovers was that I didn't sink into depression. I exercised, rode bikes and kayaked with Jimmy, and even did a little fishing with Captain Rick. I've never been much of a fisherman, and Rick was determined to change that.

I agreed to go fishing with him one morning, but he could tell I was reluctant as we were loading the gear into his skiff.

"Will, you like to eat fish, so you ought to be okay catching them."

"I eat beef too, but I don't want to slaughter a cow."

He looked exasperated. "Don't be a wuss. Fish slime washes off, okay?"

I held up my rubber gloves. "Not a problem if you don't touch them."

He rolled his eyes, but then started the boat and we headed out. By noon, we'd caught several redfish and a couple of black drum. Rick was pleased.

"See, this hasn't been bad, has it, Will?"

"No, I admit that I've enjoyed it. At least we're catching good eating fish. Too many times I see people out fishing and all they're doing is sitting and staring at the water."

"Ah, but that's part of the charm! Meditating on the water." He lifted a light beer can. "With beer, of course."

I wasn't totally convinced, but I clinked cans with him. "To meditating on the water." Then I added, "And you get to clean the fish."

Rick wasn't the only one trying to keep my spirits up. Callie had moved out of Pastor Marlee's RV and into an apartment after she finally accepted the fact that we weren't getting back together. Now Marlee had invited me to dinner.

I arrived at 5:30, and was met at the door by the rambunctious, bouncing Shih Tzu, Zoe.

"Hey, Zoe, how's our little hero tonight?"

Marlee said, "Watch out, you'll give her a big head."

I scratched the little dog behind both ears. "Well, she did bail us out of a tough situation."

Marlee laughed. "All she did was jump at him the same way she jumps at me. Zoe just wanted attention."

"Doesn't matter what her motivation was, she got us out of a jam. She's aces in my book."

Zoe responded to the praise by rolling over and presenting her tummy for a belly rub. I obliged, and Marlee shook her head. "Zoe, you are shameless!" She looked at me then, and said, "I'm happy to see you doing so well."

"You mean because of Callie?"

"Yes. I'll admit that I thought you'd take her back."

I sat on the couch and accepted the glass of wine she handed me. After a sip, I said, "I surprised myself by saying no to getting back together. I do miss her, but I don't need to be in a relationship with someone who could leave that easily. She was already moving on before she got kidnapped. I think she was disappointed that Alvaro didn't fight to save her, so she came running back to me. Not a very good reason to stay together."

She said, "I'm just pleased that you aren't depressed. You actually seem happy these days."

"You know, I *am* happy, Marlee. Callie stayed with me longer than my other girlfriends, but she also made me realize that I don't *need* to have a woman in my life. I have lots of friends, both male and female. I think I'll take my time before jumping into another relationship."

She gave me a mischievous look. "Sure you'll be able to resist finding one to take to bed?"

I feigned shock. "Why *Pastor*, I can't believe you said that!"

She laughed, and said, "Sorry, but you do have to admit that you tend to find women who jump right into bed with you."

"That's not *completely* true. Sandy and I were friends for months before we got physical, and I dated Hanna for a few months without ever going to bed with her."

"Only because she wouldn't."

"Well..."

"I'm not picking on you, Will, but I know that you like having a woman in your bed, not just someone to go out with."

She had me squirming. "Pastor Marlee, I'll admit I prefer being in a relationship where the woman is as interested in that kind of intimacy as I am."

She howled with laughter. "Will! Easy there, I'm not being critical. All I'm saying is that I have a tough time imagining you being celibate for long."

"Um, how do you, I mean, you know, since you became a pastor..."

"Will Harper! I'm a Lutheran Pastor, not a nun! We don't take vows of celibacy."

"Sorry, I just thought..."

Smiling, she said, "I need to give you a book on what Lutherans believe. Martin Luther was married to a former nun, and they had *lots* of children. Definitely not celibate."

"I didn't know."

With a twinkle in her eye, Marlee said, "Obviously."

Somehow, that awkward conversation took the edge off the evening, and we had a delightful dinner with sparkling conversation. When it was time to go, Marlee gave me a hug.

"I'm glad you're doing so well. I thought Callie might be the one for you, but I'm glad she hasn't broken your heart."

"Nah, she dinged it a little, but I think it's getting tougher."

She kissed me on the cheek. "Don't give up. The right girl for you is out there."

"Thanks, Marlee. You're a good friend."

"I'm here when you need me, Will."
As I drove away, I wondered, "What did she mean by that?"

Chapter Thirty-Two

A ll of my friends continued to work at keeping me occupied, but I didn't feel like I needed distraction. I wrote a final wrap-up on the three siblings and their immigrant status, and I was happy to report that they'd received at least temporary refugee status. I knew I'd need to do regular follow-ups to keep them from being quietly deported if no one was paying attention.

Immigrants were being demonized by the current government, never mind that our country was built through immigration. Now, with the immigration crackdown, the US population is in danger of shrinking rather than growing for the first time in history. Low birth rate, and only a trickle of immigrants. Go figure.

There were lots of related bits of information in the news. The explosion of the *PlayTime* was deemed an accident, in part because a propane tank blew when the boat exploded. The boat itself was diesel powered, and the tank was for the galley stove. No explanation was given for what caused the propane to blow, but no connection was ever made to the Russian mob either.

The tomato picking operation was raided by ICE, who took dozens of illegals into custody. No one who ran the tomato farm was prosecuted. Boss John was charged with home invasion and assault with a firearm for his visit to Pastor Marlee's motorhome, but no one was ever charged with enslaving anyone.

The trucking company that had been the entry point to Florida for many of the illegal immigrants who were sold as slaves was closed down. There were some human trafficking charges filed, but all were pleaded down to lesser offenses.

It seemed like the whole thing was getting swept under the rug.

I was pretty disgusted, but there was one bright spot. Eduardo Alvarez was charged with kidnapping and reckless endangerment. He was also charged with manslaughter over the death of his security staff member during Callie's rescue. He was subsequently forced to resign as head of the sugar company he'd run for many years.

Alvarez was out on bail while recovering from a broken arm, which had required surgery and the insertion of pins to hold it together. Seems that when he tried to ram us with the golf cart and ran into the curved tunnel wall, it flipped on top of him. When his security guy tried to lift the cart off of him, the cart shifted, throwing the man into the wall and smashing the back of his head. He was the dead man who floated out with the cart.

Alvarez was now unwelcome in Palm Beach society, and his mansion was for sale. The city had declared his beach tunnel improperly constructed and without the proper permits and had ordered its removal. *It's nice to see somebody at least pay a price for what they did.*

Callie had begun to earn her own bylines, and I was happy for her. Really.

Sometimes I missed her, but I was glad I'd been able to let go. My mother was a strong woman, and she'd taught me to both treasure and respect women. Because of my mom, I grew up believing that women were just as capable as men. I never

understood why anyone would think differently. The last thing I wanted was to hold Callie back.

It didn't keep me from missing female companionship, and I decided to remedy that. I walked next door to my neighbor Bev's old ChrisCraft cabin cruiser and knocked on the hull.

"Hey, Bev!"

A minute passed, then her cabin door opened. "Hi, Will, what can I do for you?"

"It's a beautiful day, and I'm bored. I was thinking about taking the *WanderLust* for a spin. Are you up for a boat ride?"

Her face lit up. "Oh, *hell* yes! I haven't been out on the water in months. This old tub still runs, but I don't trust it enough to get too far from the dock. Can I bring anything?"

"Just yourself. I have beer, wine and snacks, and I didn't want to go by myself."

"Terrific. Give me about ten minutes to feed the cats and put on a swimsuit. I'll come over when I'm ready."

I felt better already. A day on the water is better than a day just about anywhere else. I returned to the *WanderLust*, unhooked the water and power, and waited for Bev to come over. She arrived soon after I got the lines readied and the engines turning over.

"Ahoy the boat!"

"Come aboard, Bev. Thanks for joining me. I was starting to feel dock-bound."

I helped her on deck, and she handed me her bag. "Don't tell me about being stuck at the dock. I haven't had my boat out in over a year. Of course, part of the problem is the cats. They go berserk when I start the engines. They think it's an earthquake."

"Well, I don't have any pets, so it's no sweat to take the boat out. I'm glad you could join me."

"My pleasure. What can I help with?"

"I've got the lines singled up. If you could cast off the port bow, I'll be ready to back out when you toss the starboard line."

She grinned at me. "Aye Aye, captain." She handled the lines, and we were soon heading out towards the bay at idle speed. She joined me on the flybridge as I stood at the helm. "You're really getting into the nautical lingo, Will."

"It's hard to live at the marina without picking up the terminology."

"You sound like a professional."

I laughed. "Glad I can fake it well."

"Hey, I've seen you dock this behemoth. You're better at this than I ever was."

"It's nice of you to say that, Bev. I've gotten a crash course in a lot of stuff the last couple of years."

We cruised in silence for a moment, then she said, "I was sorry to hear about you and Callie splitting up."

"Yeah, I didn't really expect that. Guess I wasn't paying attention. In hindsight, I should have seen it coming. "

"I really liked her. I thought she might stick around."

"So did I."

She put a hand on my arm. "Sorry to bring up a sore subject."

"No worries, Bev. I'm not letting it get me down. If I start feeling low, I just invite my neighbors for a boat ride."

She smiled at me. "Well, this neighbor is always ready for a ride."

It was a beautiful day, and I had nothing to complain about. A boat on the water and a friend to keep me company. Bev is a bit older than me, and there had been no sparks between us, but spending a few hours with someone softer than Captain Rick or Jimmy Wilkins was a nice change of pace. No offense to any of them.

We cruised into the waters off Anna Maria Island to Egmont Key, one of my favorite spots to anchor out. I enjoyed Bev's reaction.

"Oh look, there's a lighthouse! I love those." She picked up my binoculars from the dashboard and looked towards the tower. "That's odd. It looks like there's no top to it."

"You're right. The top and the Fresnel lens were removed in 1944, and replaced with a rotating beacon."

"That's a shame. Seems like they could have left it intact."

"Hey, it could be worse. That tower is over 170 years old. A lot of old lighthouses were torn down. The Egmont Key light is still a functioning beacon."

"Well, the tower is nice, and the island looks gorgeous. I'm glad you invited me out here."

"Bev, you've lived at the marina for years. Are you telling me you've never been out here before?"

"Sure haven't. I told you I never take my old houseboat far from the dock, and I don't have a skiff for running around the marina like you do."

"You're welcome to use it anytime when the *WanderLust* is at the dock. I'll get you a key."

"That's awfully nice of you. It would be fun to do a little puttering around the islands here. It all looks so different from the water."

"No problem. It'll do the motor good to get some running time. When Mack Wilson restored the Whaler as a gift for me, he bought the old Evinrude outboard. It gets gummed up when it's not run enough."

"That would be my pleasure, thanks, Will."

"You're most welcome." I got the anchor set, and we took a swim before laying out in the sun. It reminded me of doing this same kind of trip with Bonnie, but she didn't believe in swimsuits. She was an *au natural* girl. Bev looked good in her one piece suit, but I wasn't out here looking for romance, just for a friend to hang out with.

I think she knew I wasn't in the market for a girlfriend, and that suited both of us.

After an hour in the sun we were baked front and back, so we decided to move to the shade of the stern deck. "Whoa, it's gotten hot out here. That's the most sun time I've gotten lately."

She poked a finger on her arm and watched the light spot it left on her pink skin fade.

"Yeah, I'm about medium rare. Can I get you a beer?"

"Sure. There's plenty in the galley fridge."

She was gone a long time to get the beers, and when she came back, she was carrying two plates with sandwiches from cold cuts and a bag of chips.

"Hope you don't mind, I found stuff in the fridge, so I made us some sandwiches. The swimming made me hungry."

"That's fine, but what happened to the beers?"

"Oh crap, I forgot them!" She rushed back into the boat and came out soon after carrying two Red Stripes. "Here you go. I'm glad to see you have good beer aboard."

"I could have come and helped, you know."

"It wasn't a big deal. Here's one for you."

They were icy cold, just the way I like my beers. "Ahh, that's good on a hot day."

She laughed. "A cold beer is good *any* day."

"You're my kind of woman, Bev." I toasted her with the bottle, then realized she looked stricken. "Did I say something wrong?"

"Will, it's just..." She was struggling to find words.

"Hey, my comment was just on what you said about beer. I didn't mean anything more, okay?"

She let out the breath she'd been holding. "I'm sorry, I over-reacted."

"Are you okay?"

"Just give me a second, Will."

I watched her make a visible effort to calm herself. When she was breathing normally, she spoke again.

"Whew! I haven't done that in a long time."

"Done what?"

"I was on the verge of a panic attack. I'm okay now."

"What triggered you?"

She gave me a sickly grin. "When you said I was your kind of woman."

I began to protest, and she said, "Will, what you said was fine. I reacted because Roy, my ex, used to say that to me all the time. 'You're my kind of woman.' He didn't mean it in a nice way, either. He usually said it when he'd been using me, taking advantage of me, grabbing me..."

"I'm so sorry, Bev. I didn't know."

She sighed. "No reason you should have. Please don't stress over it."

"How long have you been divorced?"

"We were never married. He didn't see the need. He got everything he wanted from me without it."

"Listen, any time you want to talk about it, I've sure had my share of broken relationships."

She put a hand on mine. "Thanks, Will. I might take you up on it sometime. But not today."

We finished lunch and drank our beers, but the mood of the beautiful day had slipped away.

After we cleaned up from lunch, she said, "Mind if we head back to the dock?"

"No, I'll crank the engines and pull the anchor."

We made the short trip back to the slip, and I did a double-take.

Bonnie was sitting on my dock box.

David Crosby

Epilogue

I was more than a little surprised to see her. Bev recognized her right away.

"Oh my. Were you expecting Bonnie?"

"Not even a little." I steered the boat into the slip, reversed the engines to stop, and then Bev and I made short work of tying it up and hooking up the power. Bonnie waved, but stayed seated on the dock box.

Bev thanked me for the outing and lunch, hugged me and said her goodbyes. "Hey, Bonnie, good to see you."

"You too, Bev."

I walked to the dock box, and Bonnie stood.

"Hi, Will."

"Hello, Bonnie. It's good to see you." I was surprised at just how good it was.

"Sorry to show up unannounced. I was in the neighborhood."

"Really?" I was grinning when I said it. She had moved back to her home in Charlotte, North Carolina, last I'd heard.

"Yes. I've been, um, in Sarasota the last few months."

Wow, didn't see that coming. "Sarasota?"

"I've been there trying to help my Uncle Roger. His older daughter, Stephanie, called me and asked me to come."

"I thought your brother, Andy, was your last close relative?" Andy had been murdered over his knowledge of the scam the City of Dolphin River used to take over my friend Sandy's marina.

"No, he was the last of my immediate family. My mom and dad died a few years back, but I've always been close to my Uncle Roger and Aunt Martha. She died a year and a half ago."

"Sorry to hear that."

"Thanks. She had a great life, and she was eighty-two years old, but I sure miss her."

"Has he been okay without her?"

She looked angry. "That's the problem. He made it a year with his daughters Vanessa and Stephanie helping, but he wanted more."

"More?"

"He wanted a sex partner."

"How old is your uncle?"

"He's seventy-six years old!"

"Wow. I hope I have the stamina for sex when I'm that old." Then I saw the look on her face. *Oops. Wrong thing to say.*

She spat out the response. "I'd rather he'd hired a hooker!"

Uh oh. "What happened?"

"He got married."

"And that's a problem?"

"She's awful."

"Is she mean to him?"

"No! She sucks up to him, pampers him, and probably screws him blind!"

"And that's bad?"

"Yes! She's the biggest phony I ever met."

"What's she doing that's so bad?"

"She's shutting the family out of their lives!"

"Bonnie, calm down. I'm on your side."

She took a deep breath. "Sorry. I just hate what she's doing."

"Why don't we go in the boat? It's pretty hot out here."

"Oh, sure, I'm sorry. This whole thing has me rattled."

I can see that.

She picked up her bag from the dock and followed me into the *WanderLust*. When we got inside, I needed to ask her. "So, where are you staying?" I knew it was a tricky question.

Bonnie looked uncharacteristically shy. She said it quietly. "Here? Is that okay?"

I took her hand. "Of course, you know you're always welcome on my boat."

She looked relieved. "Thanks. I'll try not to be too much trouble."

It was probably a mistake, but I couldn't help myself. I took her in my arms. "Bonnie. You are never too much trouble. I love having you here. I'm so glad you came."

She sniffled as I held her. "Thank you." After a moment she pulled away.

I said, "Tell me what happened with your uncle."

"What happened to him is a horrible woman. Her name is Millie Potts. Uncle Roger was so sad after Aunt Martha died. They'd been married over fifty years. He'd rarely been alone all those years. Then she died, and he was alone for most of every day. His daughters hired a home-care worker to come spend the daytime with him, and they actually got pretty friendly. Then all of a sudden he said he was going to try online dating."

"That's pretty bold at his age."

"Vanessa and Stephanie were shocked, but he seemed determined. The problem was that the first woman he went out with was Millie. He spent the day with her, then announced they were getting married!"

"After one day? That seems kind of crazy."

"I know it. When his daughters asked him to slow down and not rush things, he said it didn't pay to wait at his age."

"I understand why you were worried. So, they got married then?"

"Yes, a month after they met. She lived two hours away from him, and the first time she came to visit, she took one look at his house and moved in. She never left."

"Is his house all that enticing?"

"It's no mansion, but the house is 3500 square-feet with a pool. She lived in a tiny apartment before."

"Ah, I can see the attraction. Did you have her checked out by anyone?"

"No, dammit. We were going to, but she volunteered to do a prenup. Millie's no spring chicken herself. She's fifty-nine, and she plays the sweet older lady role really well. She told us, 'All I want from this family is *love*.'" She sighed. "We bought her act. Dumb."

"I'm confused. What is she doing that's so awful?"

"The first thing she did was fire Betty, the home-health lady. Then she took every single picture of Aunt Martha off the walls."

"Maybe she's a little insecure?"

"They were married more than fifty years!"

"Bonnie, calm down, I'm on your side, okay?"

"Sorry. This just makes me so damn mad."

"Anyway, we didn't like that she took the photos down, but it didn't seem worth fighting about. Then she took down every single photo of our families off the wall. Even pictures of his late sister and parents came down and got stuffed in the attic."

"Okay, that's a little weird. Didn't your uncle have any say in it?"

"She leads him around like he's on a leash. I swear, I think she's drugging him."

"Oh, come on, that's a little melodramatic."

"Will, I'm serious. She's had him sign things that he doesn't even remember signing. She had him convinced that they'd never gotten around to signing the prenup. It's a good thing Stephanie kept a signed copy in her files."

"Is Millie taking over his finances?"

"Big time. She's gotten herself put on all of his bank accounts, and I found out recently that she's trying to get him to change his will."

"Change it how?"

"To leave her his house and all of his money and to give her power of attorney. I found notes about it on his desk while she was in the bathroom."

"But what about the prenup?"

"If he puts a bequest in his will, that's outside of the prenuptial agreement. I asked a lawyer."

"Are you sure about this, Bonnie?"

"Very. His daughters met with their dad, Millie and the attorneys. Uncle Roger announced he was setting up a $200,000 trust in her name. So she'd be 'taken care of' when he's gone."

"Well, you're right. This sounds pretty bad. What can I do?"

"Find out where she came from, track her background. I'm betting she's done this before."

"I'll be glad to help if I can. How long do you plan to be in town?"

"Until I find a way to stop her." She looked at me, and said, "Don't worry, I know you and Hanna started dating when I left. If she doesn't want me on your boat, I can get a motel room."

I grinned at her. "You *have* been gone a while."

"What did I miss?"

"Things never went anywhere with Hanna. We're still friends, but she was looking for marriage, kids and a picket fence. That's just not me."

"Whoa! I guess not. That would scare me off too. Okay, but I'm guessing you haven't been a monk since then?"

"Not exactly. I met a woman named Callie when we were doing an investigation in Clewiston last year. She moved here and had been staying on the *WanderLust* with me."

"Had?"

"Yeah. Things were going really well until the last few months. I got invited by Dillon Haverhill to be a sort of special correspondent to the *Bradenton Journal*, and they hired Callie to work with me."

"Dillon Haverhill, the billionaire?"

"Yes. He bought the *Journal* and wanted to push investigative reporting for the paper."

"Wow. I can't believe you took a job."

"Well, it's not exactly a job. I can write about anything I want, with no assignments, no deadlines, and no office hours."

She grinned. "Sounds like my kind of job."

"That's why I agreed to do it. The problem started when Callie jumped in headfirst."

"I thought you said she was hired to help you?"

"That's what I thought too. She didn't think I was taking the job seriously, so she started working with a young guy at the paper."

"Ah, the plot thickens."

"Right. She started spending nights at his apartment. We split up after that."

She shook her head. "I swear, Will, you *do* have the worst luck with women."

"Yeah, it sure feels that way."

"So..."

"Yes?"

"I'm not stepping on anyone's toes by being here? Like maybe, Bev?"

"Nope. Not a soul. We're just neighbors and friends."

"And it's okay if I stay with you while I try to help my uncle and cousins?"

"I'd love to have your company."

"And you'll help?"

"Bonnie, you knew that all along."

She hugged me. "Thanks, Will."

Here we go again.

Postscript

Like all of the other Will Harper Novels, *Deadly Traffic* has a factual background. Florida is a hotspot for human trafficking, and yes, that means slavery. The three immigrant siblings in this book are fictional, but their stories are based on true experiences of immigrants who are sold as housemaids, tomato pickers and sex workers.

There are too many stories to reference here, but run a Google search for human trafficking in Florida, and you'll quickly get an idea of the scope of the problem. The solutions aren't simple, but a great start would be for the congress and the president to work together to pass humane immigration reform. By humane, I don't mean close the border and send everyone back. This country was built on immigration. Immigrants pick our fruits and vegetables, staff our restaurant kitchens and care for our children. They are also doctors, nurses and medical workers in our health-care system. Keeping them out is counter-productive.

David Crosby

A Favor, Please...

Thanks for reading my book, "Deadly Traffic". The best compliment you can give an Indie author is to post a review. I'd be very grateful if you would leave a review on the book's Amazon page. If you have any trouble finding it there, here's a link to my Author Central page: https://bit.ly/DavidCrosbyAuthor.

Select the book you want to review and click on it, then look for the number of ratings and click on that. The option to write a review is in a gray bar to your left on the page. The review can be as long or short as you like and will be much appreciated. It helps me to reach other readers and to be able to keep writing, so *Thank You* in advance!

I'm currently hard at work on the next title in the Will Harper series, and if you'd be interested in hearing when it's completed, e-mail me at david@crosbystills.com. Also feel free to write me if you have comments or questions about the book, or if there are any errors I have missed that you'd like to point out. Authors and editors can't catch everything, so thanks for spotting them.

Happy Reading,

David Crosby

Writing from breezy Zephyrhills, Florida

Made in the USA
Columbia, SC
20 May 2024

35755417R00157